By
Tom Barber

*****

Linda,

Very much hope you
enjoy the following -
you have a wonderful
daughter.

Best wishes,

Tim Byd

1

One Way
Copyright: Archway Productions
Published: 11th May 2013

The Sam Archer thriller series
by
Tom Barber

NINE LIVES

26 year old Sam Archer has just been selected to
join a new counter-terrorist squad, the Armed
Response Unit. And they have their first case. A
team of suicide bombers are planning to attack
London on New Year's Eve. The problem?
No one knows where any of them are.

THE GETAWAY

Archer is in New York City for a funeral. After
the service, an old familiar face approaches him
with a proposition. A team of bank robbers are
tearing the city apart, robbing it for millions.
The FBI agent needs Archer to go undercover and
try to stop them.

BLACKOUT

Three men have been killed in the UK and USA
in one morning. The deaths take place thousands
of miles apart, yet are connected by an event
fifteen years ago. Before long, Archer and the
ARU are drawn into the violent fray. And there's
a problem.
One of their own men is on the extermination list.

SILENT NIGHT

A dead body is found in Central Park, a man who
was killed by a deadly virus. Someone out there

has more of the substance and is planning to use it. Archer must find where this virus came from and secure it before any more is released.
But he is already too late.

ONE WAY

On his way home, Archer saves a team of US Marshals from a violent ambush in the middle of the Upper West Side. The group are forced to take cover in a tenement block in Harlem. But there are more killers on the way to finish the job.
And Archer feels there's something about the group of Marshals that isn't quite right.

RETURN FIRE

Four months after they first encountered one another, Sam Archer and Alice Vargas are both working in the NYPD Counter-Terrorism Bureau and also living together. But a week after Vargas leaves for a trip to Europe, Archer gets a knock on his front door.
Apparently Vargas has completely disappeared.
And it appears she's been abducted.

GREEN LIGHT

A nineteen year old woman is gunned down in a Queens car park, the latest victim in a brutal gang turf war that goes back almost a century.
Suspended from duty, his badge and gun confiscated, Archer is nevertheless drawn into the fray as he seeks justice for the girl. People are going missing, all over New York.
And soon, so does he.

Also:
CONDITION BLACK (A novella)
In the year 2113, a US 101st Airborne soldier
wakes up after crash landing on a moon
somewhere in space. All but two of his squad are
dead. He has no idea where he is, or who shot
him down.
But he quickly learns that some nightmares don't
stop when you wake up.

For Suzanne, Nancy, Pat, Judith and Shannon.

ONE

Two officers from East Hampton Town PD took the call. Both male, they'd joined the Department fresh from the Suffolk County Police Academy three years ago, and after a twelve-week orientation and on-the-job training programme, had been partners ever since.

East Hampton Town PD is made up of fifty-six officers who perform all of the law-enforcement tasks the area requires. The Hamptons are a group of villages forming a part of Long Island that everyone associates with wealth; the rich and famous frequently choose to vacation there, some renting places for the season and others just buying them outright to save hassle. Whichever option they take, the Hamptons contain some of the most expensive residential properties not just on the East Coast, but in all of the United States. There was a reason the region served as a setting in *The Great Gatsby;* the area evokes the glamour and sophistication of a prosperous present and romanticised past.

Given the demographic and the amount of zeroes a person needs in their bank account just to rent a place there, crime is low. Most of those who vacation and live in the Hamptons are the business and social crème de la crème, so any illegal activity tends to be either petty stuff or at the opposite end of the spectrum, serious accounting, fraud or business transgressions which an FBI or a Financial Crimes task force from the city handles. The most common illegal deed is burglary, thieves capitalising on properties mothballed for long periods out of season or when the residents are out of town, making the most of their absence to help themselves to expensive furniture, art and jewellery.

Murder in East Hampton Town is almost unheard of. Until that Saturday afternoon, there hadn't been a single case in the area in over nine years. The PD has no homicide division, which means in the extremely rare event of an unexplained death, a Department squad car answers the call.

In their three years together, the two young men on their way to the callout that day had never attended a murder scene.

But what they found at the villa significantly changed that.

It had just gone 3pm on a beautiful Saturday in early March. The air was warm, the sun shining, summer missing the memo and arriving three months early. The address the two officers were given by Dispatch was a prestigious beach villa an hour's drive from the city. A delivery man had called it in fifteen minutes ago. He'd been sent out to deliver a few additional cases of wine for a party and after no-one had responded to his repeated knocking on the front door, he'd gone around the back.

Inside an East Hampton Town PD Ford Interceptor, the two cops swung into the drive, pulling up beside an ambulance and seeing the delivery man sitting in the back. His own van was parked on the side of the road outside the gates, the rear doors still open. The man had an oxygen

8

mask over his face and was being attended to by a couple of paramedics inside the ambulance.

He was staring straight ahead, his eyes glazed, and didn't seem to notice the two cops arrive.

Sliding on the handbrake and switching off the engine, the two police officers stepped out of their vehicle and slammed the doors. Both were dressed in the dark blue EHT PD police uniform, and were carrying a pistol, cuffs, radio and nightstick on their belts.

The medics looked over at them but didn't say anything, concentrating on their patient.

Approaching the entrance to the house, the officers saw the front door was shut, several cases of wine on a wheeled dolly beside it, the booze abandoned by the delivery guy.

Looking at the door, one of the officers turned and walked over to the ambulance.

'Got a glove?' he asked quietly.

The medic closest to him pulled a latex one from a box, passing it over. Snapping it onto his hand with a silent nod of thanks, the officer re-joined his partner. With the glove protecting against fingerprints, he tried the handle.

It twisted and the door opened.

He eased it back to reveal the interior of the villa.

The house had a Mediterranean feel, light, open and airy with a polished tile floor which would keep the place cool in the hot weather. There were impressive paintings on the walls either side of the hallway, an ornate mirror hanging above a gold gilt marble-topped table to the right, a large crystal lamp and vase of flowers placed on the top.

The two cops stepped inside slowly, taking care not to touch or disturb anything. They made their way down the corridor and passed through an open door to arrive at what was the main living area.

It was spacious and open-plan, conjoined with a large kitchen and separated by a long granite-topped counter. Matching the exterior of the house, the walls were painted white and cream.

It meant the blood spattered all over them stood out starkly.

There were bodies strewn everywhere. Men. Women. Children. It was clear from the remaining foodstuffs on the counter and on a dining table that they'd been killed at or just prior to lunchtime.

Bowls of salad and plates of sliced cold-cuts were sitting abandoned.

Glasses and plates were shattered all over the floor, shards of glass and pieces of bone china lying amongst spilt food.

Bottles of wine and beer had either been fragmented by gunfire or were lying smashed on the counter, table and floor, the liquid mixing with the food and blood.

Deep black bullet holes riddled the light walls and scores of copper shell casings were scattered everywhere, lying amongst the bodies and debris.

The villa had a terrible stillness.

It looked more like an abattoir than a holiday home.

Both cops stood frozen in the doorway. It took each of them a moment to recover from the initial shock. As one stared in horror at the carnage in front of him, the other looked out onto the veranda directly in front of them.

The windows were all intact. One of the doors was pulled open, and the thin cream curtains fluttered gently in the breeze.

The only movement in an otherwise motionless house.

They heard a set of wind-chimes, tinkling softly from somewhere outside as they made gentle contact in the light wind. The villa was on the edge of the beach so the two men could see and hear the waves as they rolled in, seagulls calling from somewhere nearby, the air salty.

The cop to the right stepped forward, picking his way slowly and cautiously round the edge of the room, taking great care not to tread on any evidence. It was easier said than done. When he made it to the window, he drew his nightstick and used the club to push the gently billowing curtains to one side, examining the sand visible beyond the veranda.

There were a series of children's footprints visible, coming back and forth from the water.

But there were also a set of four, maybe five, definite adult prints, leading from the sea to the villa and back again.

He looked up but saw nothing except clear blue sea and horizon.

No ships, no sailboats.

No people.

Whoever did this was long gone.

He turned away from the window and re-joined his partner, who still hadn't moved as he stared at the massacre. He sensed his partner watching him and they made eye contact.

Their priority now was to clear the rest of the residence.

The two men pulled their side-arms and split up, following protocol, checking the villa quickly. They moved fast but worked thoroughly, both of them on edge, inspecting every room. The rest of the house was equally lavish, each room beautifully decorated and well-appointed with expensive furniture. Whoever owned the property was damn wealthy, that was for sure.

It was clear as daylight they also had enemies.

Soon after, the two officers met up again outside the main room. The man who'd stepped up to the window holstered his side-arm and swallowed, his throat dry.

'Found two more upstairs. Both shot in the head.'

'Was this a robbery?'

His partner stared at the blood-stained and bullet-riddled walls around them.

'No. This was an execution.'

The other man looked down at the corpses. The body closest to his feet was a big man in shorts and a white shirt, lying flat on his back. He had a gold chain around his neck, thick chest hair protruding through the gap in the fabric, his hair combed back.

He'd been shot three times in the chest. Blood had dried around him, his lifeless eyes staring up vacantly at the ceiling.

Shifting his gaze, a body ten feet away caught the officer's eye. The guy had a pistol in a holster on his hip, lying face down in a pool of his own blood.

He wasn't the only corpse in the room who had a weapon.

Staying where they were, the two cops both heard the sound of wailing sirens somewhere in the distance. Back up was almost here.

Then a noise came from inside the house.

The two men froze. They pulled their side arms again and looked at each other.

It had come from one of the rooms along the corridor.

They lifted their pistols and stood there, listening.

They heard it again.

A rustle.

Movement.

Keeping their weapons in the aim, the two men moved down the corridor slowly as the sirens outside grew louder. There was the sound of a series of cars screeching to a halt in the drive, the quiet villa about to become a hell of a lot busier.

Behind the two cops, the thin curtains rippled gently in the sea breeze.

And the tinkling of the wind chimes echoed through the house.

*

Two weeks later and almost fourteen hundred miles south of East Hampton, a man twisted a key in a lock and pushed open the door to his second-floor apartment. He lived alone and had just come back from a long day's work. He'd been having a rough time at the office lately and today had been especially gruelling, full of questions and not many answers. He felt like a boxer with his back to the ropes, taking an onslaught of punches, desperately trying to make it to the bell and back to his corner. He was hanging in there.

Just.

Closing the door behind him and ensuring it was locked, the man laid the keys on the side, along with a pistol he pulled from his belt and a cell phone he drew from his pocket. Walking over to the fridge, he yanked the door open and took out a cold Corona from the shelf, unscrewing the cap and tossing it at the trash. Scooping up a take-out menu, he wandered into the lounge and collapsed onto a chair, tired and pissed off in equal measure.

He grabbed the remote control from the arm beside him and flicked on the television, taking a long pull of cold beer. The last thing he felt like doing was concentrating on anything right now, but considering what he did for a living, it was important to stay abreast of current affairs.

He also wanted to see if he or anyone he knew had made the headlines.

He flicked onto CNN and took another swig of icy beer, looking at the take-out menu and thinking about what to order. He glanced at the screen again.

And he froze.

The footage was of a small girl leaving an urban Police Department Plaza in what had to be Washington or Philadelphia or maybe New York. She was being moved quickly, escorted fast by a male and female security team, reporters and journalists being kept well back.

The man scanned the banner headline and the images.

Slamming his beer on the table beside him, he jumped up from the chair and rushed across the room, grabbing his cell phone. Dialling a number, he moved back in front of the television and continued watching the screen, at the little girl being ushered towards a blacked-out car.

Someone picked up the other end.

'Yeah?'

'It's me!' the man said hurriedly.

'What is it?'

'You're not going to believe who I'm looking at right now.'

'Who?'

'CNN, right now. *Now!'*

'OK. Hang on.' There was a pause. A shuffling the other end of the line. 'Hurry!'

Another pause.

Then the man the other end came back.

'Holy shit.'

'It's her,' the man said, staring at the screen. 'It's her.'

TWO

'C'mon, push!' 3rd Grade NYPD Detective Josh Blake ordered, standing inside a gym eight days later in New York City. 'Push! Let's see some effort!'

'What do you think this is?' his detective partner hissed through gritted teeth, fighting with a barbell on a bench underneath. The weighted bar in his hands was halfway up but it wasn't moving fast, two hundred and twenty five pounds of nothing but solid metallic resistance.

'Sometime this week would be nice,' Josh said, watching him struggle.

Gritting his teeth, the blond man on the bench eventually locked out his arms and exhaled, the repetition complete. Josh nodded, helping him rack the barbell and the man sat up, wiping sweat off his brow and glancing around.

The gym was an upmarket one, located on the Upper West Side of Manhattan. It was late afternoon on a Sunday but there were still a few people around the place, some working hard on treadmills and stair climbers, others using the weight stations. The cost of a month's membership here equalled the blond man's rent in Queens for the same period, but Josh had paid for the year and was allowed to bring a guest every now and then.

He was a great advertisement for the gym, the fruits of his labours clear in his physique. Black and just turned thirty, Josh was built like a Sherman tank or someone who stood outside a club with his arms folded asking to see some ID.

Despite looking so physically intimidating, he possessed an even temperament and an even cooler head, and was one of the nicest people you could ever hope to meet. He and the blond man on the bench had been NYPD partners for eight months, and had become great friends outside of the Department.

'Getting there,' Josh said.

The other man nodded, rising from the bench, and took a seat on another positioned near the window.

His name was Sam Archer; twenty eight years old, he was also a 3rd Grade Detective and worked with Josh in the NYPD's Counter Terrorism Bureau, a division formed recently in the last couple of years. A hair over six foot and a hundred and eighty five pounds, Archer was blond with blue eyes and had a face that looked more suited to magazine covers than law enforcement, a fact he was constantly ribbed about by his colleagues.

However, like many before them, they'd quickly learned not to judge a book by its cover where he was concerned. He may have looked like a movie star but he was as tough as nails, carving out a damn good reputation in the short time he'd been an NYPD Detective. The two men operated in a five-man field team based out of the CT Bureau's headquarters across the East River in Queens. However, Archer had spent the last three months trapped behind a desk whilst he recovered from a broken ankle and a nasty case of pneumonia after an unexpected hard fall into a freezing river at Christmas.

What had started out as an irritating chesty cough at the beginning of January which he'd ignored had eventually landed him in hospital and being pumped full of antibiotics for two weeks. He'd lost twenty pounds in weight and felt about as strong as a new born puppy once he got back on his feet, not aided by the broken ankle which had complicated his recovery. He'd finally ditched the cast and the crutches five weeks ago, and had been doing intense physiotherapy ever since, working on getting the strength and mobility back in the damaged joint.

Between physio sessions he'd spent much of his spare time in the gym either out in Queens or here under Josh's expert tutelage, trying to get back to full physical health. It had been tough going, but muscle memory had kicked in and he'd regained the weight he'd lost and most of his power. He'd just been assessed and finally cleared for field work again, starting officially tomorrow morning, the best news he'd heard all year. Considering the types of people the Counter Terrorism Bureau were tasked to deal with, he had to be in peak physical condition to do his job. Now, he felt he was pretty much there.

Opening a bottle of water and taking a drink, he watched as Josh slapped an extra plate on each side of the barbell, slid on the clips, then moved around to the bench and lay back. He unracked the bar as if there was nothing on it and started pushing out repetitions, each one controlled and smooth. Archer stayed where he was, watching; Josh didn't need a spot. He'd recently recovered from an injury himself, a gunshot wound to his arm. Josh had always looked as if he'd started life with a barbell in his crib but the bullet he'd taken had forced him to lay off the iron for a while. He'd been hitting it ferociously since he got the green light from the doctor six weeks ago and now looked even bigger than he had before he took the round.

Josh's recovery was ahead of Archer's so he'd already been working on the street for six weeks but he readily admitted that it didn't feel right unless Archer was beside him. He was almost as keen for his partner to return as the man was himself. Archer had been off his feet once before when he'd broken his ankle a couple of years ago at the end of an operation back in the UK when he was a cop in the Armed Response Unit, the premier counter-terrorist task force in London. Back then every day off duty had felt like a week, tedious and boring as hell. This time around had been no different.

Finishing his set, Josh racked the barbell and sat up. Archer suddenly felt a cough coming on and hacked a few times, a deep chesty noise that came straight from the lungs and resonated around the gym, the last remnants of his chest infection. Physical exertion still brought it out every now and then.

A personal trainer nearby paused to look over but Josh caught his eye. The man turned back to his client.

'The cough still bothering you?' Josh asked.

Archer shrugged. 'Not like it used to. How's the arm, Popeye?'

Josh looked down. There was a white scar from the 9mm round, a small silver crescent moon. 'Pretty good,' he said, flexing his considerable

19

bicep. Archer rolled his eyes and coughed again. The trainer looked over again, and this time couldn't bite his tongue.

'C'mon man, this is a gym, not the infirmary,' he said. 'Don't come here sick.'

Another look from Josh sent him a clear message. Archer wiped his forehead with the sleeve of his t-shirt as Josh rose from the bench and walked over to sit beside him, drinking from his own bottle of water.

The two men watched the activity in the gym. Behind them the late afternoon sun poured in through the windows, warming their backs and lighting up the room with a golden glow.

'So is Chalky coming back any time soon?' Josh asked.

Archer grinned. 'I hope not, for both our sakes. I think once a year is enough.'

Chalky was Archer's best friend and an old police teammate in London at the Armed Response Unit. When Archer's ankle was fresh on the mend from the break in December, his friend had shown up on New Year's Eve, unannounced and totally out of the blue. Having never been to the States, he'd insisted on Archer and Josh showing him the city that weekend and they'd ended up partying for almost 72 hours straight.

With Archer's ankle newly immobilised in a cast, Chalky, by means known only to himself, had got his hands on a wheelchair which he'd used to ferry Archer around the bars in the Village. The leader of their five-man detail at the Bureau, Sergeant Matt Shepherd, had been keeping close tabs on the pair's recovery, insisting they eat well, rest up and slowly build their strength. Both of them had agreed they would never mention that particular New Year's weekend to him. Fortunately for the sake of their health and Josh's marriage, Chalky's trip had been a brief one and he'd returned to the UK, threatening to return in the not too distant future. Nevertheless, both men were sad to see him go. He was definitely a one-off.

Archer smiled, thinking of his friend and those three days of mayhem. Beside him, Josh drained his water then looked at the bottle.

'Big day tomorrow.'

Archer nodded. 'I'm nervous. Is that bad?'

'No. No way. Nerves keep us focused. How long has it been, three months?'

Archer nodded. 'Feels like three years.'

He drank some more water as Josh checked his watch.

'Shit, I need to go pick up the kids,' he said. 'Their movie will be ending soon.'

'Which one was it?'

'The new Disney film. Something about a fish. I expect I'm going to hear all about it; ask me again tomorrow and I'll recite the plot.'

Archer grinned, but felt another cough building. He noted the snarky personal trainer watching him, waiting for it to happen.

'Let's get out of here.'

Not far downtown, a tall, grey-haired man peered out of a window through a small gap in a set of shutters. He was on the 3rd floor of an apartment building on Central Park West, just off West 89th

Street. He scanned the area below for anything suspect with a practised and experienced eye.

Activity in the street was routine, cars passing each way, pedestrians enjoying the warm weather, many of them wandering in and out of the Park.

He searched for anyone who seemed suspicious, anyone who looked nervous or out of place. There were always tell-tale signs if you knew what to look out for.

But there was nothing.

Everything seemed fine.

His name was John Foster. Fifty five years old, he was a Chief Deputy US Marshal for the United States Department of Justice. Foster was built like an oak door, six foot four and with the sinewy but thick muscle that only a lifetime of physical activity gives a person. Born and bred in Oklahoma, Foster had grown up on a busy farm and consequently had developed two things: an impeccable work ethic, and a desire to see the world outside of Shawnee. His father had served in the 101st Airborne during the Second World War and his stories from his time in Normandy had painted a picture of a world far beyond the State borders of Oklahoma.

They'd had a direct effect; before his time working for the Department of Justice, Foster had served in the US Army for twenty two years, completing tours in Iraq, Afghanistan, Bosnia and in Gulf One and Two, the Middle Eastern heat giving him a baked leanness that he'd never lost, even since he mustered out. He'd entered the Army as a twenty two year old Private and left a forty four year old Major. He'd been shot almost as many times as he'd been divorced and he was one of the best and most respected guys the DOJ had at their disposal.

The US Marshals service was the oldest Federal law enforcement office in the United States, created way back in 1789. With almost five thousand employees spread out across the country, the Marshals performed a variety of vital tasks, such as hunting down and apprehending wanted fugitives, transporting Federal prisoners, protecting endangered witnesses and managing assets seized from criminal enterprises. Their success rate was outstanding; in 2012, they captured over thirty six thousand Federal fugitives and cleared over thirty nine thousand felony warrants. In eleven years, Foster had either on his own, or with a squad, apprehended over 4,000 criminals on the run, most of them armed and extremely dangerous. Add the captures to his time in the Army and it was one hell of a résumé Foster had.

However, the clock on his career was ticking. Mandatory retirement age for a Federal Marshal was fifty seven. Well aware that he was twenty two months away from that particular milestone, Foster knew many guys his age in the Service were either already retired or very much looking forward to it, a chance to put their feet up and go on long vacations, finally fully enjoy a life outside work and reap the rewards of their well-padded pension funds.

But Foster would never willingly retire, not until they packed up his desk for him and marched him out of the DOJ Headquarters or lowered him into the ground inside a wooden box. He'd spent his life facing off against an enemy, from his early days in the school yard in Shawnee, through the plains of the Middle East, all the way to the last eleven years as a US Marshal.

It was the reason he was looking through this particular window in this particular apartment on this particular evening. He didn't know how to live any other way, something his trio of ex-wives had never known how to deal with.

Relax wasn't a word in John Foster's dictionary.

Neither was *surrender*.

As a Chief Deputy, Foster led a small team that had a damn good reputation as a direct consequence of the work they'd done for the DOJ. He insisted on the highest of standards; he expected his two guys to maintain peak physical fitness, never smoke and carry two handguns with them at all times, including off duty. Hits had been ordered on Federal Marshals in the past and Foster knew there wasn't an agent in the Service who could ever be certain their name wasn't on a similar list. The Marshal issue sidearm was a Glock 22 or 23 handgun, a dependable modern pistol with seventeen rounds in the magazine, but that was Foster's back up. He was old school and liked the old school weapons. He carried a Smith and Wesson .44 six shooter in a shoulder holster that was more field cannon than handgun, but it matched his personality to a tee. If people were guns, Foster would be the .44 Magnum; seasoned, resilient, tough as a cactus in the desert and just as prickly. The younger Marshals preferred the semi-automatics, citing the increased quantity of ammunition and rate of fire as the reason why, but Foster couldn't be swayed. .44 Magnums didn't jam and also packed some serious firepower; he was fairly sure he could put down a charging rhino with the handgun if he had to.

Turning from the shutters, he opened a bottle of water and took a sip. Staying hydrated in the field was important, although too much fluid intake meant bathroom breaks and moments of vulnerability. Given his days in the military and on long patrols, Foster had it down to a science. He could sip on water all day and only have to use the bathroom once in the evening, a skill which was especially vital for witness protection. Turning his back for just one instant was an opportunity for someone to get to the target.

Foster knew the kind of people they were dealing with on this particular operation.

They were the type who would only need seconds to get the job done.

The 3rd floor Central Park-facing apartment he was standing in had been hired out by the DOJ. He looked at the four other people in the room with him, each keeping themselves occupied. Two of them were his men, US Deputy Marshals Jack Carson and Jared Barlow. Carson was sitting at the kitchen table facing Foster, Barlow across the room to the left and opening up a brown bag of fast food he'd just picked up from down the street. Both of them had a shoulder holster holding a Glock and a pancake holster on their right hip carrying a Heckler and Koch USP and two spare clips.

Foster had worked with Carson for five years and Barlow for four. Being together much of the time meant he'd got to know the two men as if they were family; he knew them inside out. Like any family, they shared some similarities and many differences. Both men were in their early thirties and now unmarried, both were dark-featured, handsome guys and both were pretty damn good at what they did.

However, their temperaments were polar opposites, just like the positive and negative signs on a battery. Carson was a light-hearted guy, never slow to crack a joke or a smile, able to lighten the mood on any occasion no matter how serious. Barlow had a much sourer disposition and complained like a landlord with late rent, but Foster didn't suffer fools. He wouldn't have had him around unless he could get shit done which was why he was on his team.

Nevertheless, Foster had pulled Barlow to one side about a month ago and told him his attitude needed to change; interestingly, the talk seemed to have had an effect. On this operation he'd been much better, even making a few jokes which had been followed by periods of complete silence, Foster and Carson staring at him, stunned. The jokes hadn't been funny but hell, for him it was a start.

The trio had either chased down on their own or assisted on 998 warrants and had protected 17 State witnesses from some of the most dangerous people not only in the United States but also from abroad. Many of the people the Marshals service guarded were involved in the drug trade in some capacity, and the cartels they were betraying would go to hideously violent lengths to ensure their silence. Foster, Carson and Barlow were all in impressive physical shape; they knew how each other thought and how they would each react to a situation, like an NFL quarterback who could pass a ball to his wide receivers without even looking. Hesitation equalled death in their world. Foster couldn't work with someone he couldn't totally rely on. For that reason alone, he'd let Barlow complain as he so often liked to do before he'd sorted out his act. He'd stick with a guy he could trust implicitly over someone he didn't know well ten times out of ten, even if the guy in question could be a pain in the ass.

As the thought crossed his mind, he flicked his eyes over to the third member of his group. She was female, twenty seven years old, with black hair, brown eyes and tanned light brown skin. She was carrying one handgun, not two.

Her name was Deputy Marshal Alice Vargas.

On operations like this, Foster, Carson and Barlow always worked as a three and none of them felt any real empathy towards the newcomer. When he'd been presented with this case, Foster had flat out refused to take on an extra Marshal; to work on a job of this nature you needed to know and trust the team beside you one hundred per cent. One mistake or lapse in judgement could get everyone killed and none of them felt like being saddled with extra weight, especially a hundred and eighteen pound inexperienced woman still in her twenties.

After doing some digging around, Foster had discovered she was also fresh out of the Marshals Academy, which he really wasn't happy with; not on a task like this. *It's too soon for her,* he told his superior, Deputy Supervisor James Dalton.

He'd been vehement in his opposition. Many people would have viewed Foster's attitude as abrasive and unnecessarily hostile but he'd spent his entire adult life either in the army being shot at or chasing down some of the most wanted criminals in the country. It didn't encourage the warm and fuzzy approach and he sure as hell wasn't going to risk people's lives by sparing this girl's feelings. Trust and experience were like solid gold in these parts.

Hurt feelings could recover. Hurt physical bodies, not so much.

He'd aired his concerns and displeasure at Vargas joining his team when he'd been assigned the case but he'd been told bluntly to shut up and put up. Given the person they were protecting, Dalton felt a female presence was mandatory and ordered Foster to deal with it and ask no further questions.

He shifted his gaze from Vargas and looked over at the last member of the group. She was a seven year old girl named Jennifer who was sitting at the table playing with Carson and Vargas, her feet hanging down from the chair and swinging as she concentrated. Spending prolonged time with some witnesses was like having a tooth gradually pulled, but Foster had spent the last eight days with the girl and had been surprised to find it wasn't the chore he expected. Some people were born more resilient than others and despite being a kid, the girl certainly had that strength of spirit in spades. She didn't whine, she didn't complain and she'd adjusted to her new situation quickly. She was only upset occasionally, and that was where

Vargas stepped in, comforting her and distracting her, calming the child down.

He watched her playing, using some kind of make-up as she painted Carson's face with a brush. She seemed happy enough. *I wonder what's going on under the surface though,* he thought. Foster had witnessed post-traumatic stress disorder a number of times. He'd suffered a bout of it himself after his first tour in the Gulf in '91, and was something that had taken all of his mental strength to defeat. He'd learned early how dangerous and unforgettably gruesome life could be on the frontline and he knew a number of soldiers, some of them good friends of his, who'd returned from combat and never shaken that thousand-yard stare, a look only people who'd witnessed some terrible things possessed.

He recognised the tell-tale signs; often they could be delayed, triggered by the strangest of things, but so far the disorder hadn't seemed to have manifested itself in the girl. Children's imaginations meant they could often filter things in a way adults couldn't, protecting them and cushioning them from the brutal realities of life. Foster had four kids himself, all boys, who were grown up now and living their own lives. He liked children; they were innocent. Having spent most of his life engaged with people who represented the worst side of human nature, he found a child's perspective of the world refreshing. Untainted. Honest.

As the thought crossed his mind, his eyes narrowed.

The same couldn't be said for the people hunting her.

She'd been placed in protective custody as a standard precaution, but particular measures were being taken on this operation considering who she was. There was bound to be a large street bounty on her head and there would be people out there right now trying to claim it. However, Foster had the upper hand. He, his team and the girl could be in any city in the United States and the five boroughs of New York City alone covered 468 square miles, with over eight million people living in them.

It was conceivable that the men after the child had guessed Foster wouldn't want to travel too far and would go to ground, remaining in their own back yard. However, Manhattan was a big place, full of tall buildings and apartment complexes with a sea of people, not to mention the possibility that they could be hiding out somewhere in The Bronx, Queens, Brooklyn or Staten Island. A concrete maze of potential hiding places. One small girl amongst eight million people; a true needle in a haystack. If you knew what you were doing, it was pretty easy to hide out in New York.

If you were as experienced as Foster, you could just disappear.

Across the room, sitting in his chair, Barlow had finished some fries and was now eating a burger out of a greasy wrapper, his leg jiggling out of boredom and pent-up energy, not enjoying being cooped up inside. They were all dressed in casual clothes, jeans, t-shirts and shirts to cover the holsters on their hips and around their shoulders. Vargas was sitting beside the child and talking with her while she worked on Carson.

Something she said made the girl giggle. Even though he didn't know or fully trust her, Foster had to admit that having the woman as part of his team for the last eight days had been helpful. She'd struck up a real rapport with the child in a way neither he nor Barlow or Carson could have done. She was also in charge of the girl's medication; Jennifer was epileptic and needed to take some tablets each morning and night, a process Vargas ensured happened right on schedule.

She'd stepped out earlier to collect some things from CVS to entertain the kid and the girl was now using whatever Vargas had picked up on Carson, giving him a makeover. Across the table, he had his eyes closed, patiently waiting as she applied makeup to his face, her brow furrowed in concentration.

Foster shook his head and hid a smile; Carson looked ridiculous, the small powdery brush catching in the stubble on his cheeks, glitter around his eyes. However, it was keeping the child occupied so he didn't intrude or say anything.

Considering everything she'd been through in the past few weeks, any moment she was happy was a good one.

He shot his cuff and checked his Tag. *1745.* They were due to drive to a safe house in Spokane, Virginia shortly, getting the girl out of the city. They'd only been in New York for the past three days but despite it being a great place to go to ground, Foster had a bad feeling in his gut which life and experience had taught him to never ignore. He was looking forward to getting out of Manhattan; it was probably safe here, but it was claustrophobic and was also the stomping ground of the men who would be hunting the girl. According to official protocol, Foster and his team were scheduled to head to a DOJ place in Baltimore tonight but Foster was calling an audible and taking the girl to a safe house no-one other than he knew about. Aside from the fact there had been leaks inside the Service before and people had been killed as a result, this was the first time in his career that Foster had protected a child; it was making him extra cautious. He often did this, going off grid with a witness.

That was why he was so good at his job. That was why he'd survived for so long.

Apart from Carson and Barlow, he didn't trust anybody.

In a car on the Park-side of the street below, two men sat side by side in the front seats in silence, facing uptown. Dressed in baggy jeans and loose tops, they were both armed with steel handguns, held low against their thighs, full magazines slotted into the base of each weapon.

The guy behind the wheel was lean, brown-skinned and tall, with thick blond dreadlocks hanging down his back and over his shoulders. He was currently the lead suspect in three city homicides without sufficient evidence to charge, and had committed almost a dozen others that the NYPD had no idea he was connected to.

He was the leader.

His name was Braeten.

He didn't view himself as a murderer per se. He was more of a problem solver, willing to do work that others couldn't either out of fear, or for moral reasons. He didn't suffer from either, so if you wanted someone gone, he and his four other guys would make it happen for the right price. He'd been hired by a variety of clients in the past; city gangs, the Mob, cartels. Even a businessman who was screwing some guy's wife and wanted her husband out of the picture for good.

New York was a city built on competition, money and greed, which meant there would always be a call for teams like Braeten's. Somewhere in the five boroughs, there was always someone who wanted someone else killed.

That was where Braeten and his crew came in.

He'd have preferred to get this particular job done indoors, out of sight and at close quarters. Manhattan was always crawling with cops and the people they were dealing with here were trained professionals, armed and more than prepared. They also needed surprise on their side; trying to force entry against this group wouldn't work. They'd be ready for that. Also, they'd be checking the street constantly. If Braeten and his crew walked into the apartment building they might as well have rung ahead and scheduled an appointment.

He'd settled on an ambush in the street. Not ideal, but the best they could do given the circumstances and timescale. They'd have to get it done hard and fast, and be gone before the pigs showed up. Eye witnesses would be plentiful but Braeten was planning to lay low and get out of New York for a while anyway. He could certainly afford it now after the down-payment he'd received for this gig.

He glanced at the pistol in his hand, resting against his thigh. He'd wanted some heavier fire power, something automatic like an Uzi or an assault rifle, but he'd only been called twenty four hours ago which had left him little time to sufficiently prepare. Even from a short distance, handguns required aim and precision; considering three of his team were prolific cocaine abusers, they'd have to get up close and personal to be accurate. Normally, that wasn't a problem, the killings taking place in tight proximity, often with a blade or a bat or a length of wire. This time, however, it could well be.

Beside him, right on cue, he heard a snort and saw the guy beside him taking a quick upper from a key. He had a small open bag on his lap, full of shitty low grade powder, and the end of the key was dusty white. They all normally did some before a job, getting psyched and pumped up. Today, Braeten was giving it a miss.

'Hey,' he said. 'Save it for later.'

The guy ignored him and did another, snorting the cocaine and recoiling as it hit his sinuses.

'Asshole. I said cut it out.'

'Relax.'

Braeten swallowed down his anger and looked up at the apartment across the street, focusing on the task at hand.

He saw the shutters move again.

He swallowed in anticipation, tightening his grip on the pistol by his thigh.

I know you're in there, he thought.

And he also knew they'd be coming out soon.

THREE

Eleven blocks uptown, Archer and Josh walked out of the gym on West 100ᵗʰ, the doors sliding apart, the dance music and cool air conditioning replaced by musky city heat and the sound of traffic.

Checking the time again, Josh patted Archer on the shoulder. 'See you tomorrow.'

Archer nodded. 'Take it easy.'

Watching Josh head across the street towards his car, Archer stayed where he was for a moment, enjoying the scenery around him.

From where he was standing, facing south, he could see the long path of Central Park West, heading all the way down towards the low West 60 Streets. The sun was sinking towards the horizon but the air was still charged with warmth, the concrete absorbing all the heat from the day and releasing it back into the air come dusk and nightfall. Archer had changed out of his gym gear and was wearing blue jeans and a white t-shirt under a red and white flannel shirt, a pair of black and white Converse sneakers on his feet, a bag slung over his shoulder containing his workout clothes.

Sliding a set of sunglasses over his nose, he made a decision. At the time it seemed so inconsequential.

Later, his thoughts on that would change.

He decided to take a walk.

He crossed the street and headed south, Central Park to his immediate left, vehicles passing each way to his right. Feeling the last of the sun for the day on him, he smiled, rolling his sleeves up towards his elbows. He was a sucker for warm weather and was one of those people who could get a tan in a couple of hours. He was already sporting a bronze tone that many would pay damn good money for, but the walk was for more than just soaking up some rays.

He'd been using every opportunity he'd had lately to build strength both in his right leg and also his lungs. He felt pretty good, full of oxygenated blood from his workout, but tired. Being bedridden with pneumonia and on crutches for so long had until very recently left him feeling weak and feeble, two words that no-one would ever normally associate with him. Like most people his age he took his robust health and stamina for granted; having had it taken from him for a brief period, he was more than grateful to have it back.

Just as the thought crossed his mind, some dust caught in his throat and he coughed again.

Well, almost back.

He hadn't been a detective in New York for long, less than a year in fact. He'd arrived here at the beginning of last summer, having just left the task force of the ARU, a senior counter terrorist police team in London. His mother was English but his father was American and had been a cop here himself when Archer was a kid. Although both of them were now gone, Archer had always been curious about what it would be like to work for the NYPD, whether it would match up to all those stories he'd heard as a boy. Last May, he'd packed his bags to find out once and for all, and with a stroke of good luck and timing, his old boss Cobb and the head of the Counter Terrorism Bureau, Jim Franklin, had worked out a deal. An NYPD detective had headed across the Atlantic to the ARU, serving as an extra set of eyes and tripwire for the Department. In return, Archer had joined the NYPD as a 3rd Grade Detective once he passed the training programme in Georgia.

Almost a year into the experience, it had definitely been a journey. Looking at the Park to his left, his mind was filled with memories.

Some of them were more pleasant than others.

He'd collected a fair few scars and broken several bones since he'd first signed up for police training ten years ago, not to mention coming face to face with suicide bombers, bank robbers, Special Forces soldiers and Neo-Nazi terrorists to name but a few. His personal life had been equally turbulent, his parents long gone and no woman in his life staying around for long, unable to adjust to his work patterns and the fact that right now his job always came first.

The only real family he had left was a sister who lived in DC and she lived a structured and regular existence as a lawyer. It was certainly a long way and very different life from his, which seemed to be just the way she liked it.

At only twenty eight years old, Sam Archer had definitely been through his share, more than a lot of men his age. However, despite the toll it had taken on his personal life and the injuries he'd sustained, he loved his job; he knew without a doubt that it was what he was meant to do. Being aware of that gave him comfort during times when things weren't so easy, when he felt a loneliness that he found hard to shake. Out here, he'd started a new life but it was one that sometimes felt isolated. He'd had a good thing going at the ARU, working with his best friend Chalky and a score of other men and women he'd do almost anything for.

Leaving all that behind was proving harder than he thought it would be.

Nevertheless, he couldn't complain. He worked in a Bureau which many police officers in New York would give their front teeth to join. He was almost back to his peak physical fitness, having survived ordeals that by all accounts should have killed him. All that personal stuff could wait. Life was pretty damn good.

He wandered on and glanced at a street sign to his right. *West 91st.* He loved the Upper West Side. Apart from the convenient fact that you could walk all the way down Park West to Columbus Circle totally uninterrupted aside from one street crossing, every neighbourhood in New York had its own personality and up here it was one of relaxed affluence. You didn't live in these parts unless you were doing seriously well in life. There was no frantic hustle as there was in Midtown, none of the suited bustling or jostling that surrounded you in the Financial District, no claustrophobic mayhem like in Chinatown. If Manhattan was a sports game, this part of the city would be the time-out zone.

It was an idyllic place to take a stroll; with the setting sun bathing the area in an orange glow, it was too good not to stop to take a seat and make the most of the last warmth of the day. Archer glanced at his Casio. *5:47 pm.* He was in no rush.

Anyway, he could hop on a train to Queens and get home in half an hour. Shower, grab some dinner, then get a good night's sleep before the big day tomorrow.

There was a hot dog stand just ahead to his left. He approached it and ordered a can of Sprite that came straight from the ice box. Paying the man and thanking him, he took a seat on an empty bench and laid his bag beside him, his back to Central Park.

In front of him, the streets were busy without being crowded. People were walking past in each direction, all of them relaxed, talking with companions, enjoying the last few hours of Sunday 24th March. He saw different ethnicities and clothes, guys in t-shirts, women wearing summer dresses three months ahead of time. He pushed his sunglasses onto his head, then pulled the ring on the cold can and took a long refreshing drink, leaning back.

Tomorrow he'd be doing field work for the first time this year. His recovery should have taken longer but he'd worked as hard as he could, fighting his way back to full fitness and shaving a couple of weeks off the expected timeline.

The thought of getting back out there gave his stomach another jolt of nervous energy but he grinned to himself.

Damn, he'd missed that feeling.

Finally, I'm back, he thought.

Up in the 3rd floor apartment across the street, Foster used his forefinger to part the shutters a fraction and look out of the window again.

Down below, activity still looked routine. Cars were parked on either side of the road, traffic moving both ways past them, people using the sidewalks, the atmosphere just about as relaxed as a Sunday afternoon in a city could be.

He noticed that a young blond guy had just taken a seat on a bench across the street near a Sabrett hot dog stand. The man looked chilled out and was drinking a soda. He had a bag beside him which Foster focused on, watching to see if the guy had his hand hovering near the zip.

Examining the loose body language, he realised the guy wasn't a threat.

If he was waiting for Foster and his team to bring out the girl, there'd be signs of tension or anticipation.

Shifting his attention from the man, he scanned the rest of the street one last time. It looked safe.

He turned from the window.

'Time to go.'

His team nodded. Barlow rolled up the wrapper from his burger, tossing it in the trash, then rose and pulled a shirt over his t-shirt, covering the Glock and holster around his shoulders and the USP, cuffs and Marshal's badge on his hip. Vargas started clearing up all the stuff on the table, pulling on her own shirt and helping Jennifer down.

Foster looked at Carson, who rose from his chair. He had make-up and fairy dust all over his face; the girl had given him a complete makeover. He looked like a Disney princess with hormonal problems.

Carson saw the expression on Foster's face and didn't need to qualify for Mensa to interpret it.

'I'll go wash my face.'

'Good idea.'

In the car ten feet from the hot dog stand, the two guys watching the apartment had just seen the shutters flicker again.

Braeten glanced at the time on the dashboard clock.

5:50 pm.

'Get ready.'

The man beside him nodded and took one last hit of coke. As he sealed the bag and stuffed it in his pocket, Braeten took out his cell phone with his free hand and dialled a number. Trapping the phone between his ear and shoulder, he pulled the slide on his handgun back, loading a round into the chamber.

Beside him, the other man did the same, his leg jiggling with cocaine-fuelled anticipation, getting fired up.

The call connected.

'Get ready,' Braeten said. 'They'll be out any minute.'

FOUR

Everyone has instincts.

Most are there for our survival, like anticipating danger. Others are more superficial, like hearing a phone ring and knowing who's calling before you pick it up. Many can't be explained, like sensing when you are being watched.

But being a cop for almost a decade sharpens these instincts.

Very often they make the difference between life and death.

And that meant despite being totally relaxed, Archer saw the gun in the man's hand before anyone else on the street.

The guy carrying it looked about nineteen or twenty, Hispanic, dressed in baggy jeans with a stringy white vest hanging off his shoulders. He'd just stepped out of a car on Archer's side of the street, about fifteen feet away, and was headed across the road in a break in the traffic. The man's hand was tucked against the side of his thigh.

The black handgun was nestled by his hamstring against the baggy jeans.

Above the pistol, the man's wiry arm was tense, the sinews and muscles pronounced and hardened. His body was pumped full of adrenaline and probably something else. Beside him was another guy wearing the same kind of jeans, brown-skinned with thick blond dreadlocks and wearing a grey t-shirt instead of a vest. He'd climbed out on the driver's side, slamming the door. Archer couldn't see a gun in his hand but he made out the tell-tale shape in the back of the waistband of his jeans.

They were walking with intent and purpose, moving fast across the road.

Someone was about to get killed.

In that split-second, Archer flicked his eyes ahead of the pair.

On the other side of the street was a black 4x4 Tahoe pulled up to the kerb, facing downtown. Three men, a woman and a small child were climbing into the car. All five were dressed similarly in casual clothes but didn't have the look of a family. One of the men was older, a big guy with short-cut grey hair, and the other two were about twenty years younger with dark looks but no family resemblance. The woman had a light-brown complexion and long black hair.

The child was a little girl, maybe six or seven.

She was being helped into the car. It seemed the two younger men would be sitting either side of her, one of them already around the road side of the car and reaching for the handle. The woman was on the kerb-side, climbing into the front passenger seat.

The grey-haired guy was reaching for the handle of the driver's seat, this side of the vehicle.

Archer was already on his feet, leaving his gym bag and drink on the bench.

He reached to his hip instinctively but all his hand met was shirt fabric and jean. *Shit*; he'd left his Department issue Sig Sauer P226 at home

43

with his badge. He always liked to be prepared but hadn't thought he'd need a pistol for the gym.

The two men with guns were halfway across the street.

Then the guy on the right suddenly raised his pistol as the dreadlocked man drew his.

'Look out!' Archer shouted.

The group at the car heard him and turned.

They reacted fast. They all ducked for cover save for one of the younger men, the guy climbing into the backseat, who was the road side of the car and had nothing to protect him.

He swung round to face the threat, but it was already too late.

The sinewy gunman in the white vest fired. The round hit the man in the torso and knocked him back; he thudded into the Tahoe and slumped to the road.

The gunman fired twice more erratically, working the trigger fast, smashing two windows on the car. The gunshots echoed around the street; people started running for cover, many of them screaming, the peace and quiet of the neighbourhood suddenly shattered.

As traffic screeched to a halt around him, Archer ran towards the two gunmen. They'd heard his shout and swung round, raising their pistols. Archer veered to the right and threw himself behind a car that had just stopped his side of the road, his sunglasses falling off his head to the ground. As he went down, he saw one of the two gunmen suddenly get punched off his feet, blood spraying into the air as a huge gunshot echoed around the street.

He pitched back to the concrete, dead, his weapon spilling out of his hand and clattering onto the road.

Archer looked over the front of the car and saw the grey-haired man holding a large six-shooter in his hand, kneeling by the front of the Tahoe. The other gunman, the guy with blond dreadlocks, had already gone for cover behind a pulled-up car and the grey-haired man fired twice more, just missing him and blowing out a front tyre on the car he'd taken refuge behind, the driver ducking down in terror.

Scrambling to his feet, Archer started running across the road, making a beeline towards the man by the car who'd been shot. He saw the guy with the .44 swing it in his direction, pointing the weapon straight at him. Archer stopped in his tracks, putting his hands up.

'*NYPD!*' he shouted.

After a moment's pause, he took a chance and moved forward, keeping his hands up, desperate to get to the wounded man and help him. The grey-haired man didn't fire, possibly because he could see Archer wasn't carrying, probably because the guy with dreadlocks had just fired back. He shifted his aim back in the direction of the immediate threat and squeezed off another round, the huge *crack* echoing around the surrounding buildings over the screams.

Archer arrived by the gunshot victim. He had dark hair, freshly wetted, and looked in his early thirties; bizarrely, Archer noticed he had some kind of glitter or dust on his neck and collar. Both his hands were clutching his torso, blood staining his shirt and soaking through his fingers, his eyes

45

wide with shock, his breathing ragged as the sounds of screams filled the street. The dark-haired woman and the other younger man had already bundled the girl into the car, pushing her to the floor and jumping in after her, one on each side, keeping her low and forming a protective shield either side.

The grey-haired man who'd killed the gunman in the vest squeezed off another round then moved over to join Archer and the wounded man, keeping his weapon trained on the car providing cover for the man with dreadlocks. He had short, buzz cut grey hair and had the lean, sinewy toughness that screamed ex-military.

He glanced at the wounded man quickly, assessing his condition.

'Hang on, Carson,' he said. 'That's an order.'

Suddenly there were more gunshots and one of the windows above them smashed, showering the trio with glass.

'Shit!'

Archer turned and saw three more men with guns had appeared from downtown, moving up the middle of the street. Each was carrying a pistol and had appeared out of nowhere. They were all dressed in jeans and dirty tops like the other two, part of the same crew.

This wasn't a car-jacking.

This was an orchestrated ambush.

The grey-haired man raised his Smith and Wesson and fired back, forcing the advancing trio to take cover, the deafening echo of the weapon firing filling the street. By now, every member of the public was hiding behind something or lying as low as they could on the ground as bullets hit cars, the echoes of the shots reverberating off the buildings.

Archer tore open the back door of the Tahoe; the man and woman reached over and grabbed the wounded man, hauling him across their seat by his collar. The girl in the footwell still had her hands over her ears and looked up in terror at the wounded man as he was dragged in beside her. More gunfire smashed the remaining intact window above them and the group jerked down instinctively, the little girl screaming.

Archer slammed the door. The grey-haired man had maintained his fire, pinning down the gunmen whilst climbing into the driver's seat. Squeezing off a sixth round, he ducked in and fired the engine, pulling his door shut.

On the road side of the car, Archer was already unprotected. Once the Tahoe left, he'd be target practice for the quartet of gunmen. The grey-haired man saw the situation.

'Get in!' he shouted.

Archer didn't need to be told twice, racing around the car and jumping into the front passenger seat. Before he'd shut his door, the grey-haired man beside him floored it, the tyres squealing as the Tahoe jerked forwards.

They pulled a fast U-turn in the middle of the street and took off uptown.

Dragging his door shut and staying low, bullets smashing into the rear windshield and riddling the 4x4, Archer sneaked a glance behind them and saw the trio of gunmen piling into a car, the man with long blond dreadlocks moving out from his cover and racing to join them.

They were already giving chase before their doors had shut.

FIVE

The grey-haired guy drove like a wheelman. He weaved in and out of traffic, torching his way uptown, streets and landmarks flashing past on both sides. The gunfire had smashed out two windows and put holes in all the others, and wind whistled through the car as they burned up the Upper West Side. The Tahoe was a big vehicle but he handled it expertly, avoiding other cars by a hair's breadth.

West 94th, 96th, 98th. West 100th.

Archer checked behind them and could see the pursuing car keeping pace, the four guys visible inside. Their driver was nowhere near as proficient as the man beside Archer and they smashed into vehicles as they forced their way through, unaware and uncaring of anyone in their way.

However, they were staying with them.

'Who the hell are you?' the grey-haired man shouted at Archer, putting his foot down.

'NYPD.'

'Show me a badge!'

'Watch the road!' Archer shouted, pointing.

The grey-haired man swerved around a truck emerging from a side street and accelerated forward, pushing the horn and cutting a red light, pedestrians leaping back as the car scorched past just inches from them. They were now in the triple digits; he cut a hard left down Cathedral Parkway and then turned right onto Amsterdam

Avenue, the streets ticking past, West 104th, West 106th, 108th, 110th.

'Hang in there, Carson!' the grey-haired man shouted, his giant hands wrapped tightly around the wheel as they raced on, approaching Harlem.

Archer twisted in his seat and saw the wounded man, Carson, in the back. He was lying across the third man and dark-haired woman, blood all over his hands and staining his white t-shirt. He'd been shot in the stomach and his body was contorted in pain, his eyes as wide as saucers as he stared up at the interior of the roof in shock.

They roared on up the street, the streets flashing by, moving further and further uptown. There was a screech of tyres as the pursuing car kept up behind them, right on their tail. They couldn't shake them.

Suddenly there was a *Bam* and a wheeze as one of the Tahoe's tyres blew out, a gunshot echoing in the street. The grey-haired man fought with the wheel but the car starting drifting unresponsively to the left. There was another *Bam* as another tyre was hit and they slammed hard into a fire hydrant, throwing everyone in the car forward, Carson coughing in pain and the little girl yelping in the rear footwell.

The ruptured hydrant started spraying water into the air and onto the front of the vehicle, people around them on the street stopping momentarily, shocked at the sudden crash.

The grey-haired man tried the ignition frantically but the 4x4 wouldn't start.

They were stuck.

'Shit!'

There was the screech of the pursuing car pulling up.

'Everybody out!' the grey-haired man shouted, pushing open his door.

Archer climbed over to the driver's side, diving out after him, and crouched down behind the 4x4. He saw the driver pull a second weapon from a pancake holster on his belt, a Glock. As the man and woman in the back started to manoeuvre themselves, the child and Carson out of the wrecked Tahoe, their driver started to fire over the bonnet, the four gunmen diving down behind their own car as passers-by screamed and ran for cover. The uninjured younger man drew his own pistol and joined the grey-haired guy firing from behind the 4x4.

The woman pulled the child and then Carson out of the car who was clutching his belly, his face twisted in agony. The four gunmen were gathered behind their vehicle, the Glock fire smashing out the windows, shell casings rattling and bouncing onto the concrete. The street around them started to clear as drivers braked hard and reversed fast, pedestrians flat on the ground or scrabbling for safety behind any form of cover.

The enemy gunmen started to return fire, the pace of it increasing dramatically, bullets ripping into the Tahoe and forcing them all down behind it, spraying them with smashed glass as the remaining pieces of window were destroyed. One of the gunmen had an assault rifle.

As bullets smashed into the car, tearing it to pieces, the group sheltering behind it looked at each other. They were pinned down, one of them

51

was already hit and the Tahoe wasn't going to last long under that kind of firepower.

If they stayed where they were, the enemy assault rifle would shred them apart like a wood-chipper.

Their only option was to retreat.

Turning, Archer saw there was a tall tenement building behind them, just past the corner of West 135th.

The grey-haired man squeezed off two rounds, then looked over his shoulder and saw the block too.

'Fall back!' he shouted, jerking his head at the entrance of the building. *'Get inside!'*

Staying low behind the vehicle, Archer grabbed Carson under his armpits and pulled him backwards towards the door as the other two men rose and fired at their pursuers, pinning them down behind the other car.

The dark-haired woman scooped up the small girl and followed Archer quickly, who'd made it to the entrance.

Pushing the handle down with his elbow, Archer kicked the door back and dragged Carson inside, the gunfight in front of them intensifying as their attackers saw what they were doing and tried to take them out before they had a chance to get inside the building.

The grey-haired man returned rapid fire with the Glock, then snatched a quick glance over his shoulder. Seeing the door behind them was open, he shouted to the uninjured man beside him.

'Barlow, move!'

The two men edged back, keeping up their fire, and stumbled inside, bullets kicking up brick dust around the entrance as they fell into the large lobby. The grey-haired guy recovered quickly, rolling to his feet, then reached forward and twisted the lock. The moment he did, one of the windows next to the door was blown out, causing him to recoil, the glass spraying into the air and cutting his face.

Behind him, there was an elevator in the middle of the large lobby. Archer was desperately pushing the button but nothing was happening.

'Shit!'

He knew they didn't have long.

The dark-haired woman saw the elevator wasn't coming, and without a word she pulled open a door on the left and ran into a stairwell. Archer bent down and hoisted Carson into a fireman's carry, then moved to the stairs and followed the woman as she took the lead, holding the girl's hand who was running alongside her.

As they headed up the flights, Archer heard thumping at the door in the lobby as the gunmen tried to force their way in. The pounding was matching the speed of his heart rate; although he was just about back to full fitness, he was carrying a grown man on his shoulders up a flight of stairs, having just come from a strenuous workout at the gym and been in the midst of a savage gunfight with no weapon.

Another burst of adrenaline kicked in and he followed the woman and child, the other two men bringing up the rear, Carson's weight draped across his shoulders.

They'd just made it to 5 when they heard the door downstairs give way and smash open. The dark-haired woman immediately ducked through the open door to the floor and ran down the corridor, still holding the girl's hand tightly.

She came to a halt outside a random apartment and knocked frantically, looking back at the way she'd come.

No-one opened up.

She turned and desperately pounded on another door across the hall. At the same time, a door behind Archer opened, on the south-east corner of the building. A middle-aged, comely-looking woman looked out, having heard the commotion. She looked shocked when she saw Carson lying across Archer's shoulders, clearly wounded and in bad shape.

The dark-haired woman saw her and immediately ran back to where she was standing, pushing her way inside the apartment past the female resident without waiting for an invitation. The other woman didn't try to stop her and stood back, confused but not objecting, still staring at Carson.

Hearing feet pounding up the stairwell, Archer glanced quickly back from where they'd just come and saw with relief that they hadn't left a blood trail. Most of Carson's blood was on his shirt, or now on him, warm and wet on his front and side.

He and the other two men didn't waste a second, following the woman and child into the apartment.

The moment they were all inside, the grey-haired man quickly pushed the door shut behind him and locked it.

Seconds later, two of the gunmen appeared on the 5th floor corridor, panting, each holding a pistol, their eyes and movements jerky and hyped up.

They checked up the stairwell and down the corridor but there was no sign of the group.

They'd disappeared.

'Shit!' one of them said, kicking the wall.

Behind them, Braeten and the man with the AK-47 raced into view. Taking some deep breaths, Braeten stood and stared down the corridor. It had a door at the front, but it had been jammed open with a wedge, revealing the length of hallway all the way to another stairwell on the other side of the building. There was music and noise coming from some of the apartments, the residents unaware of what was happening.

'Did they go down here?' Braeten asked.

'I don't know. Just missed them. Could be up a level.'

'I'll check it,' the man with the AK47 said, pushing the magazine release catch and reaching into a bag across his shoulders. He pulled out a fresh clip and slapped it into the weapon, pulling the cocking handle.

'When the hell did you get that?' Braeten asked, looking at the rifle.

'This morning.'

'Good. Go put it to use.'

The other three turned and ran back into the stairwell, heading up to the next floor.

Watching them go, Braeten pulled his cell phone and dialled a number, looking down the 5th floor corridor. Two Broadway-side doors had opened, residents peering out after hearing the commotion, but they shut quickly when they saw the man with blond dreadlocks and the pistol in his hand. He saw that none of them were the Marshals but they'd be hiding, not opening doors and peering out.

Turning, Braeten moved into the stairwell, waiting for the call to connect. This wasn't good. Hawking and spitting, he cursed, pissed off and thirsty for blood. What just went down was a disaster. He never left contracts unfulfilled; a reliable reputation was essential in his line of work.

And considering the clients he had, failure meant he could easily be joining those he'd been assigned to kill.

He headed back down the stairs, deciding to check the 4th floor.

Wherever they were hiding, the group would probably be thinking they'd got away and were safe.

But this was only just getting started.

SIX

Inside the apartment to the immediate right of the stairwell, the group were standing back from the door, all of them breathing hard from exertion and anxiety as they stared at the wooden frame, listening, waiting.

Three handguns were trained on the wood; if someone tried to get in, it would be the last thing they ever did.

They waited.

No-one came.

Momentarily satisfied the gunmen weren't about to burst in, Archer tore his gaze from the door and looked behind him.

The wounded man, Carson, was flat on his back on the floor and writhing in agony, his head in the dark-haired woman's lap who had one hand on his brow and the other holding her pistol, aimed at the door. Blood was spread all over the front of Carson's white t-shirt, his eyes screwed tight, his teeth gritted together as shock wore off and pain kicked in.

Standing beside them were the small girl and the unwounded man from the car. The man was watching the door whilst the girl watched Carson, her face pale, tears in her eyes.

The owner of the apartment was a middle-aged slightly faded blonde. She was dressed in an old pair of jeans and a grey, long-sleeved t-shirt with the logo of some baseball team on the front. She was standing to one side, staring at the group who'd invaded her space but particularly at the wounded man bleeding out on her floor.

However, she wasn't making a fuss or more importantly, any noise.

To Archer's right, the grey-haired man reloaded his .44 with another six shells. Tucking the empty copper casings into his pocket quietly, he flicked the cylinder into place then pulled a black badge from his belt and showed it to the homeowner. Archer instantly recognised the steel star surrounded by a circle.

This man was a US Marshal.

'Is there a room we can use?' he asked quietly.

She nodded, staying silent.

He turned to the dark-haired woman.

'Vargas, get the girl.' He shifted his attention to the uninjured man. 'Barlow, watch the door.'

Both of them nodded. Easing Carson's head off her lap and carefully lowering it to the floor, the woman called Vargas rose and took the child's hand as the grey-haired man holstered his .44 and bent down, gripping Carson's armpits. Archer stepped forward and took hold of the man's legs, not waiting to be asked. Together the two of them heaved him up and following the blonde homeowner, carried him through a door to the right.

They entered a sitting room which looked drab and dreary. There was a TV on a stand in the corner, a couch, several armchairs and a few lamps dotted around on small tables. There were also some photo frames containing the standard family snaps and a few ornaments on a bookshelf fixed to the wall. The floor was carpeted but the place had definitely seen better days. The homeowner rushed off, retrieving some towels from the bathroom then returning, and threw them over the couch in an attempt to protect it from any blood.

The two men placed Carson down carefully on the cushions. He was whimpering in agony, drawing ragged breaths as the blood continued to seep sluggishly from the wound to his stomach. Across the room, Vargas was sitting with the girl, distracting her and keeping her turned away from the gunshot man bleeding on the couch as they both caught their breath and recovered from what had just happened.

Once he'd deposited Carson, the big grey-haired US Marshal ducked back next door. Following him to the doorway, Archer watched as he reached behind the apartment refrigerator, unplugging it, then dragged it in front of the door as quickly and quietly as he could, forming a makeshift barrier.

If someone wanted to get in it wouldn't stop them, but the improvised blockade would buy them all a few valuable extra seconds.

Once the refrigerator was in place, the Marshal stepped back and headed back to the sitting room, passing the other uninjured man, who'd kept his weapon trained on the door the entire time.

'Barlow, in here.'

He followed and joined the others in the sitting room.

Once Barlow was inside, the grey-haired man shut the door.

In the south stairwell beside the 4th floor, Braeten ended the call as the other three gunmen reappeared from above. The sounds of shouts and music coming from apartments in the building echoed around them, the long funnelled flight of stairs carrying the noise from above. Several more residents had stuck their heads out of east-side facing apartments on the 4th floor moments ago, the same as had happened on 5, having heard the gunshots from out on the street and the noise inside the building. Braeten had ignored them, focusing on the call, giving a complete update on what had just happened to his client the other end of the line and not enjoying it at all.

Pocketing the cell phone, he turned to his guys. 'Anything?'

They shook their heads.

'They disappeared,' one of them said, talking fast. He sniffed and looked up the stairwell.

'Not for long,' Braeten said, reloading his pistol with a fresh clip, letting the empty magazine fall to the floor. 'Back up is on the way.'

'What? Who?'

He pulled the slide. 'The clients. They're sending help.'

One of them went to speak but they heard the sound of sirens from the street outside.

The four men paused momentarily, looking at each other.

Then they took off down the stairs back to the ground floor.

The first call to the NYPD's emergency hotline had occurred less than thirty seconds after the initial shots were fired on West 89th. Officers already in the area had either heard the weapons' reports and were already on their way, or had been ordered to the scene immediately by Dispatch, their phone lines suddenly inundated with crisis calls.

By the time any of them made it to the scene, the Tahoe and the pursuit car were already racing away through the streets, heading uptown through the Upper West and on into Harlem. The two cars had carved through three different NYPD areas, which meant there were now scores of blue and white NYPD vehicles converging from all directions on the scene from the 24th, 26th and 30th Precincts. Jurisdiction was collective here; these assholes had opened fire on the street in one of the safest neighbourhoods in the city. Right now, it was open season.

The squad cars were all arriving outside the tenement on West 135th around the same time, lights flashing and sirens wailing as they screeched to a halt. The officers immediately saw the two abandoned cars from the chase, both of them shot up with all the doors open. One of the vehicles was a black Tahoe which had slammed into a fire hydrant on the corner, water spraying up high into the air.

To the left of the abandoned 4x4, the front door of a tall tenement block was hanging open, the lock smashed, bits of chalk and brickwork scattered in front of it. Some of the arriving officers pulled their side-arms and immediately positioned themselves behind their cars, covering colleagues who were quickly pushing curious members of the public back and securing the area.

Suddenly one of the cops went down with a shout of pain as a gunshot echoed around the street. He clutched his thigh as two more shots hit the police car behind him.

The cops ducked down behind cover as more gunfire erupted from the entrance of the building, muzzle flashes lighting up the street. One of the officers crawled around the side of his car and managed to drag his injured partner back, bullets ripping into the vehicle, smashing glass and riddling the blue and white with holes.

The rate of fire suddenly went up a hundred notches, the terrifying echo of an assault rifle filling the Avenue as bullets shredded into the cop cars, showering the officers ducked behind with glass and shrapnel. Pulling open the door of his vehicle, the officer who'd saved his partner reached inside and grabbed both the Mossberg riot gun from its position between the front seats and the radio receiver, jerking as the window above his head was blown out.

Beside him, the wounded cop lay to one side, clutching his leg in agony as other officers started to return fire at whoever was shooting from inside the entrance of the building.

SEVEN

Upstairs, the group in the apartment heard the shots, but seeing as they were on the south-east side, their view of the front of the building was limited. They looked down from the window and saw a series of NYPD cop cars pulled up in the street, others screeching into position as the officers took cover from gunfire that ripped into their vehicles.

They watched as the cops fired back, the street transformed into another violent battle but with them as onlookers this time instead of participants. The barrelling sound of the AK-47 echoed above the other gunshots as they watched the side of a squad car get shredded to pieces by the rifle, the officers behind crowding down for cover.

'Jesus,' Barlow said. 'It's World War Three down there. These guys aren't backing down.'

Beside him, Archer observed the activity below but didn't speak. The grey-haired Marshal studied the street for moment through the same window, then turned and moved over to the couch.

Carson was lying there twisting in pain, blood all over the front of his shirt and hands, the sinews of his neck pronounced and visible as he gritted his teeth. The big man knelt down but couldn't check the wound due to the blood and Carson's hands covering it.

Behind him, the blonde apartment owner stepped forward.

'Let me look at him,' she said, the first words she'd spoken since they'd barged in.

The grey-haired man turned, about to refuse.

'I'm a nurse,' she said. 'Let me look at him.'

Hearing that, the man relented and stepped back, allowing her to examine Carson. He shifted his attention to Archer, who'd turned from the window, studying him, the next problem on his mental checklist.

'Who are you?' he asked.

'Sam Archer. NYPD.'

'Division?'

'Counter Terrorism.'

'Rank?'

'Detective. 3rd Grade.'

The Marshal looked at his waist. 'Where's your badge and piece?'

'At home. I'm off duty. Just came from the gym.'

Pause. The man looked at him for a long moment, weighing him up.

'I saw you. Before it went down. You were on the bench by the Park. What were you doing?'

'Relaxing after a workout. Having a drink.'

'Why'd you help?'

'It's my job. Wouldn't you?'

The Marshal continued to look at him closely. After a long pause, he nodded.

'I'm Foster,' he said, offering his hand. 'First name John. Thank you for what you did. Looks like we're stuck together for the time being.'

Archer stepped forward and shook it. Foster jabbed a finger towards the window at the uninjured man, who was still watching the action down on the street, his pistol clutched in his right hand.

'That's Barlow. The guy on the couch is Carson.' He pointed to the dark-haired woman, who was sitting with the girl, holding her close. 'That's Vargas. They're all my people.'

Archer nodded a greeting to them, which Vargas returned. Barlow ignored him.

'What now, boss?' he asked Foster instead. 'The cops are keeping the gunmen busy.'

'Now they get annihilated,' he said, taking out his cell phone and dialling a number.

He walked forward and peered out of the window again, the gunfight between the cops and the four men continuing unabated. He watched as an arriving NYPD squad car was ripped apart, automatic gunfire smashing into it, a brutal onslaught, the windows and fender smashing, the lights on the roof torn to pieces. Whoever was armed with the assault rifle sure as hell had plenty of spare ammunition and seriously bad intentions to go with it.

'Dalton, it's me,' Foster said into the cell, once the call connected. 'We've got a situation here.'

The noise of the initial gunfight had attracted the attention of a number of residents in the building. The full-on war that was going out there right now got scores of them coming out of their apartments.

Some were going downstairs to see what was happening but quickly retreated when they saw the quartet in the lobby ducked down by the windows and firing at police outside. Many of them weren't as surprised as might have been expected; this part of Harlem wasn't the most savoury place in Manhattan and shootings weren't uncommon around here.

However, this still looked pretty heavy and most of them decided to stay out of it, heading back up the stairs as quickly as they'd come down.

The guy with the AK stepped in front of the smashed window and squeezed off an entire magazine, shell casings spraying from the ejection port, everyone on the street pinned down. When the rifle clicked dry, he ducked back and reloaded, pulling another from the bag over his shoulder, the barrel of the weapon smoking. He'd brought more than a couple of spares. Last night, after Braeten told them about the job, he'd spoken with the guy he sourced his weapons from. The man had offered him an AK-47 and seven extended magazines; it had been already used in a gang shooting in the Bronx, and he was keen to get it off his hands. They agreed on five hundred bucks for the lot. Right now, that decision was proving to have been a worthwhile investment. None of the pigs outside had that kind of firepower at their disposal.

Standing behind him and seeing some onlookers on the stairs, Braeten wracked his brains, considering their next best move.

He looked around the lobby, thinking.

Then his eyes settled on something which gave him an idea.

Upstairs, Foster was in the corner of the sitting room, talking on the phone quietly while constantly checking the situation on the street below.

The homeowner was tending to Carson, his back arching in pain from the gunshot wound. Across the room, Barlow watched them every now and then, switching his attention back and forth from Carson to the street. Vargas had just stepped outside the room with the girl to avoid her watching the gunshot wounded man and further upsetting her. Knowing he could do nothing else to help him either right now, Archer followed and joined them in the kitchen.

He used the moment to check the layout of the apartment. It was a relatively small, compact place. He'd just stepped out of the sitting room, positioned on the right of the apartment, and was now in the kitchen; to the left was a bathroom, the door open through which he could see a tiled wall and bathtub, some bottles and a bar of soap sitting in a cluster on the side of the tub.

To his right, the little girl was sitting on the edge of the kitchen table as Vargas poured her a glass of water from the sink across the room. She walked forward and passed it to the girl, watching her drink and keeping close tabs on her. Given it was the first moment of calm in a while, Archer used the opportunity to get a good look at the female Marshal.

She was petite, dark-featured and slim, with jet black hair and hazel eyes. She was dressed in a white top and black jeans; she'd been wearing a cream-coloured shirt when he'd first seen her down on the street but it had been used in the Tahoe to staunch the blood flow from the wound to Carson's gut. She had what looked like a

Glock 22 in a holster on her hip beside her badge, cuffs and two spare clips, a small black satchel bag resting beside them with the strap over her opposite shoulder. He'd noticed Foster, Barlow and Carson all had two guns, whereas she only had one.

She was extremely attractive and looked young, in her late twenties, but there was definitely a layer of steel underneath all that beauty. There would have to be for her to qualify as a US Marshal; their training programme and day-to-day work were notoriously hard. She was calm, focusing on the child and didn't seem overly worried about their current predicament. There was definitely more to this woman than first met the eye. He figured there would be a few guys out there somewhere who'd learnt that the hard way.

Switching his attention to the little girl, he smiled. She had similar colouring to Vargas but Archer guessed they weren't related. They didn't look sufficiently alike, not to mention that Vargas wouldn't be bringing her daughter on operations. She looked maybe six or seven, dressed in a black t-shirt and jeans, white sneakers on her feet with the laces double-tied. Her presence here was confusing and raised a number of questions in his mind, but for the moment he left them alone.

The child took another sip of water from the glass, then looked over at him.

'What's your name?' he asked her.

She flicked a glance at Vargas.

'Jennifer,' she said, after a moment's hesitation. Her eyes were red rimmed with tears and she kept glancing at the sitting room door, Carson's occasional groans of pain audible through the thin wall.

'I'm Archer,' he said, trying to distract her. 'You're being very brave.'

She sniffed and nodded but didn't respond.

The sitting room door beside them opened and Foster appeared; he glanced back over his shoulder.

'Barlow, watch Jack.'

Closing the door, he walked forward and approached the girl. 'Are you OK?'

She nodded, looking up at the huge man, who dwarfed her.

'What's the situation?' Vargas asked.

'I called Dalton and told him what happened. He'd already seen it on the tube and is on his way.' He looked at Archer. 'Agency task force. Ten or twenty strong. They'll be here within half an hour. They'll get us out quickly.'

He stepped forward and glanced out of the kitchen window, looking down at the street again. The gunfight between the cops and the gunmen who'd ambushed Foster and his team had lessened in severity slightly, but it was still going on, occasional shots fired, everyone still taking cover. It was a sea of blue and red flashing lights down there, officers behind vehicles with handguns and Mossbergs aimed at the entrance of the building, none of them risking coming anywhere closer.

'A stand-off,' he said.

'Don't think they'll be getting in any time soon,' Archer said. 'One of the gunmen had an assault rifle.'

Foster nodded. 'AK. Cop killer. I saw it.'

He stepped back from the window.

'Sons of bitches. I knew they'd try. I could sense it.'

'How the hell did they know where we were?' Vargas said.

Foster didn't reply. The door to the sitting room opened and the homeowner appeared, looking grim, wiping off her hands on a small flannel. She had crows-feet around her eyes and a worn expression on her face, her hair half-tied back with some loose strands hanging down either side. She looked a bit unsteady, but not from fear. Archer had spotted an open, half-full bottle of Southern Comfort and a glass on the kitchen counter when he'd walked out here. She'd have been settling down for the evening, not expecting visitors; especially not ones with gunshot wounds to the stomach and carrying pistols. She closed the door behind her.

'How's he doing?' Foster asked her.

'Not good,' she said. 'Not good at all. The bullet hit him in the gut. He needs help immediately.'

'Back up is on the way. He just needs to hang on for an hour.'

She shook her head. 'He might not have an hour.'

'He's tough. He'll make it.'

Pause.

'I'm Helen,' the woman said, sighing and running her hand through her hair worriedly.

'Foster. Thank you for your help.'

'You mind telling me what this is about?'

70

Foster hesitated.

She saw the look on his face.

'You just dragged a seriously wounded man into my apartment, who is currently bleeding out all over my couch. There's a gunfight going on downstairs and police surrounding the building. You've barricaded the door with my refrigerator and you're all carrying guns. I don't think an explanation is too much to ask. Do you?'

Foster looked at her, then nodded.

'We're Federal Marshals. Carson, Barlow and Vargas are my people.'

'You already said that.'

'Where were you headed?' Archer asked.

Foster turned to him. 'What?'

'You were getting into a car. Where were you going?'

'Spokane.'

'Safe house?'

Foster nodded slowly. Observing him, Archer noticed his reticence, reluctant to give anything away, even his own name. He looked tough as teak; drawing information from him was like getting blood from a stone. He had an aura of strength. Archer liked him already.

Helen went to ask something else but suddenly a shrill sound filled the building, a wailing siren.

The fire alarm.

The unexpected noise made them all jump. Foster pulled his .44 as Vargas drew her Glock and drew Jennifer behind her, all of them staring in the direction of the refrigerator and instantly back on edge.

The alarm quickly got people opening their doors all over the building. Braeten had found the switch downstairs on the wall beside an emergency panel and pulled it. He and two of the others had split up and were now working their way through the block, searching the corridors and everyone they passed on the stairs for the Marshals.

They were sticking to the lower floors; the group wouldn't have had time to go anywhere higher. He'd guess they were somewhere between 1 and 6. If they emptied at least the lower portion of the tenement block, it would be far easier to hunt them down once everyone was gone.

Downstairs, the front door was being held open, the lock broken from when they'd smashed their way inside. The man with the AK was guarding it, forcing the residents out as soon as they appeared from the stairwells, responding to the alarm. Across the street, the NYPD had held their fire, unwilling to take the risk of hitting any of the people who were now streaming out of the building, urged on by the man holding the assault rifle.

'Everybody out!' he shouted. *'Let's go! Right now!'*

People continued to flood into the lobby, many of them half-dressed. They all jerked to a stop when they saw the smashed glass and the man with the Kalashnikov, people piling up behind them, but he kept the weapon on them and pulled the cocking handle for effect, a shell jumping out of the ejection port.

'Get the hell out!'

As the alarm continued to ring, Foster kept his Magnum trained on the refrigerator, looking down the sights of the large handgun, waiting for one of the assholes to try and break in. He'd already taken out one of their group, the kid who'd shot Carson, putting one of the .44 bullets in the middle of his chest when they'd been jumped in the street. His friends could join him.

'Did they start a fire?' Helen asked, loudly enough so the others could hear.

Archer shook his head, reading the situation and feeling uneasy.

They're clearing the building, he thought. *And they're not giving up.*

EIGHT

Shortly afterwards, two things happened. The alarm finally died and Foster's phone rang. In the new quiet, the alarm still ringing in their ears, he took the call, keeping his Magnum in his hand and one eye on the door. In the meantime, Helen disappeared back into the sitting room to tend to Carson and Barlow joined the others in the kitchen, watching the action in the street below through the kitchen window with Archer and Vargas.

From their position on the south-east corner, they could see scores of residents pouring out of the block, NYPD officers hustling them to safety, the gunfight momentarily paused. As Foster talked on the phone, he moved towards them to take a look himself and give an update.

Archer stepped away to make room and turned to Vargas

'Are you guys New York based?' he asked quietly.

She nodded.

'What's Marshal procedure for a situation like this?' Archer added.

'Task force,' she said. 'Ten, fifteen or twenty man team. Bulletproof vests and assault weapons. They'll take over from your people on the street when they get here. They'll access building blueprints, assess the situation, then breach and enter. Take down the enemy and secure our team.'

'And get Jack to a doctor,' Barlow said, over his shoulder.

'It's still a stand-off down there, sir,' Foster said on the call, examining the scene and standing beside Barlow. 'The NYPD are outside. The men who attacked us are holding the door.'

Pause.

'I don't know. They set off the fire alarm; it's doing its job. Most of the residents seem to be outside with the police. I guess they're trying to clear the building to make it easier to find us.'

Pause.

'Heavily,' he said. 'One of them has a Kalashnikov.'

He listened.

'Don't worry, I'll check it.'

Pause.

'It's not a problem. They won't get the drop on me again.'

During the call, Helen had reappeared in the doorway. They could all hear Carson's groans and gasps of pain in the room behind her. Foster ended the call and turned to her, tucking the phone back into his pocket.

'Tell me about this place,' he asked her. 'How many floors are there?'

'Twenty two.'

'I saw an elevator.'

'Doesn't work. Been busted for weeks.'

'Are you sure?'

'Yes, I'm sure.'

'What if you live at the top of the building?'

'You either don't go out, or you walk.'

'No-one's repaired it?'

75

'What do you think this is, the Waldorf?'

'How many stairwells?'

'Two. North and south. You headed up the south.'

'Exits?'

'Just the one. A set of double doors downstairs on the ground floor. One way in. One way out.'

'What are you thinking?' Vargas asked Foster.

'Dalton's on his way; he'll be here any minute. He said our quartet will be focused on holding the lobby, the only access point.'

'On foot,' she finished.

He nodded. 'Back up will probably have to come in from the sky. I'm going up to check the roof and if necessary, keep it secure until they get here.'

'Are you crazy?' Helen said.

'No-one else is getting hurt on my watch tonight. That includes the rescue team.'

'You can't leave. What about us?'

'I won't be long. I want to make sure there's nobody up there waiting, especially not the kid with the AK. No more surprises.'

Helen stared at him. Archer knew what she was thinking and feeling. Unlike Foster, this was the first time she'd ever been in a situation like this. As the obvious leader of the group, his presence was reassuring.

'You can't go out there,' she said.

'No better time than right now. They'll be near the lobby, focused on getting people out and keeping the cops back.'

'They're armed.'

76

'So am I. This is a big building and I've been in worse situations. And these idiots have no idea what they're doing. They're not professionals.'

'They managed to shoot your friend,' Helen said, indicating next door.

'They got lucky. That's not happening again.'

Silence. The window reflected on-off flashes of red and blue from the police lights five floors down. In the quiet, Foster holstered his Magnum then pulled his Glock and replaced the magazine, tucking the back-up shooter back into the pancake holster on his hip.

Taking one last glance out of the window, he checked the time on his wrist then drew the .44 again, ready to go.

'I'll come with you,' Vargas said.

Foster shook his head, pointing at Jennifer. 'I need you and Barlow here with her. I'll go alone.'

Beside him, Archer shook his head.

'No way. I'm coming too.'

Foster was about to say *no,* but Archer didn't let him.

'Think about it, John,' he told him. 'This entire building is made up of corridors. At every moment, you're going to have your back turned to an access point. Someone needs to watch it for you.'

Foster stared at him, examining him like a road map.

Then, without speaking, he moved next door and reappeared a few moments later with a black handgun, which he passed to Archer grip first.

'Carson's back-up weapon. He didn't fire it on the street. Fifteen in the mag, one in the chamber.'

'Thanks,' Archer said, taking it. He pulled back the slide halfway just to check and saw a round already in the pipe. There was a smear of blood on the grip; Archer wiped his palm on his jeans.

Meanwhile, Foster turned to Vargas, who'd taken Jennifer by the hand.

'Get the girl next door. Once we're gone, you and Barlow drag the refrigerator back. We'll be back soon. I'll tap four times quietly and say my name. If someone doesn't do that and tries to come in, whoever they are, don't hesitate. Drop them like a bad habit.'

'Yes, sir. Be careful.'

Foster nodded, looking at Jennifer.

'You too.'

*

Across the Hudson River, in a safe house on the outskirts of New Jersey, a response team had already moved into action.

There were ten of them there in total. After they'd learned of the Upper West Side gunfight and car chase, they'd been monitoring the situation on a television in the corner of the room. They'd watched footage of a ferocious gunfight between the NYPD and some gunmen inside a Hamilton Heights tenement block on 135th and Amsterdam. Now scores of residents were emptying out of the building and flooding into the street, the fire alarm that had prompted their exit dying off a few minutes ago. Despite a fleet of NYPD squad cars surrounding the building, the armed gunmen inside were managing to hold the officers at bay. NY ONE were covering the scene but so far they didn't have specifics on what was happening.

The response team were carrying out final checks of their equipment, working quickly but methodically. They'd done this scores of times in the past, and this was what they were here for, after all.

The leader of the group slid a thirty round magazine into a black assault rifle then checked his watch. They were always prepared for any kind of situation but if their ideal plan was an alphabet this would have been Plan X, Y or Z. A tenement building, hostiles inside, unknown layout and access points. Even though residents were leaving, there were bound to be others still inside who hadn't responded to the alarm.

He slapped forward the stock on the rifle, then whistled, jabbing his thumb at the door.

They didn't have a moment to waste.

The ten man team scooped up their weapons and bags of equipment then followed him out of the room. Outside, they loped across some tarmac towards a large black helicopter, the rotors gathering speed as the vessel warmed up.

The man pulled open the door and his team started climbing in, ready to go.

NINE

There was a scraping sound on the 5th floor corridor of the tenement block.

Then it stopped.

There was the soft *click* of a door being unlocked. The handle of 5B turned slowly and the door eased back an inch.

Foster listened for a moment then pulled it back further, not all the way but enough for him to check what he could see of the corridor.

There was no-one out there, hostile or otherwise.

It seemed the floor had been cleared.

He eased his large frame out through the gap, immediately followed by Archer, who felt his heart thumping like the bass drum on a dance track as he aimed the pistol in his hands. *For Christ's sake, get a grip,* Archer told himself. *It's not like you've never done this before.* Foster glanced back at him as the door was closed and secured.

Archer hid his uncharacteristic nerves and nodded, adopting his best poker face.

With Foster's back turned, clearing the corridor ahead with his .44, Archer took a deep breath, angry at himself. Just three months out of the field and it was like starting all over again. The workout at the gym, the sudden ambush on the street and all that had followed since had taken more out of him than he realised. He felt like one of those video game characters with their life down to 15 or 20 per cent. It wasn't pleasant.

Telling Foster he'd join him had been an instinctive response but standing there outside the apartment, he hadn't expected to feel so on edge. Particularly as they weren't exactly dealing with high-level opposition here judging from the haphazard way their attackers had behaved since the ambush. Given their sloppy shooting and what he'd seen on the street, Archer figured the four gang members had to be coked up or on some other kind of substance, maybe angel dust. If so, their aim would be all over the place; shooting a gun with a heart rate that erratic was a recipe for disaster and increased the odds in his and Foster's favour. However one of them still managed to hit Carson, he reminded himself.

And handgun bullets didn't offer a lot of second chances.

He forced the negative thoughts from his mind. They could get him killed. Shifting his focus from himself to the situation, he looked down the sights of the pistol at the empty stairwell behind them. The weapon in his hands was a Heckler and Koch USP 9mm, a German semi-automatic with a built-in recoil reduction system which greatly reduced the kick. He'd fired this weapon before on the gun range the ARU used in North London; it was a solid shooter and had good stopping power. A small blessing of the corridors in this building meant the enemy would be funnelled too if they tried another ambush, the confined space restricting their movement unlike the street, where they'd attacked from all directions. If Archer had a choice in a situation like this, a USP would be near the top of the list.

And unlike the enemy, he wasn't a guy who needed luck to put someone down with a pistol.

Helen's apartment was next to the south stairwell, but Foster pointed down the corridor towards the north side. Archer guessed he wanted to check out the rest of the floor and clear it before heading upstairs. A smart precaution. *No more surprises.*

Foster took the lead, his .44 going everywhere his eyes went, Archer covering his back with the USP, the two men moving quickly down the hallway. This wasn't a job that Foster could sensibly have done alone. Not with a long corridor accessible from both ends. Some of the apartments were still occupied; Archer heard music and the sounds of televisions from a few of the rooms. People were still here, either not hearing the alarm for some reason or just deciding to ignore it.

He didn't know if that was a good or bad thing yet.

Without mincing words, the apartment block was a dump. The walls had been a dark cream colour once but over time had faded to more of a light brown. The entire corridor was about forty five or fifty feet long. Helen had said there were twenty two floors. With twelve apartments on each floor, that was over two hundred and sixty apartments to search, which would buy the group hiding out in 5B a little time, even if the gunmen started to work their way up systematically from the ground floor. Plus, at least one or two of them would have to stay in the lobby covering the entrance, otherwise the NYPD could walk straight in, so their numbers would be lessened.

All he, Foster and the others had to do was hang on. Federal backup was already on its way and when it came to siege and entry, they never messed around. In the meantime, the NYPD would be planning their own assault. Four coked-up gang members were no match for that kind of professional operation and firepower. This thing would be over before too long. Archer had done his part and would gladly stay the hell out of the rest of it.

The two men moved up the corridor. They passed the elevator on their right halfway down the hallway. Helen said it hadn't been used in weeks and she hadn't been lying. A piece of paper with *Out of Order* printed on it in black marker pen had been stuck across the doors with a few choice extra four-letter words scribbled underneath, no doubt by disgruntled and pissed-off residents who wanted it fixed.

There was a long window panel on each door. As he passed, walking backwards, Archer peered through one of them but all he saw was darkness. The door to the apartment just past the elevator had been left open. Glancing inside, Archer saw a pair of feet slumped over the edge of a couch, the owner fast asleep. He also noticed an open black leather case on a table beside the man with some items spread out on top. The guy was going to be out cold for a while.

They arrived at the door to the north stairwell. Foster eased it back and the two men slid through the gap, covering both sides of the stairs with their handguns.

The stairwell had a railing-protected space in the middle that ran all the way up and all the way down. The two men paused, listening. Archer peered up through the gap and saw flights of stairs ascending upwards as far as he could see, all the way to the 22nd floor. He did the same the other way, carefully looking down. There was the sound of movement both above and below, people making their way down to the entrance in delayed response to the fire alarm. With an elevator that was out of action, if the residents wanted to get out, they'd be walking. Archer guessed some would be staying put, probably assuming it wasn't a real fire, just some punk who'd set it off for a prank. It was a hell of a long way to walk down for nothing.

Three people suddenly appeared on the landing above. Foster and Archer snapped around, but they weren't the gunmen, just three residents shuffling down, all of them looking pretty pissed off. Keeping their handguns tucked by their jeans, the two men stepped back and let them pass, none of the trio giving them a second glance.

Watching them go, Archer looked at Foster, who nodded.

The older man took the lead and the pair quietly started making their way up the stairs.

Across the Hudson, the rotors of the response team's helicopter were spinning in a blur. Inside the cabin, the whine from the vessel was intense and killed any conversation.

The ten men were sitting across from each other, each grim-faced and focused.

They all wanted to get the job done as quickly as possible, secure the building and take care of the enemy inside.

They were carrying an assortment of automatic weapons, pistols in holsters on their thighs, combat overalls covering their legs and torsos, the ends of their trousers tucked into thick black boots. There were also a series of black holdalls stowed to one side, packed with other equipment they would need for this kind of aerial assault. They were an eleven man team in total but one of their guys was already on his way to the scene by car. He wasn't going inside the building, but he would be an essential part of the operation nonetheless.

The pilot did his final checks then twisted in his seat and gave the thumbs up to the men in the back.

As the helicopter lifted into the air, the leader of the group pulled a balaclava down over his face.

The other men did the same.

TEN

As Helen said, there were twenty two floors. Archer and Foster encountered eleven stragglers walking down as they headed up, none of them their friends from the street but each giving them an unpleasant moment when they appeared. Despite his age, Foster was in good cardiovascular shape and set a brisk pace. By the time they arrived on 17, both men were breathing hard, their thighs burning. When they made it to 22, they both needed a few moments to catch their breath.

Pulling open the stairwell door to 22, they quickly cleared the corridor and found another door halfway along, the entrance to the roof. Archer pulled it back and Foster took the lead, moving up a short flight of steps and taking a deep breath of night air, Archer following close behind.

It was a flat roof, constructed with reinforced concrete and covered in loose grit with just a brick ledge acting as a perimeter. There was some trash, empty beer cans and cigarette butts scattered on the surface, and it smelt of old tar softened by the daytime sun. The west side of the building overlooked the Hudson River and New Jersey on the other side of the water. Although the sun had gone down, the night was warm with a slight whisper of wind which ruffled both men's hair, helping Carson's blood dry on Archer's flannel shirt.

After a quick check around with their handguns in the aim, they confirmed there was no-one else up here. The north side of the roof had several large air vents humming away side-by-side, providing potential cover or a hiding place, but no-one was lurking behind them. It looked as if the four gunmen were all downstairs in or around the lobby, holding the front door while they cleared the place out.

The roof was clear.

Foster pulled his cell phone again as Archer moved over to the east side of the building, looking down. He saw scores of blue and red flashing lights far below, the streets now cordoned off, cops and detectives crouched behind their vehicles and watching the door to the tenement. Foster's Tahoe was still rammed up against the fire hydrant, water continuing to spray everywhere. Scores of residents were gathered south of the building in huddles, police officers and detectives beside them, no doubt asking them what happened inside and who they saw.

He suddenly realised in the frenzy of activity and danger that he hadn't made any calls himself. Keeping one eye on the door to the roof and the USP tight in his hand, he lifted his Nokia from his pocket and scrolled through his *Call History*.

Downtown on 78th Street, Josh walked in through the front door with his three kids, having just picked them up from the Loews at Lincoln Square. Just as expected, the cartoon fish movie had gone down a hit and the kids had spent the entire ride home quoting lines and going over the best scenes in detail. They'd been caught in Sunday night traffic, and the journey had taken longer than expected, so needless to say Josh was happy to be back, feeling that he now probably knew the film better than the director himself.

Dropping his gym bag by the door, Josh followed the trio into the kitchen and kissed his wife Michelle. She was standing by the cooker in the midst of preparing dinner, but had paused in her work, watching the television, a big metal spoon in her hand.

'Have you seen this?' she said.

'What's that?' Josh said, going to the refrigerator and grabbing a bottle of water.

'This. Josh, look.'

He turned and examined the screen. The shots were of a tenement block somewhere in the city, a male reporter giving an update, scores of cops and detectives visible behind him, crouched behind NYPD vehicles. Josh scanned the headline.

Breaking News: Gunfight and car chase on Upper West Side. Four men occupy Harlem building on West 135th and fire at NYPD officers arriving at scene. At least one officer injured.

'What the hell?' Josh said, frowning and looking closer.

'Apparently one of the gunmen got shot in the street. They hit a cop too.'

'Jesus. What's it about?'

Before she could reply, the cell phone in his pocket started ringing. Watching the screen, he pulled it from his pocket and answered it, not looking at the display and keeping his eyes on the television.

'Yeah?'

'It's me,' Archer said.

'Hey. You watching the news?'

'*Not right now. So you're not going to believe this...*'

ELEVEN

Down in the lobby of the building, the four gunmen had sealed and barricaded the front door. Smashing their way in earlier had annihilated the lock, so they'd improvised. Whilst Braeten and the man with the Kalashnikov held the entrance and continued to herd the stragglers still appearing from the stairwells out through the door, the other two went upstairs and came back with a thick, heavy desk from a maintenance office on the 1st floor. Shoving out the remaining residents, they'd shut the door and rammed the desk up against it.

The residents who'd responded to the fire alarm had mostly all been evacuated, the majority completely overwhelmed when they saw the scores of cop cars and weapons trained on the entrance as they were hustled out of the door. However, a few latecomers had only just arrived in the lobby, wanting to get out too. Braeten gave them a simple choice; *go back upstairs and stay in your apartment or I'll shoot you.* The pistol he'd aimed at them had been persuasive and they hadn't needed to be told twice.

Now the stragglers had disappeared back up the stairs, the lobby was empty apart from the four gunmen. The fire alarm had done its job and they weren't going to open up for anyone else; no-one was getting in or out.

Braeten peered around the edge of the broken window beside the door and checked out the scores of NYPD squad cars. Officers were aiming directly at them over the front of their cars or from behind their doors, some with pistols, many with shotguns.

One of his other men joined him, taking a look.

'Jesus Christ. Every cop in Manhattan is out there,' he said, echoing Braeten's thoughts. 'How the hell are we going to get out of here?'

Braeten didn't reply, stepping back from the door. The other two guys were leaning against the wall beside the elevator and taking a moment's respite. The guy with the AK-47 pulled a bag of coke from his pocket, his eyes already wide, his t-shirt ringed with sweat from the muggy night air. Braeten lost his cool.

'How the hell did you all miss?' he said. 'We had clear shots. They had no idea we were coming.'

'We put one down,' one of them said.

'No, dumbass, Hayes put him down. Now he's dead.'

None of them responded. Braeten swore, frustrated, and shook his head.

'Shit,' he said. 'This is bad.'

'We emptied the building out,' the guy with the Kalashnikov said. 'So let's start looking.'

'There are four of us,' Braeten fumed, turning on him. 'They could be anywhere in this place. And you think the pigs are gonna wait outside all night so we can take a look around?'

'They can't hide out forever, and one of them is hit. You said back up is on the way. They'll take care of it.'

Braeten didn't respond. *And maybe take care of us*, he thought. They were in deep, deep shit and it was getting worse by the minute. He looked at

91

the idiot with the bag of cocaine, his temper worsening by the second.

'Don't do that when they get here,' he said. 'Not if you want to survive tonight.'

It took Archer and Foster much less time to head back to the 5th floor then it had taken to get up to the roof. Moving down gave them a far greater advantage than coming in from below, standard tactical philosophy, and having confirmed the roof was clear they both wanted to get out of sight and re-join the rest of the group. They used the south stairwell this time to give them a complete picture of the geography of the building, which was very straightforward and just as Helen had described. They moved quickly, and this time didn't encounter anyone on their way.

Once Vargas let them into the apartment and they'd shifted the refrigerator back into position, they all reassembled in the sitting room.

'Any trouble?' Vargas asked Archer, as Foster knelt down to check on Carson.

He shook his head.

'We passed some residents heading out. Most of them seem to be gone, but a few are still here. The roof's clear.'

'The gunmen?'

'No sign of them. They'll be downstairs, guarding the lobby.'

On the sofa, Carson coughed and groaned, blood around his lips. He was trying not to make too much noise but he was in excruciating pain. Some towels and Vargas's shirt had been packed on his stomach to try and staunch the bleeding but he was in agony, grabbing Foster's arm as he gritted his teeth. Foster looked down at his wounded Marshal and gripped his arm back.

'Hang on, Jack. Just hang on a bit longer. Dalton will be here any minute. Then we'll get you to a doctor.'

Carson didn't reply, nodding weakly, coughing. Foster watched him for a few seconds longer, then rose. Helen motioned with her head and he joined her by the window, Carson's groans filling the room.

'Forget *any minute*. He needs a doctor right now,' she said quietly. 'He's losing too much blood.'

'We can't go anywhere yet. We need to stay here until help arrives. We try to get him out, there'll be more than one of us bleeding.'

'He doesn't have much time.'

'He'll have to hang on.'

'He needs an IV and surgery to get the bullet out.'

'He'll have to wait.'

Helen shook her head, frustrated. '*Listen to me. Have you been shot before?'

'Occasionally.'

'Was it ever in the gut?'

Foster paused; he shook his head. 'No.'

'Try to imagine the most excruciating pain you've ever been in. Then double it. Then you'll have a vague idea of what every second is like for him right now.'

'We can't leave yet.' He pointed at Jennifer. 'Her safety is my priority. Jack's tough. He'll make it.'

93

She exhaled sharply, exasperated. He wasn't going to budge.

'Well if we can't leave, he needs pain relief,' she said.

'Oh, right. You happen to have any morphine handy?' Barlow asked sarcastically, from across the room.

'No. I don't,' she fired back, turning to him. 'Excuse me for trying to think of a solution.'

'Do you have anything we could give him?' Foster asked.

She shrugged. 'I wasn't exactly expecting this. All I have is a first aid kit, some cough syrup and some band aids.'

'Marvellous,' Barlow muttered.

'No, there is something,' Archer said from the window.

'What would that be?' Barlow asked. 'Aspirin?'

'Not here. Outside. I saw some gear down the hallway when we were clearing the corridor,' Archer said, looking at Foster and ignoring Barlow.

'What do you mean, gear?'

Pause.

'Heroin.'

'*What?*' Vargas said.

'Heroin. We could give it to him. It'll take away the pain.'

'Are you crazy?' Vargas said. 'We can't dose him up with heroin.'

Archer motioned at Carson.

'Helen's right. I don't know about the rest of you, but I can't just stand here and watch him go through that without trying to do something. Plus, he's making a hell of a lot of noise. These guys will be searching for us. We're near the stairwell; they walk past, they're going to hear him.'

Vargas stared at him, then shook her head. She looked at Foster, who thought for a moment.

'Where did you see this?' he asked Archer.

'Down the corridor on this floor, alongside the elevator. One of the apartments was open. There was a guy laid out on the couch, a pack on the table beside him. I saw what it was.'

'You're sure it was heroin?'

'I'm a cop. I'm sure.'

'There's a first aid kit in the bathroom,' Helen said, seemingly on board. 'There're two clean syringes inside.'

Archer nodded, looking at Foster. 'Decision time. He's your man.'

There was a pause. Carson's hacks and grunts of pain filled it.

Foster relented. 'OK. Let's do it.'

Down on the street, Josh had just arrived. He was still in his gym clothes, having burnt fifty one blocks uptown as if they were five. The moment Archer had started to explain what had happened, Josh had grabbed his badge and gun and raced out of his apartment, Michelle totally confused and watching him go. He'd fired up the engine to his Ford and sped up here, parking as close as he could get which was on 133rd by City College.

Dressed in a pair of black sweats and a white t-shirt, the holster of his pistol clipped to his hip, he approached the barriers, pushing his way through the crowd. An NYPD officer tried to block him

95

but Josh showed him his badge and the man stood back, letting him past with a nod. Tucking the Counter Terrorism badge back into its home beside the holster, he joined a mass of other officers and detectives, staring up at the tall building. There was a ring of blue and white squad cars acting as a makeshift cordon in front of them all, also acting as a front-side barrier.

This neighbourhood, Hamilton Heights, was not considered safe by any means. New Yorker knowledge decreed that 125th to 145th in Harlem was up there with the roughest spots in Manhattan, and this building was right in the middle of that area. Using a vehicle as cover, Josh examined the run-down tenement block. There looked to be about twenty or so floors. Many of the windows were half-open, shutters or blinds either concealing lights or half-revealing them depending on your point of view. Each apartment had a small concrete balcony, a few with laundry drying on them, most with air-conditioning units. Archer had said he and the group were on the 5th floor, south side. He tried to pick out which apartment contained the Marshals, the child and his friend.

In front of him, scores of officers in uniform were leaning over the front of the cop cars hastily pulled up across the street, the first responders. They were armed with handguns and shotguns, all of them aimed at the front of the building. He noticed many of the vehicles had smashed windows and bullet holes punched in the sides, shell casings and empty shotgun shells beside the officers on the road.

He looked over at the main door of the building; the windows beside it had been blown out and there was substantial damage to the brickwork around the entrance. He caught a brief glimpse of a figure inside, but it was gone in an instant. Archer had mentioned there'd been a stand-off and that the men who ambushed the Marshals weren't giving in. There must have been a hell of a fire-fight.

An ambulance was parked behind him to his left, two medics treating a cop, loading the man up on a gurney and feeding him oxygen through a mask. It appeared he'd been shot in the leg. Behind them, beyond the blue wooden barriers, were scores of what had to be occupants of the building, passing on statements and witness reports of what they'd seen inside. Archer said the four shooters used the fire alarm to try and get all the residents out of the building; there were a significant number here, many half-dressed and being given NYPD coats or jackets to wear. A lot of them looked rough and tough as hell, ranting at cops and detectives, lots of four letter words being used, furious at being turfed out of their apartment block on a Sunday night. This was a definitely dangerous part of the city; the look of many of the people standing there reinforced that fact.

Watching them, he remembered Archer mentioning there were still some people inside who'd ignored the alarm. Despite the number of residents out here, the building they'd vacated was by no means empty. ESU had arrived in their black and white truck, parked inside the wooden barriers beside the ambulance. They were the

NYPD's SWAT team, trained and equipped for this kind of situation. The officers were already in their gear and standing in a group, looking up at the building and talking in low voices, keeping to themselves.

Stepping his way past people and heading downtown, Josh came to a halt in the middle of the cross street, facing the south side of the building which was thirty five or so yards away. Three cop cars were pulled across the street and would protect him from any sudden gunfire from the lobby.

Looking up, he reached for his phone to call Archer but heard someone shout his name somewhere behind him. He turned and saw two familiar faces stepping out of a car pulled up to the kerb beyond the barriers.

Matt Shepherd and Lisa Marquez had just arrived.

Shepherd was Sergeant of his and Archer's Counter-Terrorism detail, a family man who'd been in the Department for almost fifteen years. Beside him was Marquez, a Latina 3rd Grade Detective in her early thirties who was as dependable as the sun going down each night. Both of them were in jeans and loose tops, Shepherd a blue shirt, Marquez a cropped t-shirt; they were off duty today, but he saw both had their side-arm and badge with them. Once Archer had filled him in on the situation, Josh had immediately called his boss and then Marquez, asking them to meet him up here, saying Archer was in deep shit but saving the specifics.

They were supposed to be a five-man team, but since the departure of Marquez's old partner

Jorgensen a few months ago, they'd managed as a four until Shepherd was satisfied he'd identified a suitable replacement. They worked well together as a team, and Shepherd was determined not to upset the balance.

Josh walked over, greeting the pair quickly, then the trio looked up at the tall tenement building.

'What's the situation?' Shepherd asked.

'Archer and a group of US Marshals are inside on the 5th floor. There's an armed gang hunting them. They're trying to get to a witness the Marshals are protecting.'

The two newcomers looked over at the Tahoe rammed into the fire hydrant, water erupting up like a geyser onto the street. As they watched, someone must have killed the pressure somehow as the flow of water suddenly stopped, the plume of water dying away to a trickle.

'What the hell happened?' Marquez asked.

'A group of gunmen jumped the Marshals as they were getting into their car on West 89th and Central Park West,' Josh said, pointing downtown. 'Foster, the lead Marshal, fired back and killed one. They managed to escape but were chased up here. Their tyres were shot out and they crashed. They had to retreat into the building.'

'And Archer?'

'He was passing by when it went down. You know what his luck's like.'

Shepherd shook his head. 'Jesus Christ, did he do something in a past life? He only just got fit again.'

Pause.

'Is he armed?'

'No, sir. He came straight from the gym.'

'The enemy?'

'There are four left. Three handguns and an AK-47. I called CSU; the man who Foster killed is already at the lab being dusted for prints and background checked. But there's another problem.'

'What's that?' Shepherd asked.

'As I said, one of the Marshals was shot in the gut. Archer said it's bad. The gunmen are controlling the lobby and there's no other exit. He's running out of time.'

'Shit.'

'So who's running the show down here?' Marquez asked, casting her eyes down to the street. 'Let's figure out an entry and get in there.'

Josh went to reply but something interrupted him. Behind the trio, a loud argument had broken out between two men by the ESU truck. One of them was in a dark suit and blue tie, the other an ESU Lieutenant in navy-blue fatigues. Josh had seen the ESU man before on an operation around Christmas; his name was Hobbs. He'd also seen him a lot calmer.

They were face to face, their argument causing people to turn and stare.

'Don't forget where you are!' Hobbs said to the other man, jabbing his finger at him.

'Don't forget who the hell is in there!' the other man fired back.

'This is our turf, asshole! Your team caused a daylight gun fight in one of our safest neighbourhoods.'

'I'm sorry, did they start this?'

'We're calling the shots here.'

'Like hell you are! This is a Federal situation. So make yourself useful; go get me a donut.'

That lit the keg. Hobbs stepped forward but one of his officers held him back, people from both sides intervening as the two men glared at each other. Cursing, Hobbs turned and stalked away as Shepherd, Josh and Marquez watched it all unfold.

The man in the suit pulled his cell phone, shaking his head, then dialled a number as he walked away.

'Well that was cute,' Marquez said.

Behind the detectives, emergency services and assembled police cars crowded together thirty yards from the tenement block, officers were containing the public and gathered news teams behind a series of hastily-erected wooden barriers. The stand-off was still volatile, and more gunfire could erupt at any moment.

Amongst the throng of people, a man in a black shirt and blue jeans stood still, looking up at the building. He was light-haired and tanned with a nondescript face, blending in with the crowd. Like everyone else down there, he was watching the situation unfold with interest, listening to the conversations and rumours being passed around.

Turning, he pushed his way through the gathered mass of people and headed south, a briefcase in his hand.

Crossing the street, he walked downtown on the sidewalk for several minutes, police and detective cars racing past the other way, people passing him in the opposite direction as they walked towards the scene, curious, wanting to see what was happening.

He arrived at an office building about eighty yards from the apartment building, on West 133rd.

The man glanced over his shoulder, then pushed his way through the revolving doors and walked inside.

TWELVE

Inside the tenement block, Archer eased the apartment door shut behind him then moved down the 5th floor corridor quickly, his back to the wall, checking left and right constantly with Carson's USP in his hand.

All of a sudden the stretch of corridor seemed a hell of a lot longer than it had with Foster watching his back.

John had been coming with him but had just received a call from his superior, Dalton, and been forced to hold up. Vargas and Barlow weren't going anywhere, staying with Jennifer who was the priority and guarding Carson as Helen did her best to comfort him and keep him quiet. He needed pain relief and he needed it now. This couldn't wait.

It meant Archer was momentarily on his own.

Keeping the USP trained on the end of the corridor, he worked his way along the hall, passing the closed apartment doors either side. Moving past the elevator, he finally arrived by the room with the unconscious guy on the couch and ducked inside, relieved to be out of the hallway. He stood motionless for a second, listening, then stepped further into the room.

The man slumped on the cushions was still out cold, his head lolled to one side, his eyes shut. He was a black guy, wearing a string vest, and was painfully thin. A needle was jutting out of his arm, a tourniquet wrapped around his lower bicep. Given that the door had been left open, Archer figured a buddy of his had heard the alarm and left, probably unable to wake the guy on the couch and then just leaving him behind. He'd encountered heavy drug users before on raids, but most of the time the doors in front of such activity were closed. Helen's voice echoed in his mind.

What do you think this is, the Waldorf?

Archer stared at the unconscious man for a moment then switched his attention to the table. There was an open leather pack, a junkie kit. He saw several packets of foil tucked inside. He reached forward and picked one up, opening it and finding crumbly dark brown powder inside. It was heroin; this guy had just scored. Unlike the movies, he didn't need to taste it to know. No way was he putting that horrible shit in his mouth.

He closed the foil ball, tucking it back into the leather case. He picked the pack up and headed to the door to get the hell out of here.

Then he heard footsteps and voices coming from the north stairwell.

'They must have ducked down one of these floors,' Braeten said, arriving on the 5th floor and walking down the corridor. The man armed with the AK-47 was beside him.

'Why so sure?'

'I heard them going up the stairs. One of them is shot and they've got the kid. They couldn't have gone too far up, but they'd have gone as high as they could.'

'How can you know?'

'Common sense. If they were on 1 or 2, they'd know we'd find them quickly.'

They stopped outside an apartment beside the elevator. 5H. Unlike the rest of the corridor, the door was open. Looking inside, they noticed the legs of someone laid out on the couch.

Frowning, Braeten moved inside, training his pistol on the body as he approached. His companion followed him in, doing the same but with the Kalashnikov. When they got closer, they saw it was just a junkie, passed out on the couch, his head lolled to the side, his mouth open. Braeten nudged him with his sneaker but the guy didn't react.

The other man looked around the rest of the place, and saw there was no one else here.

'Want to search the next one?' he asked.

'We do that, we'll be here till next week,' Braeten said, looking around the room. He glanced at a clock on the wall, considering his next move. He shook his head. 'We need to stay on the front door for the moment. This was just a hunch. We're expecting company any minute.'

The other man nodded and went to walk out of the room.

But as they moved to the door, there was a noise from the bathroom.

Both men swung round.

To their right, the bathroom door was closed.

Stepping back, they aimed their weapons at the wood, easing their way forward. The man with the AK-47 settled into the weapon as Braeten took the lead, creeping towards the frame.

He kicked the door back as hard as he could.

The room was empty.

Braeten stepped forward and swept the shower curtain to one side, but there was no-one in the bathtub. They heard the sound again, a rattling and humming.

It was the old pipes, water flowing through them and the metal jangling and clanging in protest as it did so, an old system on its last legs.

Seeing there was no-one there, Braeten lowered his weapon and exhaled.

'Screw this. Let's get the hell out of here.'

The two men turned and walked back out through the room into the corridor and towards the north stairwell, heading down the stairs.

The apartment was still for a few moments.

Then the front door eased forward and Archer exhaled as he stepped out from his hiding place behind it.

It had been close, razor-thin; he'd only just made it behind the door before the two men entered the room. When they'd stopped on their way out and come back, he'd been on the verge of kicking back the door and firing, trying to drop them both before they had a chance to react, his heart thumping so loud he was convinced they might hear it.

Now alone, he looked down at the pack in his left hand.

They were in business.

He glanced over at the comatose man on the couch, the guy completely unaware of what had just happened, completely out of it. *Thanks*

106

buddy. When he woke up he was going to be pissed off when he found his stash was gone but at least he wouldn't be in handcuffs and a jail cell, which is exactly where he would be if Archer didn't have other priorities.

Edging round the open door, Archer checked either side of the corridor cautiously, making sure the two guys had gone, his finger on the trigger of the USP.

It was empty.

Satisfied, he slipped out of the room and quickly moved along the hallway, heading back to Helen's apartment and Carson, the leather pack of dope clutched in his left hand.

THIRTEEN

A few moments later, there was a quick knock on the door of 5B and a murmured name. Foster pulled it open, and Archer slid back into the room, relaxing slightly as the door closed behind him.

'Success?' Foster asked.

Archer nodded, holding up the pack. As the big Deputy Marshal pushed the refrigerator back into position, Archer walked into the sitting room and handed the pack to Helen, as Vargas and Barlow watched with grim curiosity.

She unzipped it and looked at the equipment inside.

There was a rusty spoon, several foil packets and some spare tubing.

She shuddered.

'I'll get the first aid kit,' she said. 'Just do him a favour and get a clean spoon from the kitchen.'

Down on the street, Shepherd approached the man in the suit who'd been arguing with Hobbs, as Josh finished filling Marquez in on the situation. He had black hair, smartly cut, and looked in his late thirties, standing beside a colleague as the two of them examined a tablet screen resting on the back of his car.

Without knowing anything about him, Shepherd was ninety nine per cent sure the man was a Federal agent; his spat with Hobbs had all but confirmed it, as did the current activity behind him. A series of other 4x4 Tahoes had just drawn up, the barriers and crowd moved out of the way so they could pass and get inside the cordon. A group of tough-looking men and women had piled out of the vehicles immediately, moving to the back of the 4x4s and pulling on bulletproof vests then loading Remington shotguns and AR-15 assault rifles. The vests had lettering printed on them.

United States Marshals.

Now this man's argument with Hobbs made total sense.

'Not now,' the guy in the suit said without looking up, as he sensed Shepherd approach.

'One of my men is in the building. He's with your group.'

The man paused; he glanced up at him.

'The cop?'

'Archer. He's one of my detectives.'

'Foster told me what he did on the street. We owe him one.'

Shepherd nodded. 'He's a good man.'

The suited man examined Shepherd for a moment. Then he took a deep breath and offered his hand.

'I'm James Dalton. Chief Deputy Marshal. The team inside are one of mine.'

'Sergeant Matt Shepherd,' he said, shaking Dalton's hand. Shepherd indicated to the pair who'd just joined him. 'These are two of my detectives, Blake and Marquez. We're with the Counter Terrorism Bureau.'

Dalton nodded a greeting to them.

'Sorry about the drama,' he said, motioning with his head to Hobbs, who noticed the gesture

109

and glared at him. He and several of his ESU men were gathered by their truck, huddled around a screen and talking quietly, mirroring Dalton and his squad.

'What's the problem?' Shepherd asked.

'Our two helicopters are tied up on the outskirts of Long Island on an operation and won't be here for another hour. He found out and figured he's taking over. He seems to think this is his fight.'

'Isn't it?'

'He doesn't know who we have inside there,' Dalton said, jabbing a forefinger at the tenement block. 'And we have jurisdiction. This is a Federal situation. He can sit and watch. That's it.'

'You New York-based?' Josh asked.

Dalton nodded. 'Pearl Street.'

'So what's the plan?' Marquez asked.

Dalton pointed at the tablet in his hand, tilting it so the trio could see. They all peered closer and saw blue and white schematics for the building.

It was a layout of the 5th floor, pulled from city files. Dalton expanded it with his thumb and forefinger, pointing at a rectangular south-side room.

It was separated into three portions; a bathroom to the left of the door, a kitchen in the middle and a sitting room to the right.

'Our team are in here,' he said, pointing at the sitting room. '5B, near the south stairwell. Four Marshals, a child, your detective and the woman who rents the apartment. They've barricaded themselves in as best they can but the situation is pretty fragile. The door isn't substantial. It's thin wood and the only thing they could use to block it is an old refrigerator. Someone finds out they're in there, it won't take them long to get in.'

'Archer said one of your Marshals was shot in the stomach,' Josh said.

Dalton nodded. 'Carson. The slug was from a .45. We'll get him out of there ASAP.'

'Do we have any idea how many residents are still inside?' Marquez asked.

Dalton shrugged. 'Can't say for sure. I think most of them got out.'

'They could be an issue. Potential casualties.'

'My task force is clinical,' Dalton said, indicating to the group of Marshals assembling behind him. 'And this time, we're not going to be taken by surprise.'

'OK, so let's get in there right now,' Shepherd said.

Dalton nodded. 'You read my mind.'

Sticking two fingers in his mouth, he whistled and beckoned the team to join him. They all hustled over, fully prepared and ready to go. Doing a quick headcount, Shepherd made fifteen of them, stern-faced and determined, people who had colleagues trapped inside and would make damn sure they made it out in one piece. He'd had experience with the Marshals service before and they didn't screw around, especially if their own people were in danger. The four thugs holding the lobby would be no match for this team.

He glanced over his shoulder at Hobbs, who was looking at the group with narrowed eyes. Turning the tablet, Dalton laid it on the front of

111

his car, tilting it up so the gathered team could see.

'Right, listen up,' he called. 'Here's the situation.'

He started his brief but then heard something that made him pause.

The noise was faint, yet increasing in volume.

Seeing him halt, Shepherd frowned, then turned his head. He also heard the sound.

It was getting closer.

Other people on the street started to look up. Dalton realised what was happening.

Swinging from his group of Marshals, he stalked towards Hobbs standing by the ESU truck.

'You son of a bitch!'

Eighty yards downtown, an office building elevator dinged on the 13th floor. The man in the black t-shirt and blue jeans with the briefcase stepped out, looking left and right, making sure he was alone.

The lights were off, the place deserted, a dark stillness filling the offices that would be a distant memory tomorrow morning.

He walked through the aisles, eventually arriving by the windows facing uptown. The tenement building was straight ahead, less than a hundred yards away. The street to the right was packed with squad and Federal vehicles along with a crowd of cops, detectives and curious bystanders.

He stood still for a moment, examining the building's exterior, all of its windows and the roof.

His position on 13 meant he was halfway up the other building, giving him a total view of the entire south side.

Then he laid his briefcase on a desk and clicked it open.

In the 5th floor apartment, Helen was just administering the dose to Carson. He had an old belt wrapped up tightly by his elbow, the needle jabbed into a prominent vein in his arm. She'd opened one of the foil packs of brown powder, tipping it onto a clean spoon with a touch of water which Foster held for her. She'd warmed the underside with a lighter, and used the syringe to suck up the resulting liquid.

She pushed the substance into Carson's bloodstream, Foster, Archer and Barlow observing in silence. Vargas had her back to the room and was looking out of the window with Jennifer by her side, pointing things out in order to distract both the child and herself.

The effect of the opiate was immediate. Carson's face, screwed up with pain, suddenly softened like butter in a pan. It was extraordinary but also disturbing. His body relaxed. His mouth opened, sucking in air like a fish, his movements slowing right down as if he'd been dropped in a vat of treacle.

Everyone else in the room save Vargas and Jennifer watched, their feelings most definitely mixed. The instant release of pain was clear and a relief to everyone, not just Carson. However, what they'd just had to do went against every instinct they had.

Withdrawing the needle slowly, Helen pressed a pad against the puncture on his arm, staying silent. Carson's groans and whimpers of pain had stopped.

'How long will it last?' Barlow asked, breaking the quiet.

'Depends on the quality,' Helen said. 'Around a couple of hours I guess.'

'At least he's out of pain,' Foster said, patting Carson on the leg.

Helen nodded. Wrapping the needle in the tissue, she took it next door and headed for the trash. On the couch, Carson's mouth was open, his eyes somewhere else and focusing on something nobody else could see, probably Pluto.

As Helen disappeared into the kitchen, a sound they'd all been vaguely aware of outside suddenly became much louder.

Everyone in the room looked towards the window; the noise was easily heard above the humming from the street below and was increasing by the second.

It was unmistakable, familiar and totally reassuring.

Standing beside Carson, Foster smiled.

'Here comes back up.'

FOURTEEN

The helicopter pilot had approached across the Hudson River and entered Manhattan over West 100th Street. He'd swept over the Upper West Side and Harlem, flying fast and low over the buildings.

Coming in from downtown, the helicopter had slowed and was now hovering over the Hamilton Heights 135th Street tenement block. The rotor wash blew away all the dust, dirt and trash on the rooftop, sending paper cans and other detritus swirling in all directions.

The doors were wrenched open. Five black ropes were slung out, tumbling down out of the vessel and hitting the roof.

Five figures slid down the ropes, followed by five more.

The group were dressed in grey, black and white fatigues and tactical vests, their sleeves rolled up as it was still warm, and wore black leather gloves to prevent rope burn. They descended quickly, their boots wrapped around the cord, their bags of equipment and weapons slung over their shoulders.

The moment after the tenth man released the rope, the helicopter rose and pulled away, the noise of the vessel instantly decreasing and the ropes hanging from the open doors like jungle vines.

As the chopper headed back across the River towards New Jersey, eight of the men ran for the door to the floor below.

The other two knelt down and began setting up some equipment on the roof.

On the street, everyone gathered was watching with interest. Everyone except Dalton.

He strode towards Hobbs; some of the ESU men saw the look on his face and stepped forward, keeping him back.

'You son of a bitch!' Dalton said. *'I ordered you to hold back!'*

Shepherd and Josh hadn't moved. They'd both watched the chopper arrive like everyone else and were replaying in their minds what they'd just seen. Marquez had rushed twenty yards to the left, watching the helicopter flying across the Hudson and examining the vessel carefully. She headed back quickly, making eye contact with Shepherd and shook her head, concern on her face.

They'd all caught a glimpse of the figures abseiling onto the roof.

They were dressed in camo fatigues, not police or Federal clothing.

They were wearing balaclavas.

The chopper was black and unmarked.

Something wasn't right.

The moment the eight men made it to the 22nd floor, they split up. Four went to the north stairwell, four the south and they started moving down the flights quickly.

With combat vests holding spare ammunition, a knife and several grenades, the men also had a pistol in a holster clipped to their right thigh.

They were each holding a Colt M4A1 Commando carbine assault rifle, thirty 5.56 mm rounds in the magazines slotted into the underside of each weapon. A descendant of the M16, the manufacturer designed this specific variant of the rifle for special operations use and *to exploit firepower capability in confined spaces where lightweight mobility, speed and violence of action rule.* Each one of those circumstances was certainly ticked off the sheet given their task at hand inside the building. Unlike other sub-machine guns and assault rifles, the M4A1 didn't have a three-round burst option. It was either safe, semi-automatic or fully automatic. Capable of unleashing anywhere from 750-900 rounds per minute, the weapon was effective at 500 to 600 metres and devastating closer. The US Rangers, Navy SEALS and the Brazilian counter-terrorist team BOPE used it with very good reason. It provided ruinous and destructive firepower at close quarters and only weighed less than six pounds.

The north stairwell team worked their way down quickly, establishing the geography of the building. On the 21st floor, two of them split away and headed down the corridor, beginning to clear the apartments one by one.

The other two, including the leader, pressed on down the stairs.

On 18, a resident from an apartment a third of the way down the corridor opened his door and peered out, catching the leader's attention as they passed in the stairwell. Without a word, the armed man moved down the hallway towards him, his compatriot beside him.

Dressed in a vest and some old sweats, the guy frowned when he saw the two men in balaclavas approaching. It wasn't unusual to see cops in the tenement block and the residents had become accustomed to it, but he noticed these two were dressed in different clothing from the usual police gear.

'Who the hell are you?' he asked.

'You're in deep shit, Hobbs,' Dalton shouted. 'This is a Federal operation!'

'It wasn't one of ours!' Hobbs shouted back.

Dalton paused. *'What?'*

Hobbs pointed up at the building. *'That wasn't our chopper!'*

The leader of the response team checked the interior of the apartment behind the man, then responded.

'Police operation, sir. Stay in your apartment.'

'You don't look like cops.'

'Get back in your apartment.'

'Listen, asshole, I-'

Without another word, the leader aimed his M4A1 at the centre of the man's torso and squeezed the trigger.

One pull, six rounds. The burst tore the man's chest apart, the bullets shredding through his body and smashing plaster from the wall the other end of the corridor. Blood sprayed onto the walls as the man collapsed to the floor, clinically dead before the third round passed through his body. His girlfriend had been inside the apartment and she ran out of the doorway, covering her mouth and screaming when she saw what had happened.

The other gunman stepped forward and put four rounds through her forehead, more blood and brains spattered to the wall, the woman slumping onto the ground and joining the dead man.

Two less people to get in their way.

Dalton had stared at Hobbs for a moment, then turned and walked away, re-joining Shepherd, Josh and Marquez, who were watching him, concerned and confused. They'd all just heard what sounded like faint automatic gunfire from inside the block.

'What on earth is going on?' Josh whispered, confused.

Then there were two more bursts, faint but definite, someone firing off a weapon inside. Together, the quartet looked up at the building, the Marshals behind them doing the same. The sound of the helicopter that had delivered the group was now gone.

'Who the hell just went in there?' Dalton said.

FIFTEEN

The ten man response team inside the West 135th apartment building were only ever meant as insurance. This whole thing should have been over before sundown without their involvement.

Four US Marshals caught unawares and a kid shouldn't have been any match for a five-man ambush with semi-automatic weapons and surprise on their side. Braeten's team had come recommended from people in the area and had been hired with specific orders under specific circumstances. However, their work today had been amateur at best. The leader of the response team had received the call from Braeten forty minutes ago telling him that they'd failed. They'd hit one of the Marshals but not the girl, and one of their own team had been killed. The Marshals had taken cover in a building in Harlem, which the remaining four gang members had sealed off, more and more cops and Feds arriving outside with every passing minute.

However, despite this unexpected development, the leader of the group had been prepared. He was a meticulous planner, almost to the point of obsession, and had only ever made one big mistake in his life, which was the reason they were all here tonight. When they'd first located the Marshals and laid out what equipment they would need if Braeten failed, his men had thought he was being unnecessarily over-cautious. He'd acquired M4A1 assault rifles, pistols, grenades, Claymore mines; even C4 plastic explosive and several M72 LAW portable rocket launchers.

He'd ordered a helicopter and pilot contact to join them and be available on 24/7 standby. He'd bought enough tactical gear and weaponry to hold off a military siege. However, once they'd flicked on the television and seen what was happening tonight, any criticism of his seemingly excessive preparations had evaporated.

Thanks to him, the team were now inside the building and armed to the teeth.

They were all equally invested in ending the girl's life tonight. If she made it out of here with air in her lungs she could still talk and therefore bury all of them like they were dead men walking. And when the cops and detectives on the street got inside, they knew there was no way anyone was getting close to the Marshals and the girl again.

They had a brief window of opportunity.

And they were going to take it.

Together with one of his men, the leader passed 7, then 6, the pair sweeping their way down silently with practised efficiency. As he took point, the leader glanced down the passing corridors. He saw most of the apartments were closed but the place was pretty silent, the building a giant cavern of nooks, crannies and potential hiding places. Most of the residents seemed to be gone.

But she was still here somewhere, the one person who could put them all away if she made it out alive.

A game of hide and seek with the deadliest of results.

He looked down the 6th corridor through the sights of his M4A1.

Come out, come out, wherever you are.

In the lobby, Braeten risked another check through the shattered front window as the other three men paced nervously behind him. They'd all heard distant gunshots from somewhere in the building above which had spooked the three guys on coke, the powder in their system not helping their nerves or their ability to think calmly. They were walking back and forth so much they were almost wearing a track into the floor, all three sweating from the drugs and the heat.

'Who's firing?' one of them said quickly. 'The Marshals?'

Just as Braeten was about to respond, the south stairwell door opened. All four men swung round and saw two figures in balaclavas and black, grey and white combat fatigues move into the lobby, stubby black assault rifles in each man's shoulder. A few moments later, the same happened from the north side, two more men arriving and walking over towards them.

The quartet ended up surrounding Braeten and his team, four assault weapons aimed straight at them. For a horrible moment Braeten thought they were going to fire, but then the weapons moved elsewhere, the men checking the rest of the large lobby.

As Braeten and his team watched in silence, one of the newcomers made sure the desk blocking off the entrance was secure, then swung a black holdall off his shoulder, laying it on the ground. Another reversed his rifle then used it to smash the glass of a glass cabinet beside the fire switch Braeten had pulled earlier. He pulled an axe out of the bracket and headed to the door that led to the basement, disappearing out of sight.

A third man moved over to his colleague by the door and pulled out an item from the open black holdall. It looked like a small wireless Internet hub. He turned and laid it down against the wall by the elevator, adjusting the small stick antenna. He flicked a switch on the gadget and a few seconds later a green light blinked on. Braeten noticed the man had a cylindrical weapon tucked in a holster on the back of his vest; it looked like a portable anti-tank weapon. A rocket launcher.

Braeten and his three men watched all this in silence. The newcomers moved with a fluency that was both impressive and unnerving, none of them speaking, each man doing his job in silence and with practised ease. They were also carrying some ferocious weaponry. Braeten's instincts were telling him these were cartel guys, but he couldn't be sure. Organisations built on drugs often employed teams like these, ex-military mercenaries used to silence witnesses and remove opposition, men who had been professionally trained to kill.

Glancing at the assault rifles the newcomers were carrying, he suddenly felt severely ill-equipped with just the pistol in his hand, well aware of the fact that the only reason these men were here was because he and his team had failed. Braeten had no idea who was bankrolling this, as was usually the way with these things, but they sure as hell had some deep pockets, whoever they were. He also didn't have a clue who these newcomers were. The balaclavas they were all were wearing meant despite the situation, that wasn't going to change.

As he watched in silence, beside him one of his guys sniffed nervously and reached into his pocket.

Braeten caught his arm, gripping it firmly.

He got the message.

Upstairs, Archer was speaking in low tones with Shepherd. Foster's phone, set to silent, had also flashed with an incoming call, Dalton on the other end. They'd heard gunfire from somewhere in the building a few minutes ago, but it was faint, nowhere near them. They figured it was probably one of the gunmen from the street getting nervous or trying to scare them out.

Archer was at the window, looking down, trying to make out where his boss, Josh and Marquez were in the crowd. Being on the south side, they had limited view of the east side of the street where most of the rescue effort was gathered.

He examined the cross street on the corner of 135th, but couldn't see them.

'Did you hear the chopper?' Shepherd asked.

'Yeah, we did,' he said. 'Was it ours, or Federal?'

'Archer, listen to me,' Shepherd said, urgency in his voice. *'They aren't-'*

Suddenly the call cut out. Archer frowned.

'Sir? Hello? Sir?'

The call was dead. Beside him, the same thing had just happened to Foster, on the line with

Dalton. Archer tried calling back but he couldn't get through.

He checked the display and saw all four bars had disappeared, no service provider.

'Shit,' he said. 'Perfect. No signal.'

Foster frowned. 'They must have disabled the cell phones.'

'How the hell could they do that?' Barlow asked. 'They're street punks.'

Foster walked over to the main phone and grabbed it off the receiver. There was no dial tone.

He glanced over at the group, who were looking at him, a hint of unease creeping into the room.

'Main line's dead too.'

Downstairs, the man from the basement reappeared without the axe, nodding towards the man who Braeten had already identified to be the leader of the response team.

'Outside line is cut. They're not gonna be talking to anyone any time soon.'

'Any other ways in down there?'

'No, sir.'

The leader walked over towards Braeten. The two men were around the same size but with his balaclava, the response team leader was anonymous and therefore more intimidating. Braeten didn't know if these were the guys who'd hired him or a secondary team sent in to finish the job, but he hid his unease. He wasn't comfortable meeting his clients in person and made it a rule never to do so. It kept things professional. He also didn't like them knowing exactly what he looked like; he was just as expendable as the guys he was hired to kill.

He looked at the man's eyes through the eyeholes of the black balaclava, which stared straight back at him impassively. He was solidly built, broader and more thickset than Braeten and his guys. The way he was staring was pissing Braeten off.

'Take a photo,' Braeten said. 'It'll last longer.'

The man frowned. 'What?'

Braeten instantly recognised his voice. He was the man from the original call, the man who'd hired him. The client.

'We did our best.'

'Is that right? Did your best include lighting up half of the Upper West Side?'

'We almost got her.'

'Instead you attracted the attention of every cop in Manhattan.'

'We tagged one of their people.'

'Is he the one I want dead?'

Braeten didn't answer. The man kept staring at him.

'You knew where they were. You had an entire afternoon to get to them. But you decided to start a gunfight in the street and then get involved in a car chase across town.'

The anonymous leader shook his head.

'I'm trying to think of a way you could have screwed this up even more. I'm struggling.'

Braeten didn't respond. He knew the man was right, but he didn't apologise. They maintained eye contact, like two fighters squaring off before the bell. The lobby had gone silent. Every man in the room listened to the exchange, their hands wrapped around pistol grips, fingers on triggers. The tension was palpable. If someone made the wrong move, the Marshal wouldn't be the only gunshot man in the building.

'The information we gave you was golden,' the leader continued. 'You knew where she'd be and what their movements would be. You think that sort of information is easy to come by?'

Braeten didn't reply.

'What more did you want? Her head on a chopping block and an axe in your hand?'

'I'm sorry,' Braeten said. 'And that's the last time I'm saying it.'

The two men stood eye to eye for a long moment.

Then the leader turned away and the room relaxed slightly. Braeten glanced at the entrance and saw one of the response team had pulled the desk back slightly and drawn a series of translucent tripwires across the front of the door. Behind the wires were five rectangular Claymore mines, anti-personnel weapons that fired hundreds of metal ball bearings. He'd placed them this side of the desk, so anyone coming in wouldn't see them before it was too late. Braeten had seen the mines before in some Russell Crowe movie; they were activated either by tripwire or clacker and made one thing certain.

Whoever was on the wrong side when they went off would have enough holes punched through them to grate cheese.

'So what now?' Braeten asked the leader, making the point that he wasn't intimidated.

The man looked at him. 'We find her. We kill her. We leave.'

'We?'

'My team. You can stay here and figure it out with the NYPD. This is your mess. We're just passing through.'

Before Braeten could reply, the leader turned to two of his men.

'Find her.'

The pair nodded and made their way to the south stairwell.

They started moving up the steps, looking through the sights of their M4A1s as they disappeared out of sight.

SIXTEEN

Upstairs, three members of the group were still trying the phones, Archer and Foster with their cells, Vargas with the land line, frustrated and confused in equal measure. Barlow had made a good point; the gunmen who'd ambushed them had to be street thugs.

How the hell would they be able to kill all cell phone signal?

Realising it was futile, Archer tucked his phone back into his pocket then looked out of the window again. He checked the sky but the chopper was gone, the sound of the rotors having disappeared into the night. Shepherd had been trying to warn him of something when he was cut off mid-sentence.

But what?

Turning, he walked across the room and opened the sitting room door, making sure the barricade was still in place and that he couldn't hear any sound of movement in the corridor outside.

He glanced over at Foster, who was standing beside Carson.

'Did you get a look at the chopper?' he asked.

Foster shook his head.

'Must be our guys though,' Barlow said. 'They'll be here any second.'

'So why would the phone lines go down?'

'Could be ESU?' Barlow suggested. 'They did it to stop the gunmen communicating?'

'Did Dalton say it was one of yours?'

'Didn't have a chance,' Foster said. 'He'd only just called before the line went dead.'

Cursing quietly, he tried redialling Dalton. No reception.

Something about this wasn't right.

He put the phone back in his pocket, then turned his attention to the group, who were looking at him.

'Listen. Right now we-'

There was a sudden, tiny smash of glass.

Foster was thumped back as a bullet hit him in the forehead, blood sprayed all over the wall behind him. As Jennifer screamed, everyone in the room recoiled in shock.

Foster dropped to the floor, dead before he got there.

'Get down!' Archer shouted, the group throwing themselves to the floor, Vargas covering Jennifer as they all stared in shock at Foster's body.

'Jesus Christ!' Vargas said. *'Where the hell did that come from?'*

Eighty yards away in the office building downtown, the man in the t-shirt and jeans watched through the scope of his rifle, snuggled in close to the stock.

He'd taken out the grey-haired Marshal and could see the back of his head blown across the wall.

The others had hit the deck and were out of sight.

He was sitting at a desk, tucked in behind a VSS Vintorez, a gas-operated silenced Russian weapon which had a ten round magazine and was the shooter the Spetsnaz, Russian Special Forces, used on their operations. The weapon consisted of three main parts and could be transported easily in the special briefcase, making it easy to conceal and carry. His prints were all over both the weapon and the case, but he would be taking them with him and would take the necessary disposal precautions later. He'd fired through an open window and with both sub-sonic ammunition and a fat black suppressor on the rifle no-one on the street would have heard the shot.

The window of the apartment he'd fired into was still intact, just a small bullet hole in the pane. Keeping the scope on the tenement block window, the sniper pushed a pressel switch laid on the desk beside his left hand. It was connected to an earpiece tucked in place over his left ear and a small Velcro tactical microphone around his neck.

'5th floor, south east side,' he said. 'Move!'

Releasing the switch, he kept the scope on the window. He focused the crosshairs on a guy lying on the couch, looking dazed, bloodied towels on his torso. He must have been the asshole tagged on the street in the gunfight.

The sniper hated Feds.

His finger tightened on the trigger.

Against the wall, the window above him, Archer stared at Foster.

He was slumped against the wall, his eyes blank and lifeless, half his head on the wall behind him, the rivulets of blood sliding down.

The bullet had hit him between the eyes and killed him instantly.

Then he suddenly realised Carson would be in the firing line.

He dove forward and dragged the doped-up injured Marshal off the couch to the ground by his feet.

A split-second later, there was another smash of glass and a whump of feathers and fabric from the couch as a round hit where his head had just been lying.

Jennifer screamed again as the group kept as low as they could.

The two men who'd just left the lobby sprinted up the south stairwell, responding to the radio call from Joker, their sniper.

Their handles tonight were Queen and Clubs. Using their real names would be more than foolish considering anyone nearby who had the skill could pick up their radio chatter, so the ten-man team had each been assigned call signs. Considering most of them were prolific gamblers, chess pieces and card suits had seemed apt.

They ran up the stairs to the 5th floor and turned out of the stairwell, coming to a halt outside 5B. Queen aimed his M4A1 at the lock and gave it a quick trigger pull, the metal and wood blowing apart and splintering, totally destroyed from the burst of assault rifle fire. Looking through the foresights of their weapons, the two men tried to

132

kick back the door but there was something blocking the way.

Clubs stepped back and rammed his shoulder into it. It wouldn't give. He tried twice more, Queen aiming down his M4A1, ready to shoot anyone inside.

The third time Clubs rammed into the door, it suddenly gave way, followed by a smash as something fell over the other side.

Forcing the door back, the two men moved into the apartment cautiously, looking through the sights of their assault rifles.

They entered straight into a kitchen with a table and two chairs ahead beside a set of windows, the curtains drawn back. The weight blocking the door from the other side had been a refrigerator; tipping it over had knocked out some of the contents, and milk was seeping onto the floor in a widening pool.

There was some blood there too, a faint but definite smear on the wooden floor.

Both a clue and confirmation.

The two men worked their way into the apartment quietly, tracing the apartment with their weapons, the underside of their boots leaving prints in the widening puddle of milk.

To the left was a bathroom. The door was open.

To the right was what had to be the sitting room.

The door was closed.

Clubs looked at Queen and nodded.

Both men aimed their weapons at the doorframe and stepped towards it.

Inside the bathroom, Archer had Carson's USP in his hand, his back against the wall.

He'd heard the lock being blown off the door and had scrambled through the kitchen, diving into the bathroom as whoever was the other side smashed the refrigerator out of the way.

Risking a look from the slightest of angles, he saw two men in combat fatigues and balaclavas with black assault rifles moving quietly towards the sitting room door, their backs to him.

They sure as hell weren't US Marshals or ESU.

He stepped out from behind the door, raising his weapon, ready to drop them both.

Then a floorboard creaked under his foot.

The other two men's senses were on a hair trigger. They wheeled round but Archer had already ducked back into the bathroom, taking cover behind the wall.

The space where he'd been standing a second earlier was torn apart by assault rifle fire. The bullets ripped into the wall above the bathtub, shredding and fragmenting the tiling into pieces, showering Archer with dust and debris as he stayed low behind the wall.

Queen and Clubs continued to fire down on the bathroom, their barrage ripping it to pieces as they advanced.

Behind them, the door to the sitting room suddenly opened and a dark-haired woman rolled out low, a pistol in her hands. Clubs saw her first but she had the drop and shot him twice in the chest, the force knocking him back and killing him instantly as he landed in the puddle of milk beside the refrigerator.

Queen spun around with his M4A1 as the woman rolled back behind the door for cover.

He fired, but his mag clicked dry.

'Shit!'

In that split-second, Archer was already moving in on the guy. He couldn't have fired from the bathroom in case he hit Vargas, so he ran out and launched himself at the man. Tying up, Archer nailed him with a head butt which crunched into the man's nose, causing him to drop his assault rifle, the weapon clattering to the deck.

They hit the wall and then the floor, rolling over the dead gunman's limp legs. The man was powerful and was going for Archer's groin and eyes. Freeing one of his hands, he pulled a knife from a sheath on his belt. Archer caught his wrist but the man was stronger, the knife moving towards his neck.

Archer forced the man's hand to one side, the blade slicing into his arm, hot white pain shooting through him.

Vargas was aiming at the two men but couldn't get a clear shot without risking hitting Archer, so she ran over and smashed her Glock into the back of the gunmen's head, pistol-whipping him as hard as she could. The guy rode the impact but it stunned him momentarily, allowing Archer to push him up and up kick him in the jaw. Vargas quickly stepped back, aiming her weapon, but then there was another smash at the window. A bullet skimmed her and hit the gunman in the back of his head, killing him instantly, spraying a small amount of blood and whatever else into the air.

As she dropped down, the dead man slumped onto the floor beside Archer. The sniper sure as hell wasn't protecting them; he'd killed his own guy trying to hit Vargas.

Neither of them waited an extra second. Staying as low as possible and out of sight of the sniper, Archer grabbed the man's assault rifle from the floor as Vargas crawled over to the man she'd shot and did the same. The gunfire would have reverberated around the building. They didn't know who the hell these guys were or how many there were, and they didn't want to hang around to find out.

'Who the hell are they?' Vargas hissed.

'I don't know. We need to get out of here right now!'

Each gunman had two spare clips in the vest on his uniform which they stuffed into their pockets. Then Archer crawled over to the kitchen windows, reaching up to pull the curtains shut as Vargas stayed low and went back into the sitting room, the M4A1 in her right hand. Barlow had already drawn the curtains in there.

Suddenly, there were two more smashes of glass as two more holes appeared in the fabric, everyone jumping.

The sniper was trying his luck.

As they all stayed down, Vargas reached for Jennifer with her free hand and headed back for the front door as Helen and Barlow followed right behind her, dragging Carson between them.

'Let's move!'

Eighty yards away, Joker cursed, searching with the crosshairs. He'd seen Patterson go down, taking two to the chest. He'd had a clear shot at the woman, but the bitch had moved at the last second and he'd hit Markowski instead.

Now they'd drawn the curtains and he couldn't see shit.

He pushed his pressel.

'All of you, 5th floor, south side. Get over there! Two men down!'

Archer was the first out of the apartment, Carson's USP in the back of his jeans, the M4A1 in his shoulder, a fresh mag slapped into the base. He was covered in dust, dried blood and specks of tile from the bathroom walls, but at least he knew the weapon fired.

He moved to the left into the stairwell and cleared it, up and down. Behind him, Carson was being carried by Barlow and Helen, Vargas holding Jennifer's hand, her USP in her other and the other stolen M4A1 slung across her shoulders.

Up above, Archer heard running footsteps from much higher up, heading down fast.

Back up was coming.

'Let's go!' he whispered.

They needed to get as far from 5 as they could without meeting the guys on their way down. They made it up another three floors, arriving on 8, the footsteps from above getting closer and closer, only five or six flights away and counting.

Archer desperately checked the 8th floor corridor as the others caught up. He was thinking about the sharpshooter who'd killed Foster. He was on the south side and therefore wouldn't be able to see them from the north, west or east. They needed to get into a room down the hall away from his line of sight.

He went to move forward but then heard shouting and noise echoing from the other stairwell.

Meanwhile, the running feet in this stairwell were almost upon them.

In moments, they were going to be trapped from both sides.

They had seconds.

Archer saw the door to the apartment to the left of the stairwell was open, on the south-west corner. It was the opposite apartment to Helen's, the other side of the stairwell, facing the Hudson but also downtown and the sniper. They had no choice. He raced forward, pushing open 8A, and checked inside, sweeping left and right. The layout of this apartment was the same as Helen's, but it was empty and by the grace of God the curtains were already drawn across the windows.

The group piled in behind him and he quickly shut the door as soon as they were all inside.

As he and Vargas dragged the refrigerator across as a makeshift barricade, Barlow and Helen carried Carson into the next room and placed him on the couch.

Breathing hard and backing up from the door, Vargas unslung her M4A1 and aimed it at the wood, Archer already doing the same.

Both of them heard shouting and footsteps sprinting down the stairwell, passing where they'd been seconds ago.

They'd made it.

Just.

SEVENTEEN

Helen and Jennifer stayed where they were inside the sitting room, scared, disorientated and tense. Helen had her arm around the child protectively, holding her close, both of them staying away from the curtain-covered window. Across the room, Carson was on the couch, totally out of it.

Barlow and Vargas were in the kitchen, standing near the bathroom door, keeping their weapons aimed at the refrigerator covering the entrance. On the opposite side, Archer was crouching in the doorway of the sitting room, his new M4A1 locked in his shoulder, waiting for someone to try and force their way in.

He heard the sound of voices and running feet echoing from the stairwell but no-one seemed to be on this corridor.

Realising he had some blood on his face from when his attacker had taken the sniper round, Archer wiped it with the sleeve of his shirt and glanced behind him. Jennifer was sniffing and crying, Helen doing her best to comfort her and try to keep her quiet. When it became clear no one was about to burst in, Archer, Barlow and Vargas relaxed very slightly, taking some deep breaths, letting the change to their situation fully sink in now Foster was dead.

Suddenly, things were looking a hell of a lot worse.

Vargas lowered her stolen assault rifle then strode across the kitchen and stepped behind Archer into the sitting room. Checking the safety, she placed the M4A1 to one side then dropped

140

down, Jennifer breaking from Helen's protective grasp and rushing forward to hug her.

'It's OK. It's OK,' she said, as Jennifer clung to her like a small koala. Barlow also moved inside the room, keeping his pistol in his hand and moving over to the couch to check on Carson.

Archer rose and leant against the doorjamb, keeping an eye on the entrance to the apartment, his newly-acquired M4A1 in his hands. He watched the door like a sentry, waiting for the lock to be blown off at any moment, wondering just what the hell was going on.

'I don't believe it,' Barlow said, pacing. 'Foster's gone. They killed him. How did that just happen?'

No-one responded. Jennifer sniffed and sobbed in the quiet.

'Jesus. Who the hell are these guys?'

'Whoever they are, the chopper must have brought them,' Vargas said, looking up from comforting the girl. 'And they've got a sniper. We underestimated this. Them.'

Archer glanced down at the M4A1 in his hands instead. It was in flawless condition. Black and compact with an adjustable strap, the weapon was high-tech and savage, not the kind of thing a street thug could get his hands on without some serious cash.

He thought back to the two intruders, the way they'd moved, their equipment, how quickly they'd followed up the sniper fire.

'Are they military?' Helen asked, echoing the thoughts in his mind.

No-one replied, because no-one knew.

Not hearing anything from the corridor, Archer laid his M4A1 to one side, ensuring the safety was on and that Vargas had charge of Jennifer. He walked across the room and joined Helen beside Carson. This time they hadn't bothered to lay any towels or blankets over the furniture.

By the looks of the rest of the apartment, the bloodstains would blend right in with the décor.

'How is he?' he asked.

'Better than the rest of us,' Helen said. Carson's eyes were open but were seeing something somewhere else, totally oblivious to his surroundings. Thankfully the gunfire and Foster's sudden death hadn't turned things sour; since he'd been a cop Archer had encountered more than a couple of heroin users and knew any negative outside stimulus could turn a good trip into a nightmare like the flick of a switch.

If he started screaming from hallucinations, they wouldn't stay hidden for long.

Archer turned his attention to Helen. 'Are you OK?'

'Yes,' she said. 'I think so.'

'Hey,' Vargas said. Archer turned. 'Your arm.'

He glanced down at his bicep and saw a growing bloodstain on the right sleeve of his red and white flannel shirt. He remembered the man cutting him with the knife, just before Vargas had pistol-whipped him and he took the sniper round in the back of the head.

Suddenly aware of the wound and as if almost on cue, it started to throb. Giving Jennifer one last reassuring hug, Vargas rose and scooped up her M4A1.

142

'Follow me,' she told him.

Knight and Bishop had arrived on the 5th floor. They'd been on 21 when they'd heard shots being fired and the situation being called in over the radio by Joker, their sniper. Queen and Clubs had taken the call, but their radios had gone dead. The piece of shit elevator was busted so they'd been forced to take the stairs, bombing down them, taking the steps two at a time.

However, by the time they'd made it down here the Marshals and the kid had disappeared. They were too late. Arriving on 5, there'd been no question which apartment had been their hideout, even without Joker telling them. The door to the right of the stairwell was ajar and they could smell the gun smoke and oil. The lock had been obliterated by a burst of gunfire.

The two men were now standing inside the apartment, looking at the bodies of their two guys. Both had been stripped of their weapons and magazines and were lying on the floor, their blood mixed with milk from the overturned refrigerator.

They'd both been shot, Clubs in the chest, Queen in the back of the head, a red hole in his balaclava and blood all over the wall.

Examining the scene without saying a word, the armed men then checked out the rest of the apartment. To the right, one of the US Marshals was slumped against the sitting room wall, half his head blown onto the plaster behind him. They recognised him as Foster, the leader of the group, a giant of a man. Although the other Marshals had escaped, at least this guy was now out of the picture. When they'd acquired the tip and extensive information on the Marshals team, they'd examined Foster's jacket and known he was going to be one hell of a challenge. The man was a goddamn terminator, military trained and survivor of numerous gunshot wounds and full-on sieges and conflicts from his time in the army. However, a bullet to the head had solved that problem. Six feet four inches and over two hundred and ten pounds of expert soldier they wouldn't need to deal with anymore. Their main human obstacle tonight was now out of the way.

That was the only bit of good news.

Knight pushed the switch on his uniform, looking at the three dead men.

'This is Knight. I'm on 5 with Bishop.'

'Report,' King said, still in the lobby. *'Is the girl dead?'*

'No. Clubs and Queen are.'

Pause. Knight could picture how the news was being received.

'How?'

'Shot. Their weapons are gone.'

Silence.

'Foster bought it too. Joker tagged him.'

'The girl?'

'She's not here. They escaped.'

There was a long pause. Knight noticed some bloodied towels and rags on the couch, some of them dragged to the floor. The injured Marshal must have been there.

'Find her. Check the rest of the floor. They can't have gone far.'

'The bodies?'

144

'We'll deal with them later.'

Knight released the switch, then looked at the two dead men, Markowski and Patterson. When the call signs had been assigned, much laughter had been had at the expense of Markowski being allocated the name Queen. He hadn't been amused, seeing as he was probably the toughest and surliest member of the group, built like a fridge-freezer and with a sense of humour as cold as the icebox.

Knight looked down at his colleague; his head was laid to the side, showing a glimpse of a huge ugly exit wound on his face from the bullet that killed him. Turning, he moved to the window and drew open the curtains. There was a small bullet hole there in the window.

'Joker, what the hell happened?' he asked, pushing his pressel.

'Clubs went down; I didn't see how. I had a shot at the woman. I took it but she moved at the last second.'

Knight looked out at the other building eighty yards south, trying to gauge where exactly Joker was.

'I hit Queen instead. I apologise, everyone. It's on me.'

Pause.

'Doesn't matter,' King's voice said, overhearing the transmission. *'We do what it takes tonight. He'd want the rest of us to get this shit done regardless. Stay focused and find her.'*

Knight nodded, and turned to Bishop, who was standing behind him. During this exchange, he'd checked out the bathroom. The wall had been annihilated by gunfire, many of the tiles smashed, half-pieces and fragments left clinging to the plaster.

'They just took this up a notch. So let's find them and use this to redecorate,' he said, patting his M4A1. Bishop nodded without a word.

Taking a last look at their two dead colleagues, the two men moved back to the door.

Down on the street, everyone had all heard the sudden automatic gunfire erupt from inside the building. It had ended as quickly as it had started and no-one had any idea what the hell was going on in there.

The sudden and unexpected arrival of the unmarked chopper and the team abseiling onto the roof had delayed the Marshals' approach and severely complicated things. They had no idea who these newcomers were and what kind of weaponry they had. Despite his team's willingness to proceed, Dalton needed to fully assess the changed situation before sending them in, so he ordered the task force to hold back for the time being. They knew the lobby would be guarded, controlling the only entrance, so a front-on entry was still a last case resort. Carson had already been hit tonight; no more Marshals were getting dropped on his watch as long as he could help it.

Standing beside Josh near the Marshals team, Shepherd looked up at the building, filled with trepidation. The automatic gunfire was raising all sorts of questions, the potential answers to which were worrying him considerably. His call with

Archer had cut out before he could tell him about the arrival of the anonymous men in the chopper.

From the sounds of things, they'd already encountered each other.

'What the hell is going on in there?' he muttered in frustration.

To his left, Josh didn't reply.

As they looked up at the building, Marquez walked over quickly and re-joined them, a brown file in her hand which she passed over to Shepherd.

'CSU just sent this over, sir. They pulled an ID on the guy who got shot in the street when they ambushed the Marshals.'

Shepherd took the folder, opening it.

'His name is Marlon Hayes,' she said, as he read. '20 years old, born and raised in Harlem. Mother died HIV, father unknown.'

'Priors?'

'Usual shit. Nothing major. Never did time aside from a stint in juvenile hall. But get this; he's a joint suspect in three unsolved homicides. Detectives from SID have him down as being a gun for hire, part of a five man team. They do wet work for people who don't want to get their hands dirty. Basically, a street thug and a killer. Shoot first, ask questions later.'

Shepherd examined the man's file. 'So he was paid to do this job. It wasn't personal.'

She nodded. 'Witnesses say there were four other men shooting down on the Marshals. Must be the rest of that suspect crew. The numbers make sense.'

'Files?'

147

'Already being drawn. We'll have them any minute.'

Shepherd nodded.

'OK, but who hired them?' Josh asked.

Marquez shrugged. 'Whoever they are, someone sure wants Dalton's witness dead.'

'OK, so who the hell is this witness?'

Shepherd turned and looked at Dalton, who was standing with his team, talking with his people.

'Only one way to find out.'

EIGHTEEN

Inside the bathroom in apartment 8A, Archer was sitting on the edge of the bathtub, which was set against the far wall and on a raised level from the rest of the floor. Helen's had been the same; it must have been the building design, some half-hearted attempt at style long ago, or maybe just so cockroaches couldn't climb into the tub without really earning it.

He'd swept an old stained shower curtain out of the way, which was gathered to his right. It might have been white once, but now had a depressing brown tinge like everything else inside the place. Glancing around the room, it seemed whoever the homeowner was, they weren't overly concerned with hygiene. The bathroom had definitely seen better days, like the rest of the building. It needed a good clean, a few layers of paint or just a demo crew to clear it out and start over.

Still wearing his white t-shirt, he'd removed his red and white flannel over-shirt and had it resting on his lap. A naked light bulb hung from the ceiling, throwing a stark and unforgiving light over everything in the room. In front of him, Vargas was kneeling on the step, examining the knife wound on his arm, the two of them alone, everyone else next door. Beside him, his M4A1 rested against the porcelain bath, the safety on.

His adrenaline had dropped and he felt nauseous. It had happened scores of times before, the inevitable response to a life-threatening situation, his body pumping the hormone into his bloodstream in an effort to keep him alive. That wasn't the first gunfight he'd been in and he knew it wouldn't be the last, but it had been a relatively long time since someone had tried to kill him and his body had reacted instantly to the stress.

Swallowing and closing his eyes, he waited for the feeling to pass, furious at himself.

He'd had the jump on two armed guys but almost got himself and everyone else killed. A creaky floorboard, for Christ's sake; hell, it all might have ended differently if it wasn't for a bullet intended for Vargas. The Archer of three months ago would have slotted those two gunmen before they'd even had a chance to turn, no hesitation, no mistakes.

With his eyes still shut, he shook his head. Errors like that were hardly ever forgiven.

He'd been lucky.

Vargas noticed the look on his face. 'Everything alright?'

He opened his eyes and nodded, looking down at her. She'd lifted the edge of the sleeve of his white t-shirt and was studying the wound, making sure it wasn't too deep. Archer glanced at it. The knife had sliced across his arm, blood leaking out and leaving a rivulet path on the skin below. It was only a superficial cut, no tendon or muscle damage, although it hurt like hell.

Knives were scary weapons; Archer couldn't stand them. They could kill with just one slice or jab and unlike guns they didn't require reloading and didn't jam. They were also silent and could be concealed easily. Archer had some unpleasant memories of knives and the type of people who used them as weapons. He had a jagged scar

150

running along his brow just under his hairline that was a constant reminder of just how dangerous they were.

'Yeah, he got you,' she said. 'An ounce more pressure, you'd be in deep shit.'

He smiled. 'Story of my life.'

She looked around the bathroom for a bandage. He read her mind and lifted his red and white flannel shirt from his lap. Carson's, his own and the other man's blood had stained the upper half, but the lower portion of the garment was relatively clean and a damn sight cleaner than anything else around the place.

'Use this.'

'It'll be ruined,' she said, taking it. 'You don't mind?'

'Gift from an ex.'

She smiled. 'Probably not what she had in mind when she gave it to you.'

Taking a pair of scissors she'd found in the kitchen, she made a cut then ripped off a long strip. She then wrapped it around the wound firmly but gently, the fabric soaking up blood the moment it touched the cut. He watched her work; the light was accentuating her cheekbones in a nice way. He suddenly had a flashback to another Latina face under a similarly harsh light; that had been very different. Examining her face, he tried to guess her heritage. Her hair and eyebrows were jet black, her eyes the colour of coffee, her skin the same but with a splash of milk.

'So what's your story?' she asked, tightening the bandage. 'You said you're NYPD.'

'That's right.'

'You don't sound American.'

'I'm half English. I used to be a cop in London. Grew up over there too.'

'Why'd you move?'

'Itchy feet.'

'You got a family?'

He nodded. 'A sister. She's a lawyer. Lives in DC.'

Pause.

'How about you?'

She smiled. 'My story's boring as hell.'

'I'd like to hear it.'

'Trust me. You wouldn't.'

She paused.

'I'm from LA. I never met my father; apparently he was Brazilian. My mother was American and raised me. She died when I was sixteen.'

'How?'

'Wrong place, wrong time. She was in a deli in Reseda when someone held it up. Shot her twice along with the cashier. He forgot to wear a mask and didn't want any witnesses.'

'I'm sorry.' Pause. 'Wrong place, wrong time. Sounds familiar.'

Finishing winding the bandage, she double tied it, then examined her work. Archer looked down at it, moving his arm around, testing the pressure. It was wrapped tight, yet was loose enough to not cut off circulation. There was no more blood leaking from the wound and staining his arm. Given the circumstances, she'd done a pretty good job.

'Thanks.'

She watched him for a moment then leaned back, rolling to her feet. They both looked around the bathroom as a silence fell.

'This must be the President's suite,' she said.

He smiled as Helen appeared in the doorway, seeing him sitting on the edge of the tub. 'All patched up?'

He nodded. 'How's Carson?'

'On Cloud Nine. Barlow's watching him and the girl.' Pause. 'So I hate to ask the obvious but who the hell were those men? Do you have any idea?'

'I don't know,' Archer said honestly, glancing at Vargas. She shook her head. 'But this is bigger than we thought. The guys on the street were amateurs. They had surprise on their side and that was it. But this group is in a different league, whoever they are and how many they are. They have high-tech weapons; they move in pairs. They arrived by helicopter and they have a sniper. They had no idea we'd end up in this building, yet they were prepared enough to be here within forty minutes and kill Foster. They're professionals.'

'And this is about Jennifer?' Helen said, lowering her voice.

Archer looked at Vargas, who nodded.

'Let's just say she's important.'

'Enough that they'll kill each other to get to us and her,' he said. 'Mind telling us who she is?'

'I can't share that,' Vargas replied.

'I can't share that,' Dalton replied outside on the street corner, unwittingly echoing Vargas.

'C'mon James, save it,' Shepherd said, frustrated. 'You heard the gunfire and saw that chopper. One of my people is in there too. We're in this together. Tell us what this is about.'

'Not going to happen,' Dalton replied. 'Save your breath, Sergeant.'

He turned to one of his team, a female Marshal in a bulletproof vest. She had a cell phone to her ear.

'Any luck?' he asked.

She shook her head. 'Still down; can't get through to any of them. Tried the 5B mainline but its dead too.'

'How could they disable the cell phones?'

The woman shrugged. 'They must have a jammer of some sort.'

As Dalton considered what she'd said, Marquez returned, carrying another folder.

'Got the four files on the other boys from the street,' she said, passing it to Shepherd. 'Check 'em out.'

He opened them, examining the files one by one. The last one caught his eye; the man in question had long blond dreadlocks with brown skin and angry eyes, holding up a placard as he was snapped for a mug shot. Apparently he was half-Colombian; his name was Zachary Braeten. In and out of juvenile facilities and prison for most of his twenty six years; Marquez was right. A detective up in Harlem had been trying to build a case against him and his friends for a series of unexplained murders, with him down as the leader. Shepherd had seen similar files before; these kind of people were killers but not trained

154

killers, men who would take life for money without a second thought. Amateurs.

But dangerous.

'You seen this?' Shepherd asked, passing it to Dalton. He took it and scanned the sheets, thumbing through them quickly. 'Someone hired them to take out your witness. But there's still a missing piece of the puzzle.'

'Let it go, Sergeant. I'm not telling you who she is.'

'But whoever she is, she's been placed in protective custody, right? Witness protection.'

Dalton nodded. 'Correct.'

'Then how the hell would they know where your Marshals were?' Josh finished, reading Shepherd's mind. 'Is your crew sloppy?'

Dalton shot him a look that could have melted ice.

'Foster and his team are the best we have.'

'Someone tipped these guys off,' Shepherd said, waving the file. 'Someone in your department?'

'No way.'

'You can be that sure?'

'Yes. Positive. No-one in my office aside from myself and Foster's team knew about this operation. It was highly confidential.'

'What about leverage, or coercion?' Marquez said. 'Doesn't matter who you are, if a man puts a gun to someone you love you have to make a choice.'

'Personal files on all Marshals are restricted. Neither Barlow or Carson have any immediate family.'

155

'What about Foster?'

'He's got four boys. Two are in the army overseas, the other two working defence contracts in the Middle East for a security firm. He's clean. Anyway, all three of my guys are tough as hell. They know the way this job goes. They wouldn't slip.'

'What about the woman?' Marquez asked. 'What's her name?'

Dalton paused. 'Vargas.'

'Can she be trusted?'

'With your life,' Dalton said, fixing her gaze. 'Trust me on that, Detective.'

Closing the folder, Shepherd exhaled, frustrated. Dalton wouldn't budge. Turning, he looked over at the ESU team twenty yards behind them. There were twelve or so of them, huddled together in a tight group, examining floor plans and schematics over by their truck.

Hobbs was in the middle, issuing orders to the group quietly.

It looked as if a briefing was coming to an end.

Dalton saw it too and walked towards them.

'Oh shit,' Josh muttered to Shepherd and Marquez, watching him go. 'Here comes Round Three.'

'Hobbs,' Dalton called.

Hobbs looked at him but didn't respond. Neither did any of his men.

'Don't even think about it, Hobbs. This is our operation.'

'Take a hike.'

'Stand down. That's an order.'

'And do what, sit here and wait?' Hobbs pointed at Dalton's team, who were standing just behind him, looking up at the building. 'Try growing a set of balls. You heard the shots fired inside. We need to get in there now, not hang around and wait for an invitation.'

'Our choppers are on the way. They'll be here soon.'

'We're going in.'

'We don't know who those people are or what kind of weaponry they have,' Dalton emphasised. 'You have no idea what you're sending your men into.'

Ignoring him, Hobbs turned to his task force. *'Clear?'* he called.

'Don't do it,' Dalton said. 'That's a Federal order.'

Ignoring him, the ESU team nodded. Gathering their gear, they climbed into their van without a word and pulled the rear doors shut behind them. A guy in the front seat fired the engine and they headed off down the street, away from the crowd. Dalton watched them go, as Shepherd, Josh and Marquez joined him.

'What's happening?' Marquez asked.

'It's show time,' Josh said quietly, watching the truck head downtown.

NINETEEN

Up in the 8th floor apartment, Archer, Vargas and Helen had re-joined Barlow and Carson in the sitting room. With the curtains drawn and only a few lights on, the place was low lit, but it was staying that way. They weren't about to switch any more lights on and risk alerting the sniper that they were in here.

As Vargas walked over to Jennifer and sat down with her, Archer took a seat against the wall away from the window, resting the M4A1 beside him and thinking about their next move after double-checking that the curtains beside him were fully drawn and had no gaps. Fortunately, the owner of the apartment hadn't opened the window behind them, meaning there was no risk of the curtains moving from the wind which could reveal their presence to the shooter, if only for a split-second. The son of a bitch wouldn't be too far away and he would be looking for another chance to take a shot and take another one of them out.

A silence fell. Archer saw the brooding expression on Barlow's face across the room and guessed what was on his mind.

Or who.

'He wouldn't have known anything about it,' Archer said. 'It was instant.'

Silence.

'I can't believe they killed him,' Barlow said. 'He was invincible. Our boss. Shit.'

'It was quick,' Vargas said.

Pause.

'We can't stay here,' Barlow said. 'Whoever these guys are, they'll find us.'

'Can we force our way out?' Helen asked.

'With a wounded man and a small girl?' Vargas said, holding Jennifer close. 'They'll cut us to pieces. And we don't even know who these men are, or how many of them are here. There could easily be a squad of them for all we know.'

'So what do we do?'

'We wait for reinforcements,' Vargas said.

'So where the hell are they?' Barlow said.

'They'll come.'

'But what if *they* find us first?'

'This is a big building,' Archer said, with more confidence than he felt. 'We could be anywhere. It'll take them time to clear it.'

There was a pause. In the silence, Carson opened his mouth like a child, staring up at the ceiling, wonderment in his eyes.

'And we're still alive,' Archer said, looking over at Jennifer. 'Let's keep it together and ensure it stays that way.'

Barlow went to reply, but suddenly there was the same noise from outside as earlier, a distant familiar thumping.

It was increasing, getting louder and closer, coming from downtown.

The group looked at each other; Vargas turned to Barlow and smiled.

'You wanted back up, Jared? Here they come.'

Down on the street, Shepherd, Marquez and Josh were standing beside Hobbs, who'd set up a

159

command post beside his Department-issue vehicle. Dalton had stopped his protestations for the moment, joining them. Although this was a Federal operation, his people didn't have immediate access to a chopper and ESU did. They were also drilled and professionally trained for an aerial assault, whereas the Marshals were primarily a ground entry team. As much as Dalton disliked this being in someone else's hands, Hobbs had a point. At the end of the day, they all wanted the same thing.

Hobbs grabbed his radio. 'Briggs, give me a sitrep.'

'*Twenty seconds, sir. Roof is clear.*'

Looking downtown, Shepherd, Josh, Marquez and Dalton saw the black shape in the early evening sky moving over the Upper West Side, coming closer and closer.

Hobbs nodded, turning to Shepherd, one NYPD man to another.

'Here we go.'

On the 16th floor, Castle was clearing an apartment alone when his earpiece suddenly went off. He was one of the two guys who'd set up some equipment on the roof, in charge of dealing with an aerial assault.

'*Chopper coming!*' Joker said. '*It's ESU!*'

Turning, Castle raced out of the apartment and down the hallway.

He sprinted up the north stairwell, taking the stairs two at a time.

Sweeping through the clammy night air, the ESU chopper slowed and hovered over the West 135th tenement block, the rotors whirring in a whumping blur, mirroring what the other chopper had done less than thirty minutes earlier.

Up front, the pilot spoke into his radio as Hobbs' ESU team sat in the back, ready and raring to go. All of them were dressed in the standard police-issue navy blue combat fatigues, helmets strapped to their heads, AR15 assault rifles slung across their backs and black gloves on their hands.

Their side doors were open, coils of rope ready to be thrown out to be used as entry points. They would start from the roof and work their way down floor by floor, taking out the enemy, locating and securing the group of Marshals and the child.

'Lieutenant, we're in position,' the pilot said.

Down on the street, Hobbs looked up. Beside him, Shepherd and Dalton didn't speak, watching in silence.

'*Go!*'

Hooked up to the same transmission, the ESU Sergeant in the back gave the thumbs up to his men.

Throwing out the ropes and checking their harnesses, they all abseiled down onto the roof, two sets of six, twelve men sliding down the cords in smooth and immaculately-drilled fashion. It took less than ten seconds, mirroring the entry of the anonymous response team earlier, and soon the entire task force were grouped on the roof of the building.

They each unslung their AR15s and knelt in firing positions, covering each other's backs.

'First Team is on the roof,' the Sergeant said into his radio.

As the helicopter rose, pulling back from the building with the ropes still hanging down from its cabin, the twelve man ESU team took a moment to take stock, aiming out in a circle, letting their senses calibrate, their eyes protected from swirling dust and grit by protective goggles.

As they did so, the officers noticed something that hadn't been visible from above.

There were six small black blankets placed around the roof, surrounding the men in a large circle.

The blankets were concealing something.

Castle burst through the entrance to the stairwell. Running up the stairs, he peered over the wall and saw the circle of ESU officers.

He dropped down and picked up a clacker he'd left on one of the steps.

Staying low behind cover, he closed his eyes and squeezed it.

Down on the street, Josh was beside Hobbs when the helicopter suddenly reared up.

There was the sound of smashing glass from windows on buildings nearby, glass raining down to the street as people ran and ducked for cover from a sudden hail of deadly shrapnel.

'Jesus Christ!' he said. *'What the hell was that?'*

'What's going on? Briggs, report!' Hobbs said into his radio, as debris continued to rain down on them.

'Sir, First Team is down!' the pilot said. *'I repeat, First Team is down!'*

'What? How many?'

'All of them!'

By the stairwell, Castle peered over the wall again.

The clacker had been rigged up to six Claymore mines he and Spades had set up when they arrived, the same weapons as those aimed at the front entrance. With black blankets draped over them, the mines were pretty much invisible from above on the dark tarred surface. Shaped in a boxy curved rectangle, each convex mine contained seven hundred steel balls buried in an epoxy resin and C4 plastic explosive. When detonated, the balls were projected into a firing line at just under four thousand feet per second. There was a reason many dirty-bomb makers imitated the design.

One Claymore could cut down an entire group of people with one push of a clacker.

Six of them daisy-chained together in a circle could shred an entire platoon.

He saw what was left of the ESU task force spread out on the roof. Twelve cops, the NYPD's finest, dropped in one moment with not a single bullet fired.

Their AR15s and equipment were scattered everywhere, a sea of bodies, weapons, blood, radios and ball bearings.

He smiled. Seeing as his own team controlled the lobby, there'd been only one other way into the building available to them and they'd acted exactly as anticipated.

Looking up, Castle saw the ESU helicopter still hovering, the pilot inside most likely reporting what had just happened and what he could see. Laying down his M4A1, Castle swung a circular tube from a holster by his left shoulder and pulled it out, the sights flipping up into place as the launcher extended.

It was an M72 LAW, a light anti-tank weapon made up of two tubes. When drawn open, the launcher armed itself, a 66m HEAT warhead primed and ready to be fired. It was easily portable and unguided, meaning whoever was firing needed to hit their target first time.

Castle lifted it to his shoulder and aimed at the vessel, narrowing his eyes as the rotors kicked up dust and grit from the roof.

It was still well within range.

He put the sights on the underbelly.

Down on the street they were brushing glass and other debris off themselves, still trying to grasp what had just happened, when there was a sudden *whoosh* in the sky and a large explosion.

Ducking for cover again, they all looked up and saw the ESU helicopter take a massive hit, a large fireball erupting from its undercarriage.

164

Recoiling from the impact, the vessel started to spin, smoke pouring from the rotor, the chopper shaking as it turned.

'Pull up, Briggs!' Hobbs screamed into his radio. '*Pull up!'*

The chopper wheeled away to the left but the vessel was heading for the other side of the building towards Riverbank State Park.

Shepherd, Josh and Marquez watched as it dropped out of sight, going down fast.

They didn't see it land but they heard the explosion.

Up on the roof, Castle heard it too and walked over to the west side of the building.

He saw the burning wreckage of the chopper in Riverbank State Park, fifty yards or so away by the Hudson River, the flames a bright and harsh orange in the dark night as thick smoke billowed up.

A helicopter and an entire ESU task force dropped in less than twenty seconds.

So much for the rescue effort.

'Castle, report,' came King's voice.

'ESU is down, sir,' he said, pushing his pressel. 'So is their chopper.'

'Excellent.'

Tossing the LAW launcher to the concrete, Castle scooped up his M4A1 from the stairs and moved back down to the door, a smile on his lips and twelve dead cops laid out on the roof behind him.

TWENTY

Down in 8A, the group had heard two explosions. Moments earlier, they'd heard the helicopter moving in close, the windows reverberating slightly as it hovered either nearby or above them.

Unnerved and confused, they glanced at each other, literally alone in the dark.

'What the hell was that?' Barlow said.

They waited. Listening.

'Maybe they're engaging them?' Vargas said.

Together, the pair of Marshals headed towards the window facing the Hudson side, Archer moving across the room and joining them. It was more than unlikely that another sharpshooter would be covering this side, considering he'd have to be hundreds of yards away the other side of the River.

Nevertheless, the trio looked down through the side of the curtains, not standing front on, sneaking quick glances at the west side of the building below.

'Holy shit,' Barlow said.

There was the burning wreckage of a helicopter in Riverbank State Park, the vessel engulfed in flames, smoke billowing up into the night. They could just make out distinctive white lettering on the tail of the wrecked burning vessel.

ESU.

'No, no,' Barlow said. 'Not good.'

The trio looked at each other, realising what had just happened. Vargas then turned to Helen, who was standing near the apartment phone.

'Is the landline still cut?'

Helen picked up the receiver from a phone on a desk and lifted it to her ear. She pushed a few buttons then nodded.

'It's dead. What's down there?'

'An ESU chopper. It's been hit.'

Helen's eyes widened. *What?* You said they were our rescue? Were there men inside?'

No-one responded; the trio withdrew from the curtains, making sure they were fully back in place. An uneasy silence filled the room. All of them were feeling increasingly trapped and increasingly worried.

This was getting worse and worse by the minute.

'We need to talk to people outside,' Vargas said. 'Inside here, with no communications, we're sitting ducks.'

She nodded at the window.

'And they're not getting to us any time soon.'

'So how do we communicate?' Barlow said. 'The phones are dead.'

Archer turned to Helen. 'Are there any other phone lines in the building? Anywhere?'

She thought about it. 'I don't know.'

'Anything?'

'I think there's an old emergency line up on 22. Don't know if it works though. Or if it's even still there.'

'An emergency line?'

'It's a fire phone, next to an extinguisher. But I don't know if it's connected. I don't think it's ever been used. It's been there for years.'

Archer glanced at Vargas, who nodded.

'Whoa, wait a minute,' Helen said, reading their minds. 'You can't go out there. We need to stay put. You don't know who these people are, or what kind of weaponry they have.'

'We have to do something. And the ESU team might have made it onto the roof before the chopper took the hit. We can meet up with them.'

'But those other men appeared out of nowhere. You don't know how many of them there are. You just said that yourselves.'

'We stay here, it's only a matter of time before they find us,' Vargas said, as Archer nodded, pulling the USP from the back of his waistband and checking the clip. 'And we're running out of options.'

Helen stared at her, the red and blue lights from below flashing through the curtains covering the south-facing window behind her, not liking the plan. Barlow didn't speak.

Whispering something to Jennifer and hugging her, Vargas scooped up the M4A1. She pulled out the magazine, a round gleaming back, then slotted it back into the weapon and looked over at Barlow.

'Can you hold the fort here?'

'Since when have you started giving orders?'

She rolled her eyes. 'OK Jared, we can swap. You can head up to 22 and I'll stay.'

He shook his head.

'No way. I'll watch the kid. I don't fancy dying tonight.'

Checking his own M4A1, Archer turned to Helen.

'Whereabouts is this phone?' he asked. 'Be specific. We won't have long up there.'

'22, middle of the corridor. Red box. You can't miss it.'

Down on the street, Hobbs was in a state of shock. Including the chopper pilot, thirteen of his people had just been killed in a matter of seconds, their rescue effort annihilated, the chopper swatted aside like an irritating fly. All of his angry defiance and hostile attitude towards Dalton had evaporated.

He was sitting by his truck, several of his remaining men with him, on the phone with one of his superiors and trying to explain what the hell had just happened. In their entire history, ESU had never lost a team like that so easily.

All of those officers had been standing here ten minutes ago.

Now, they were all dead.

Standing in the street, Dalton, Shepherd, Marquez and Josh watched him in grim silence. They could hear distant sirens of several fire trucks approaching; the group caught a glimpse of the vehicles racing up Riverside Drive a street over, headed towards the burning wreckage of the chopper. Several NYPD blue and whites had pulled round to the scene soon after it had happened, and their reports confirmed that the helicopter had been totalled, landing in the stretch of Park adjacent to the Hudson. Thankfully, no members of the public had been killed; the same couldn't be said for the pilot.

'This is unreal,' Josh muttered.

'They knew we'd try the roof,' Shepherd said. 'Hobbs' team landed right in their trap.'

Watching the shell-shocked ESU Lieutenant explaining himself on the phone, Shepherd turned to Dalton.

'No more bullshit. Men from my team just died. Time you told us who this witness is. Why are people so desperate to kill her?'

Dalton stared up at the building.

He didn't say a word.

Easing the door of 8A back almost painfully slowly, Archer checked the hallway.

It was empty.

He slid out, the assault rifle locked into his shoulder. Vargas followed, doing the same. She pulled the door shut behind them gently, and heard Barlow replacing the refrigerator the other side of the wood, shunting it back into place, the underside scraping across the floor. Barlow had his Glock, USP and two spare mags for each so Jennifer would have sufficient protection for the time being. Helen was staying close to Carson, keeping close tabs on him. Her resistance to Archer's and Vargas' course of action had continued all the way until they stepped outside.

However, the pair now outside the apartment knew they had to do something. Rescue wasn't coming anytime soon. If they were going to get out of here alive, they'd have to figure it out themselves.

If they waited, they'd be found.

And if they were found, they would almost certainly be killed.

The stairwell to their right, the main corridor stretching away to their left, the two of them stood there, waiting, listening.

Archer glanced over his shoulder at Vargas, who motioned with her head. She took point, the pair moving into the south stairwell, Archer keeping his M4A1 trained on the long corridor behind them as Vargas took the lead.

Keeping their movements slow and quiet, they checked down then looked up through the gap in the railings. Everywhere their eyes went, the M4A1s followed.

There was noise coming from the building but it was muffled shouts and rap music from somewhere, nothing threatening.

She went to start moving up but he grabbed her arm.

A few floors above, someone had just pulled open a stairwell door and stepped out.

They were coming this way.

After his work on the roof, Castle had hooked up with Spades and they'd just cleared the 10th floor, moving from the north side to the south. They'd been assigned 10 to 16, but so far, no luck, no sign of these assholes anywhere.

Heading down the south stairwell, they came to a halt on 8, the door pushed back and held in place by a door wedge.

Spades looked down the corridor. It was long and empty, a couple of apartments left open from the sudden evacuation of the building, although most of the doors were shut. Spades was a guy whose temper was always simmering, waiting to boil over.

Staring down the hallway, he hawked and spat, pissed off.

'They could be anywhere,' he said. 'They could have doubled back on us somewhere and be in a room we've already checked.'

'We'll find her,' Castle said. 'Relax.'

He pulled a pack of smokes from his overalls and offered one to Spades, who declined. Drawing one into his mouth from the pack, Castle pulled a lighter and sparked it.

'What time is it?' Spades asked.

Castle checked his watch as he took a draw on the cig, exhaling. '1938.'

'Clock's ticking. We can't hang around. We've already been here too long.'

He looked up the stairwell from where they'd just come and swore.

'We need to smoke them out.'

Castle took a long draw, then exhaled. 'Relax. I just destroyed the ESU team. We've got time. That'll hold everyone off for a while.'

'Or make them even more determined. You killed a whole squad of cops, brother. They'll want revenge for that.'

Castle shook his head, grinning. 'The next group sent in will be pissing their pants. And we'll be out of here by then anyway. We'll find her.'

'*Castle, Spades, report,*' a voice said over the radio.

Looking around, Castle pushed the pressel on his uniform.

'Nothing up here, boss.'

He released the handle, taking a last draw on the cigarette, then dropped it to the floor and stubbed it out with his boot.

'Let's go see the others. You're right; we need to think of another way.'

Spades nodded.

'We keep searching every single apartment, we'll be here till next week.'

Raising their M4A1s, the two men continued on their way, the sound of their boots clattering in the stairwell as they headed down towards the ground floor.

A few feet away, around the corner and pressed up flat against the wall, Vargas looked at Archer beside her, who waited.

They'd ducked back through the door and were the other side of the wall to the stairwell, having listened to the pair's entire conversation.

Hearing the men head off, they both remained where they were, holding their breath, making sure the men were gone.

After a few moments, hearing boots disappearing down the stairs, Archer eased away from the wall and crept back into the stairwell.

The air smelt of cigarette smoke and gun oil, a stub dropped on the floor with a spiral of smoke rising from the tip.

He and Vargas could still hear the men's footsteps, but they were fading and getting fainter, heading down, far enough away to not be an issue.

He looked over at Vargas, who nodded, determination on her face.

Then the two of them started making their way upstairs, taking extra care to tread quietly.

TWENTY ONE

It took them ten minutes to get to 22, Archer's second trip up there for the evening. They didn't encounter any remaining residents on the way and more importantly, no-one carrying a gun. They'd heard the two enemy gunmen report they'd found nothing in their area, so they guessed for the moment at least the south stairwell should be clear.

They worked their way up quickly but methodically, clearing each corridor, their fingers tense on the triggers of the M4A1s. There were no windows in the stairwell which gave them one less thing to worry about, but each corridor they passed was eerily quiet. With a possible threat lurking on every level, they couldn't be complacent or let their guard down for a second.

They could get jumped or ambushed at any moment.

As they made their way up, Archer quietly thanked God for the cardio work he'd been doing since he got off the crutches. If he'd taken his rehab slower he'd have been in seriously deep shit by now. As befitted the Marshals badge on her hip Vargas was in excellent shape, and by the time they got to 22 she was barely breathing hard.

On the top floor, they waited just inside the door in the stairwell, sneaking a glance through the glass panel.

The corridor was clear.

Vargas pulled the door open quietly and moved inside, sweeping in front of her with her assault rifle. They made their way down, looking through their sights, Archer checking behind them constantly so they couldn't get blindsided.

Halfway along, they found the red box Helen had talked about. It was exactly where she said it would be, attached to the wall, a glass square with a red phone inside and a fire extinguisher in a bracket underneath.

'Bulls eye,' Vargas said.

She reached for the handle to pull the front glass panel open but Archer stopped her.

'Let's clear the roof first.'

Castle and Spades walked into the lobby and saw the four gang members they'd hired to do this job in the first place watching King and Bishop, who were keeping tabs on the front door.

All the men turned, looking at the newcomers as they joined them.

'Anything?' King asked.

'Nothing. Not a damn thing,' said Castle. He grinned. 'The NYPD are going to need a stack of body bags for the roof though. And I saved the chopper pilot a cremation.'

'You killed the entire squad?' Braeten asked.

'Of course. We haven't found the girl yet. We need more time.'

'Now you're cop killers. You got some plan of escape?'

'They're sitting ducks,' King said, ignoring him and addressing Castle, Spades and Bishop. 'We disabled all the phone lines. One of their guys is bleeding out and might already be dead. We just took out their rescue team. It's just a matter of time.'

He pushed the pressel switch on his vest.

'Pawn, Hearts, where are you?'

'Still doing our sweep, sir. No sign of them yet.'

'Check again. They may have doubled back behind you.'

Pause.

'Yes, sir.'

He released the handle, turning to his guys. 'We'll find them. Wherever they are, they can't stay there forever. Sooner or later, they're going to make a move.'

'Then what?'

'Then they die. Every single one.'

Easing open the door to the roof, Archer crept up the last flight of concrete stairs, Vargas beside him.

When they saw what was on the surface, they both stopped dead in their tracks.

'Jesus,' Vargas whispered.

There was an entire ESU task force scattered in the middle of the roof; they'd been shredded to pieces. In a ragged circle around them were the spent cases and plates of Claymore mines, seared and torn black blankets near them. Small steel ball bearings were everywhere, many of them blackened or stained with blood.

Archer picked one up beside his foot on the step and examined it.

These men were willing to kill each other and an entire squad of police officers to get to Jennifer.

Very soon, he was going to need some answers for those questions he had about the girl.

Vargas went to move forward to look closer, but Archer grabbed her arm, keeping her low.

'The sniper.'

She remembered and nodded her thanks. Together, the two of them took a last look at the carnage.

'It was a trap,' he said. 'They never stood a chance.'

'So let's try the line and tell the people outside.'

Back in the 22nd corridor moments later, Vargas pulled the box open and scooped up the red receiver as Archer checked either side with the M4A1.

She held the phone to her ear and her eyes immediately widened.

'Dial tone.'

She started punching in a number quickly as Archer kept clearing either side of them.

The corridor was empty but he felt exposed and increasingly uneasy.

They needed to make the call and get the hell out of here.

Down on the street, Dalton was watching Hobbs when his phone started ringing. Pulling it from his pocket, he looked at the display and frowned. It wasn't a number he recognised.

'Hello?'

Beside him, Shepherd saw his expression change instantly.

'Vargas! What the hell is going on in there?'

He listened for a moment as Shepherd stepped closer. There was a pause.

'ESU were taken out with Claymores,' Dalton relayed to Shepherd, Josh and Marquez. 'The chopper dropped them off right in the target zone. The mines must have been camouflaged.'

'Archer?'

Dalton listened. 'He's OK.'

Pause.

'She says the newcomers are all heavily armed. M4A1 assault rifles. She and Archer managed to kill two of them. They were in tactical gear and balaclavas.'

Pause.

Dalton continued to listen intently.

'We saw them arrive, Vargas,' he said. 'We counted ten, not including the four remaining men who ambushed you.'

The others watched him as he listened.

His expression changed, and he suddenly hit the front of his car in anger.

'*Shit!*'

'What? What is it?' Josh asked.

Dalton shook his head, swearing again. 'One of our people is down. Foster, the team leader. Carson is still bleeding out. They doped him up to kill the pain and keep him quiet. '

Pause.

'She said soon after the first chopper arrived, all the phone lines went dead. She's using a fire phone in one of the corridors.'

'They must have a jammer,' Marquez said.

'How's the girl, Vargas?' Dalton asked, the other three watching him intently.

On 22, Archer stood point on the female US Marshal, who was talking rapidly into the phone. He made the signal to her to wrap it up. She nodded and held up her forefinger.

Almost done, the gesture said.

He looked back and forth, feeling more and more vulnerable in this corridor, well aware that there were men hunting them right now. Vargas was still talking rapidly into the phone, her M4A1 slung over her shoulder as she continued to give Dalton a sitrep.

Even though she was keeping her voice low, the silence meant her words were carrying down the corridor, further fraying Archer's nerves.

C'mon, Vargas, hurry.

'She's OK, sir,' Vargas said into the phone. 'But Carson needs to be med evac'd ASAP. He's bleeding out; he doesn't have long.'

She listened to his response as Archer cleared either side, covering her back.

Every instinct he had was screaming at him to get the hell out of here.

They'd stayed too long already.

'Let's go!' he said to her quietly.

'OK. Yes sir,' she said. Pause. 'Yes, sir. Will do.'

She put the phone back on the handle and turned to Archer, swinging her own M4A1 off the strap and back into her hands.

'Dalton said ten men abseiled in. He's got a Marshals task force with him. No more approaches from up here. They're looking at a frontal assault. Attack them head on.'

Archer went to reply, but stopped.

Two men in grey fatigues and balaclavas had suddenly appeared at the end of the corridor from the north stairwell.

They were staring at him and Vargas.

And both had assault rifles in their hands.

TWENTY TWO

The two men looked at Archer and Vargas for a split-second.

A moment that felt like a horrifying eternity.

Then they reacted.

Grabbing Vargas, who had her back turned to the men, Archer smashed into the door of the room to the right of the phone as the two gunmen snapped their rifles up.

The old wood around the lock splintered and gave way as automatic gunfire tore into the corridor behind them, the quiet hallway suddenly deafening, chips of wood and plaster around the doorframe spraying into the air from the bullets.

Falling into the apartment, Archer and Vargas scrambled to their feet. There was no-one inside. Running forward, they both dove for cover behind the kitchen counter as the two guys appeared in the doorway, firing and ripping apart the cupboards and shelves, smashing bottles, annihilating the entire kitchen.

Rolling out, Vargas fired back, forcing the two men to take cover either side of the door, the muzzle of her own M4A1 flashing as she squeezed off bursts of fire while Archer desperately looked around the room for an escape route.

Staying low, he moved to the window leading to the balcony, firing off some of his own rounds towards the door and buying them some extra seconds. The M4A1 had no triple round setting, just safety, single or fully automatic, so he used short bursts, conserving ammo. Maintaining fire, Vargas followed him, both of them managing to hold the doorway. The two gunmen had no option but to stay back, the ferocity of Archer and Vargas's assault spraying debris from the corridor and doorframe into the air.

The curtains in the room were drawn. Sweeping the left half to the side, Archer saw a small balcony with an air conditioner on the far right side, blowing cold air into the apartment through a vent to the right of the windows.

Squeezing off a burst at the door, he felt behind him, found the handle and yanked open the sliding door, Vargas keeping up her ferocious fire as she moved across the room to join him.

Suddenly, a black shape was tossed into the room as Vargas' magazine clicked dry.

Grenade.

He pulled her out onto the balcony with him, dragging the door shut and hitting the deck.

Outside in the corridor, Pawn and Hearts had ducked down, both reloading, slapping fresh magazines into the underside of the M4A1s.

The explosion smashed out any remaining glass in the room. Plaster, dust and smoke filled the air.

Moving forward carefully and not encountering any fire, the two men eased themselves into the apartment, the triggers on the M4A1s half pushed down, ready to execute, thirty fresh rounds locked and loaded in each weapon.

The place was dark and dim and smoky.

Their weapons traced through the gloom.

There was no sign of them.

Outside, Vargas took a deep breath and leapt off the balcony.

She was only in the air for a second, but for that brief moment she was over nothing but twenty two storeys of night air, the New York City street far below.

She landed on the balcony next door, re-gathering her balance then turned and looked back at Archer. Hearing footsteps crunching on debris behind him in the apartment, he stood up on the concrete edge, holding onto the wall for balance with his left hand, fresh cuts on his arms and body from the smashed glass.

Looking down, his toes were over twenty two storeys of nothing.

Far below, he saw the street. They were on the east side of the building, so he saw all the cop cars with their lights flashing down below.

'C'mon!' she hissed.

Bunching his hamstrings, Archer sprang forward and jumped.

Stepping their way over the debris on the floor, Pawn and Hearts checked behind the kitchen counter. Then they dragged the main curtains out of the way and moved out through the smashed windows onto the balcony, their boots crunching on the glass.

They swept their M4A1s up and down, left and right.

'Where the hell did they go?' said Hearts.

Six feet from them, huddled behind the concrete wall of the balcony next door and hidden from view, Archer and Vargas stayed low.

Archer eased out the magazine of his assault rifle, quietly placing the empty on the ground, and pushed in a new one with the softest of *click*s.

Suddenly, the sliding doors behind them opened. A man in a vest and underpants appeared, coughing and frowning. Judging from the dust and debris on him, the bullets and the force of the explosion had shredded apart the walls of his apartment.

He looked down at the two of them.

'*Who the hell are you?*'

They were already moving; Vargas went through the door as Archer tackled the man back into his apartment, automatic gunfire tearing into the concrete where they'd just been and smashing the glass window, shooting it out as they fell through the gap.

Pushing off the man and staggering to his feet, Archer followed Vargas, who'd wrenched open the front door and was already back out in the corridor.

Next door, Pawn and Hearts ran back through the apartment. They slowed when they got to the entrance, then edged out into the corridor and saw the door to the north stairwell swinging shut.

Reloading, the two men sprinted down the hallway after them.

The moment the first man burst through the door, Archer front kicked him as hard as he could. He'd been standing beside the doorframe, the frame just missing him as it was smashed open.

The gunman flew down the flight of stairs and hit the landing between 22 and 21 hard, the breath knocked out of him. He dropped his rifle, dazed and winded.

The other man behind him reacted fast but Vargas had been ready, coming from the other side. Considering Archer was behind the guy, Vargas couldn't shoot so she smashed the butt of her rifle into his face instead.

He shouted in pain and fell back into the corridor, trying to raise his own M4A1 through blurry vision. This time he had nothing behind him.

Vargas had no choice and fired.

On the landing in the stairwell, the other gunman had regained his senses. He lifted his rifle but Archer got there a split second ahead, putting the sights of his M4A1 on the man's upper torso.

'Drop the weapon!'

The man paused, mid-sweep, staring into Archer's eyes venomously, his face masked by the balaclava.

'Don't do it!'

Pause.

He suddenly swung the rifle up all the way.

Archer fired just before he did. The burst hit the man in the sternum and killed him instantly, his finger jerking instinctively and spraying a burst of bullets into the wall near Archer, who threw himself to one side.

Those last shots echoed down the stairwell.

Then it was silent.

Archer got back to his feet, panting as Vargas re-joined him. Both of them were bleeding from flying glass and covered in debris from the gunfight, dirty, sweaty and cut up.

Pulling up his M4A1, the barrel hot to touch, Archer aimed down the stairwell beside the dead man, waiting for his hearing to fully return and for any other gunmen to run into his sights.

He stood there, Vargas beside him, both of them taking deep breaths.

They watched and waited.

But no-one else came.

TWENTY THREE

Everyone in the lobby had heard the shots. They'd echoed down the north stairwell. King, Bishop, Castle and Spades were standing there, along with Braeten and the members of his crew, listening and hopeful.

It sure as hell sounded like someone had found the Marshals.

Then there was silence. King pushed the pressel on his uniform, walking over to the north side and pulling open the door.

'What the hell is going on up there? Give me a sitrep.'

Nothing.

'Pawn, Hearts, report.'

Nothing.

'Report.'

The man didn't have a radio; the anonymous team were communicating with earpieces and pressel switches. Archer had already pulled the earpiece from the man's ear, listening closely. *Pawn, Hearts.*

They were using call signs, chess pieces and card suits, not their real names.

'Pawn, Hearts, respond, damn it. Someone in the area check it.'

Holding the earpiece to his lobe with his right hand, Archer used his left to grab two magazines from pouches on the front of the dead man's fatigues, stuffing them into his pocket. He checked the rest of the guy's fatigues quickly but he had no ID. He pulled off his balaclava. The man had black hair and was tanned, stubble around his chin and neck; he was white and appeared to be in his thirties, tough, with a fighter's face, some scar tissue across his eyebrows.

His head lolled back as Archer released it, blood leaking out of his mouth, his eyes open. Archer looked down at the dead man.

It was you or me, buddy.

And you started this.

Suddenly, he heard a noise from the stairwell. He stood up and leant over the railing; there was the sound of running feet, and more than one pair.

It was distant, but getting closer, from about ten floors below and moving fast.

In his ear, the man's radio had gone quiet.

Scooping up the magazines and the M4A1 and letting the earpiece go, Archer ran up the last flight and joined Vargas in the hallway. She was doing the same as him, taking what she could from the dead man.

She'd also pulled off the man's balaclava and was staring at the guy when Archer joined her.

'We've got to go!' he whispered.

She didn't react. He grabbed her shoulder, which finally got her attention. Scooping up her M4A1, she also pulled two grenades from pouches on the man's tactical vest and took off down the corridor with Archer, both of them bloodied, dirtied and bruised but still alive.

Archer took point, moving out into the south stairwell. There was no-one coming up these stairs. Whoever the footsteps belonged to were

189

coming up from the north side. The doors to the corridors on the upper floors were all shut, so even if they passed the stairwell at the same time as anyone on the north they wouldn't be seen.

Vargas followed him and they started moving down, the door behind them swinging shut as they disappeared out of sight.

Moments later, Knight and Diamonds arrived at the 21st floor, having sprinted up from 11. Both men slammed to a halt, panting when they got there, and saw Pawn's body on the landing between their position and the 22nd floor. His balaclava had been pulled off, blood around his mouth; he was staring up lifelessly and was sprawled out limply across the stairwell landing. He'd been shot in the chest.

Another one of their guys down.

'Son of a bitch,' Knight muttered.

Diamonds stepped past the body carefully, carrying on up the stairs. Knight dropped to one knee and examined his dead colleague. The spare magazines for his M4A1 had been taken, the pouches empty. Blood was pooled on the floor under his body, still warm under Knight's knee. He felt his anger rise; like Markowski, Gibbons had been a close friend of his and was a tough bastard.

None of this was going to plan.

Half a flight up, Diamonds reappeared. 'They iced Taylor too. He's gone. Three in the sternum.'

'Someone, report goddammit. What the hell happened?'

Neither man responded at first. Then Knight pushed the pressel on his radio, still kneeling in Gibbons' blood.

'Sir, we've got a serious problem up here.'

*

Down in 8A again, Archer locked the door and dragged the refrigerator back into place as Vargas moved through into the sitting room, both of them relieved to be out of the stairwell and back behind the relative safety of the barricade.

Barlow, Jennifer and Helen all looked up as Vargas walked in and were immediately taken aback by her appearance. Her once-spotless white top was dirty, covered in brick dust, and she had cuts and nicks on her arms and face, her top and face blackened with smoke. Archer looked much the same as he walked in, joining her in the sitting room.

Vargas put her rifle and the two grenades she'd lifted to one side then knelt down in front of Jennifer, the girl hugging her with as much strength as she could muster. The embrace meant some of the dust and debris on Vargas' clothing was imprinted onto her own clothes and arms, but she clung on tight.

'What the hell happened up there?' Barlow said.

'We ran into company,' Archer said.

'And?'

'Two more of them are down. We found the ESU team on the roof.'

'So where are they?' Helen said, hopefully.

'They're dead. This response team took them out.'

191

'All of them?'

He nodded. 'All.'

'Were they shot?'

'No,' he said. 'Claymore mines.'

She looked blank.

'They're anti-personnel weapons that fire metal ball bearings,' he explained. 'The helicopter dropped the team off into a circle of them. One push of a clacker was all it took. The chopper got hit by an anti-tank rocket. We saw the spent launcher dumped up there.'

'Did you find the phone?' Helen asked.

Vargas nodded. 'That's the good news. I spoke to Dalton, our Supervisor. Told him the situation and what happened to Foster. The chopper earlier was this other team abseiling in. Everyone outside thought it was one of theirs, and by the time they realised it wasn't the team were already inside in the building. They counted ten of them.'

'Now there are six,' Archer said.

'Still ten,' Barlow said. 'You're forgetting the four guys from the street.'

Pause.

'What did Dalton say?'

'They're working on coming in through the front door.'

'It won't be easy.'

She shrugged. 'They'll have to duke it out. It's their only option. One way in, one way out.'

Vargas turned her focus to Jennifer, talking to her quietly. As she did so, Archer walked over to the couch, knelt and checked on Carson. Helen was sitting beside him, her hand on his brow.

'Any change?'

192

'The same,' Helen said. 'Hanging in there. But he's lost a lot of blood.'

As she spoke, she noticed something on Vargas's leg and pointed.

'As will you if you don't get that looked at.'

Archer turned and saw where Helen was indicating. There was a wound to Vargas' thigh from the gunfight upstairs, what looked like a small piece of shrapnel buried in her jeans.

She looked down at it, just as surprised as everyone else. It looked painful. Seeing the injury, Archer rose and motioned towards the kitchen with his head.

'C'mon. There's still some of my shirt left.'

In the lobby, King and his men listened to Knight's report, all of them stunned.

'Pawn and Hearts are dead, sir.'

'What?'

'There was a shootout on 22. Pawn bought it in the stairwell, Hearts in the corridor. Both took a burst to the chest. They tore up an apartment and the hallway. Looks like the fight went all over the place.'

'That's four of our guys down,' King said quietly, more to himself than anyone else. Releasing the pressel, he whirled on Castle, Spades and Bishop, who were standing behind him. 'How the hell are these people still alive?'

'It's not that easy,' Bishop said. 'This place is big. There're still residents here, too.'

'So? Are we all on the same page? Do you understand the consequences if that girl leaves this building alive?'

None of them responded.

'So what the hell are you waiting for? Get upstairs and find them!'

As they headed off, he pushed down the pressel.

'Everyone, get your shit together,' he ordered. 'Search every apartment room by room; I don't care if it takes all night. Pull your fingers out of your asses and find these people. Don't come back down here until you do.'

King released the switch, cursing again. He was left alone with the four gunmen he'd hired for the ambush on the street. They'd all listened to the exchange between King and his men, picking up on what had happened, but none of them said a word.

The man armed with the AK-47 was cautiously peering out of the shattered hole where a glass pane on the front door had been, his concerns not on finding the girl, but on figuring out an escape and getting out of here alive. It looked like most of the NYPD were outside. He had no idea how the hell he was going to get out, and the cocaine up his nose wasn't exactly helping him think clearly.

'We're running out of time,' he said. 'The pigs are gonna try to get in again soon.'

Furious, King went to reply but Braeten suddenly cut him off.

'Hold on a second,' he said sharply.

'What?' King spat back. 'Your brain finally switched on?'

Turning to him, Braeten smiled, ignoring the slight.

Something Bishop just said had given him an idea.

'I know how we can find her.'

'What?'

'I know how we can find the girl.'

TWENTY FOUR

The same as before, Archer and Vargas were back in the bathroom, but this time it was three floors higher and Vargas who was being patched up.

She was sitting on the edge of the tub, watching Archer examine the wound to her leg. He was kneeling on the step up to the bath, both their M4A1s within arm's reach, the safety on each weapon clicked on. There was a sliver of metal in her thigh, jutting out of her jeans, a circle of red around the wound. It wasn't in deep enough from what he could see to be overly concerning, but it was enough to hurt like hell.

He examined it up close. The shard was white and about the length of his index finger.

'I think it's a piece of balcony door,' he said. 'Must have come from the grenade blast.'

She didn't reply.

He looked up and saw she was staring over his head, her mind elsewhere.

'Hey? You good?'

She snapped out of it. 'Huh?'

'You OK?'

'Yeah. I'm fine.'

'I'm going to have to cut a hole in your jeans.'

'Go for it.'

Taking the scissors and a wad of gauze from a first aid kit he'd found under the basin, he snipped at the fabric, further exposing the wound. Placing the scissors to one side, he took hold of the shrapnel and looked up at her.

'Ready?'

She nodded.

A split-second later, he pulled the metal out and she exhaled sharply. Tossing the piece of shrapnel to one side, he staunched the immediate flow of blood with the gauze, keeping pressure on the wound. After a moment or two he lifted the pad and poured a small amount of antiseptic over the affected area, Vargas's body tensing from the stinging pain. It needed to be cleaned, but he hoped she'd had a tetanus shot nonetheless.

He then placed another wad of gauze over the wound, wrapping a strip from his old shirt around her thigh to hold the padding in place. He cinched and knotted it. Once it was done, he leant back and wiped antiseptic off his hands with the remains of his shirt, studying his handiwork. It sure as hell wasn't going to qualify him for a medical career, but it would do for now.

Her hair hanging down, Vargas checked out his work then looked up and smiled.

'Thank you,' she said. 'Guess that makes us even.'

'No problem.'

He thought back to the battle upstairs and how she'd acquired the injury. She'd done brilliantly. She was conservative with her ammo, not panicking in the face of a full-on attack and had kept her cool, thinking fast when she'd jumped to the next balcony. She'd also taken out one of the gunmen without hesitation; everything she'd done had been faultless, decisive and extremely impressive.

More to her than meets the eye, he'd thought earlier. That was for damn sure.

'You were great up there,' he told her.

'You too.'

'I can see why you've got that badge on your hip.'

There was a pause.

'Did you know that the Marshals service has never lost a witness under protection?' she said.

'I didn't. And that's not going to change tonight.'

They made eye contact and shared a moment.

'No. It isn't,' she said, sharing his determination.

He rose, picked up his M4A1 and moved into the kitchen, Vargas staying where she was on the edge of the bathtub. He walked up to the refrigerator rammed up against the door and stood still, listening intently for any sounds of movement in the corridor outside the apartment.

It was quiet.

He headed back into the bathroom and re-joined her, placing his rifle to one side but within reach. He leant against the basin, enjoying the moment's respite and her company. Alone together, a barricade across the door, one could almost forget the predicament they were in.

Almost.

'So how long have you been a Marshal?' he asked.

'Not long.' She noticed the way he was looking at her; he had another question on his lips. 'What?'

'Right now. You and me. This stays here. What is this about?'

She didn't react.

He pressed her. 'You can trust me, Vargas. Who's the little girl?'

She didn't reply but her manner had changed slightly. He got the impression she was just about willing to open up and offer him something. He pushed forward, seizing the opportunity. Foster had been like a brick wall the last time he'd asked this.

'Is her real name Jennifer?'

Silence.

'No,' she said. 'It's Isabel.'

He nodded. She was ready to talk.

'What did she see, Vargas?' he asked. 'Tell me.'

*

'You know much about New York family crime?' Vargas asked.

Archer shook his head. 'I'm Counter Terrorism. Our focus is elsewhere.'

'You've heard about the Five Families and the Mob stories from back in the day though?'

'I saw *The Godfather*.'

'There're a few of these families still operating like that, especially downtown. Times may have changed but crime sure as hell hasn't. In the last ten years, two dominant gangs have emerged in Tribeca: the Lombardis and the Devaneys. Italian versus Irish. They may have only come to full prominence in the last decade, but their feud goes back much further than that. This isn't any Montague and Capulet shit, either. These are rough, nasty people who'll go to any lengths to get what they want. They've put scores of each other into the ground and to the bottom of the bay over the years, fighting for control and power.'

She paused.

'Three weeks ago, the head of the Lombardis, Gino, had a family gathering at his holiday place up in the Hamptons. It was a get-together to celebrate his fifty eighth birthday. Everyone was there apart from one of his kids who couldn't make it. A hit team showed up and wasted the entire group. Machine-gunned the lot. The total body count was nineteen; men, women and children. It was the worst massacre ever recorded in the area. They hadn't even had a single homicide around there for almost a decade.'

'The trigger men?'

'Four sets of footprints in the sand.'

'How did they do it?'

'They came in from the bay. Silenced weapons; sub-machine guns. MP5s, judging from the ballistics reports. They went right inside the villa too; there were bullet holes and shell casings all over the sitting room, kitchen and upstairs. The windows were intact, meaning they had their backs to them when they fired. The shooters were clever. They waited until lunchtime, when everyone was gathered inside the house, walked up and opened fire from the doorway to the veranda.'

'Witnesses?'

'None from the water or beach. The places either side were unoccupied, the owners out of town. Someone had done their homework. The weapons were suppressed, so no-one in the area heard any weapons' reports. Most of Gino's crew were armed but they never even had a chance to fire back. They were taken completely off-guard.'

Vargas paused.

'But the four killers screwed up. They missed someone.'

'Jennifer,' Archer finished. 'I mean, Isabel.'

Vargas nodded. 'She was in the bathroom when they opened fire, washing her hands. She hid in a laundry basket and they didn't find her. But then again, no big deal, right? She's a seven year old child; what's she going to do?'

Archer waited.

'She was traumatised when two guys from East Hampton Town PD found her. They took her to the station straight away. Once they realised who she was, they contacted the city and an NYPD homicide team from the 1st Precinct who'd been building a case against the Devaney family sped up there.'

Archer nodded.

'They brought in specially-trained officers to try and find out what she saw, but the poor kid still wasn't saying much. She'd heard her entire family get murdered.'

Vargas paused.

'However, she answered *yes* to a very important question.'

'Did you see the people with the guns?'

Vargas nodded. 'And she did. She'd heard them open fire and saw them through a gap in the bathroom door before she hid. This got the 1st Precinct detectives salivating, seeing as there was only one group of suspects.'

'The Devaney gang.'

She nodded. 'The evidence from the villa was gathered and sent to forensics for analysis. Once they ran some dust over the shell casings, they found four different sets of prints. Rory Gannon, Jim O'Meara, Brian Malley and Kellan Teague. All four are enforcers for the Devaney crew. That alone was enough for a conviction. But if Isabel ID'd them as the shooters, it was a big enough case to go after the entire gang. Try and prove Devaney ordered his boys to make the move.'

'When's the trial?'

'Next week.'

He leaned back, nodding. 'So that's why she's here. These men must be from the Devaney crew. They want to silence her for good.'

Vargas shook her head.

'No, no. That's not it. You didn't let me finish.'

Archer frowned, confused. 'Did I miss something?'

'You're thinking what everyone else did. The detectives starting pushing all the mug shots of the Devaney family under Isabel's nose but they were barking up the wrong tree. The shooters weren't part of the Devaney crew.'

'What?' How is that possible? They were fingerprinted.'

She didn't reply.

'So who were the hit team?'

'A man called Mike Lombardi and three friends.'

'Lombardi?'

'Gino's son.'

Vargas paused.

'Isabel's brother.'

202

'Wait a minute; Lombardi's son?'

She nodded.

'*He killed his whole family?*' Archer whispered, in disbelief.

'The detectives conducting the interview thought the girl was muddled at first. Maybe the shock of the incident had resulted in severe trauma which was affecting her memory. But then it started to make sense, at least psychopathically. Obviously, Mike was well aware of the history between the two families. He was a part of it, for Christ's sake. He knew that the Devaney crew would be the inevitable suspects for the massacre. If they went down, it would remove both gangs, the Devaneys and the senior Lombardis. It wouldn't even matter if they never found the murder weapons; they had the shell casings.'

'Yeah, but how the hell did they get those? That's ironclad evidence, Vargas.'

'A few weeks before the incident, some of Devaney's crew were jumped down at the East Side Docks. Held up at gunpoint then worked over by four guys with knuckledusters and bats. Not enough to kill them but enough to put them in the hospital for a few days. Their weapons were taken. All 9mm pistols. Copper Parabellums inside.'

'Ammunition that would fit into a silenced MP5,' Archer said quietly. 'Smart boys. They knew Devaney's people would have prints on at least a couple of the bullets.'

She nodded. 'And in the resulting chaos, Mike could take control of the Lombardi gang.'

Archer shook his head, incredulous. 'I can't believe it. He killed his entire family? I thought the Mob was built on blood loyalty.'

'He might have the same surname, but his mother wasn't a Lombardi, only his father. Isabel is his half-sister. He was the product of an affair twenty five years ago.'

She sighed.

'The detectives had totally overlooked him, thinking just the same as you. If Isabel had been killed, they would have tried and convicted the wrong people. But by the time the truth started to emerge, the press were already on the story of the Hamptons massacre.'

She paused.

'And some idiot at East Hampton Town PD let slip that there was a survivor.'

'So that's where you, Foster, Barlow and Carson come in.'

She nodded. 'We picked her up eight days ago. The press were taking a real interest in her. If Mike had seen the reports he'd have realised that he missed someone.'

'He isn't inside?'

'The prosecution is building this case behind closed doors. That's why the press screwed it up and Isabel's gone into protection. If they hadn't reported that she was alive, Mike and his crew would have had no idea until they were arrested. Now, he'll know for sure that he missed her off his hit list.'

She shook her head.

'The trial is due to start next week. If Isabel makes it to the stand and testifies, Mike and his crew are going down. There's no death penalty in New York State anymore as you know, but they slaughtered nineteen people, with a witness seeing them open fire. They'll serve multiple life sentences, no chance of early release. And that's if they make it past the first week of their terms. Gino Lombardi had a lot of friends, and word in those circles spreads quickly. They've got a lot of enemies waiting for them in the joint.'

'And what happens to Isabel after she makes the stand?'

'Standard procedure. She's relocated to a new city, given a new identity. She's only seven so she'll be placed with a foster family. They won't even be told who she really is, the youngest daughter of a dead Mobster.'

'No relatives?'

'They're all dead apart from Mike. All of them were gunned down at the house.'

Archer thought for a moment, this new knowledge clarifying their current situation and predicament. He thought of the little girl next door, scared and vulnerable, anonymous armed men repeatedly trying to kill her.

'Jesus Christ. I knew the Mob were violent, but always thought the one thing they respected was family.'

'Mike's a different breed.' She lowered her voice. 'And forgive my honesty, but what happened to Isabel's father is no great loss. Gino Lombardi was a scumbag. He ran prostitution rings, some of the girls as young as twelve, and kept many of them doped up so they couldn't escape. His crew sold drugs and guns to kids. They've murdered scores of people over the years. Gino himself was a killer; he started out as an enforcer and worked his way up through the ranks until he took over the operation.'

Archer didn't reply. He glanced at the wound on his arm, then at the M4A1 resting by his leg, all the pieces of the story fitting together.

'All this for a child.'

Vargas nodded, looking worried. 'All this.'

Archer went to continue, but there was a sudden commotion from the hallway outside the apartment.

They both looked at each other then rose quickly, grabbing their M4A1s and moving to the door.

Across the kitchen, the sitting room door opened and Helen and Barlow appeared, Barlow aiming his USP at the main door.

Archer and Vargas did the same with their assault rifles, all of them suddenly tense again, fingers on triggers and ready to fire.

BAMBAMBAM.

Someone pounded on the wood.

'*Downstairs! Dollar opportunity,*' a harsh voice the other side shouted.

Neither Archer, Vargas or Barlow moved, keeping their weapons trained on the entrance.

They heard whoever was outside walk off, move on to the next apartment. It sounded as if others had joined him, more than one person beating on doors and shouting.

'*Who wants to make some money?*' someone called from the corridor, hitting on the doors.

His finger resting on the M4A1 trigger, looking down the sights, Archer stared at the door, puzzled.

He turned and glanced at Vargas, who looked equally nonplussed.

What the hell is going on? he thought.

Before long, thirty or so of the remaining residents had wandered down to the ground floor, gathered from all of the floors and assembling in the lobby. Most of them were men but there were a couple of women.

They all looked tough and rough, appearing from both stairwells, and examined the team of balaclava clad men in combat fatigues and assault rifles suspiciously but without any trace of fear. They were supposed to have been cleared out earlier after the fire alarm, but they either hadn't heard it for some reason or most likely just didn't give a shit. They were all dull-eyed and disinterested, hardened by life and their surroundings.

The sight of the armed men in the lobby didn't seem to faze any of them at all.

'What the hell is this about?' one of them asked.

'You want to make twenty grand?' King asked, Braeten beside him.

Castle, Spades and Bishop were behind the two men, staying silent, watching.

All murmuring in the group of residents ceased. Someone hawked and spat on the floor. King continued.

'We're looking for a group hiding out in this building,' he said. 'That's why we're here. That's what's been going on. There are four, maybe five of them. One is a kid; the others are US Marshals.'

'So?'

'So, you tell us where they are or kill any one of them, you get twenty grand.'

A few of them snorted and turned, walking back up the stairwell and disappearing out of sight, not interested. The response team let them go.

However, a large number of them remained.

'That's what all this shooting is about?' another man asked.

'Yes. You help us out, you get rich. Simple as that.'

Pause.

'Why do you wanna kill them?'

'None of your business.'

The group seemed unsure.

Several of them glanced at each other, wondering if this was a ruse.

'Bullshit. This is a set up. You're pigs.'

'No. It's not. These assholes have taken out four of my men tonight. Twenty grand for whoever locates them or gets me a body. You tag all four, you get eighty. Take it or leave it.'

The authority in his voice and force of his personality was swaying them. The rag tag group was looking more and more interested.

They started looking at each other.

'Think about it,' Braeten added. 'That's a lot of cash.'

'So where's the money?' one of the residents asked.

'You get it when you deliver.'

'Bullshit.'

King held up his M4A1 sideways so they could see it. 'Look at this. You think this hardware is cheap? Or that?'

He pointed at the Claymores aimed at the door.

'We've got the cash. Take it or leave it. I'm guessing no-one else is ever going to offer you eighty grand for twenty minutes of work again.'

'How do we know who these people are?' the man who'd first spoken asked.

'One of them is shot in the gut,' Braeten said. 'Another is a kid. A seven year old girl. Like he said, there will be four or five of them.'

'You got weapons?' Bishop asked.

Slowly but surely, interest had started to catch fire, like a single spark in a dry forest. Some of them nodded, but the front guy shook his head. Bishop pulled his sidearm from the holster on his thigh and passed it to the man, who took it. Some of the men at the back had already moved off up the stairwell, eager to get a head start. Mob fever was just starting to prickle in the air like electricity, the sparks of the fire about to turn into flames.

'Twenty grand a head,' Bishop said. 'Follow me.'

He stepped forward, closely followed by Castle; both men cut through the group, heading up the stairwell and setting the pace.

There was a brief pause.

209

Then members of the crowd started to follow quickly.

Watching them go and staying where he was, King smiled. He turned to Braeten.

'Good thinking. You just earned yourself a ride out of here.'

The rest of Braeten's crew heard this.

'What about us?' one of them asked.

'What about you?'

'We aren't staying here when this is done. No way.'

'So earn it. This is all your fault. We wouldn't be in this shit if you'd acted like professionals in the first place and hadn't screwed up.'

The three men looked at each other then moved to the stairwell quickly, joining the hunt.

Standing beside King, Braeten watched his guys leave, his arms folded, his pistol tucked into the back of his waistband.

'You're never going to pay any of them, are you?' he said quietly.

King smiled.

'Would you?'

TWENTY FIVE

Inside 8A, Archer and Helen were still in the kitchen. Vargas had taken Isabel back into the sitting room, trying to divert her mind and lighten her mood but also keep her away from the door. Barlow had joined her.

Archer was still staring at the refrigerator-covered entrance, wondering what that knock had been about and what the hell was going. Being trapped and isolated, they had no idea. The unpredictability of the last few hours had left him on edge.

So had the lack of back-up from outside.

'*Dollar opportunity,*' Helen echoed quietly. 'What the hell were they talking about?'

Archer shrugged, but didn't reply. Dragging his eyes from the door, he turned to her.

'How are you doing?'

'Well my apartment has been half destroyed. I've seen three men die tonight. There are armed men currently hunting for us and we're trapped in the building with them with no way out.'

She forced a smile.

'But apart from that, I'm fine.'

Pause. Archer smiled too.

'Sorry. Dumb question.' Pause. 'You said you're a nurse?'

She nodded.

'I work downtown. St Luke's. Been doing it for nineteen years.'

He glanced down and noticed a wedding ring on her finger for the first time.

211

'You're married.'

'I was. He left me,' she said, looking down and twisting the ring between her thumb and forefinger. The unthinking way she did it indicated she'd done it many times before. 'It happened almost five years ago. I should take this off. But I guess I keep hoping he'll come back.'

Silence.

'He was a financial planner; he used to work late. One night I went to the office to surprise him and found him there with his secretary doing everything but working. Real cliché, right? Turned out he'd been having an affair with her for over a year. A few days later, he didn't come home. Just never came back; left all his belongings. He'd quit his job and run off with her, leaving me and our son behind. The boy was only sixteen. I didn't know how to cope.'

She shook her head.

'We used to live downtown, in Chelsea. Real nice place. But once he left I couldn't afford to pay rent and was forced out. I had to keep working at the hospital of course. The only place I found that I could afford was up here.'

Pause.

She looked at him.

'I was watching you earlier. I know you saw the bottle of whiskey.'

Archer didn't respond.

'When you've got no-one and you live in a place like this, you sure as hell need something to take your mind off it. That's why I started drinking. But I took it out on my boy. He didn't deserve that. He hated it up here, and blamed it on me. His dad still called and saw him every now then. He never did with me. Somehow it ended up all being my fault.'

'So where's your son?'

'When he was eighteen he packed his things and left. The last time we spoke, he told me he never wanted to see me again. He said I'd ruined his life.'

She blinked, the fear and emotion of the day threatening to overwhelm her.

'He hates me.'

'I doubt that,' Archer said. 'When was the last time you called him?'

'Two years. He lives in Pittsburgh. I kept trying but he wouldn't answer so I gave up.'

'When we make it out of here, try him again.'

'He won't pick up.'

'I bet he will. He might even be watching this on the television and thinking about you right now. I bet he misses you as much as you miss him.'

She paused.

'*When* we make it out of here? You make it sound like a certainty.'

He nodded. 'We're not dying in here. Not tonight.'

She sniffed, and wiped her eyes. 'You seem so sure.'

Pause.

'And it shouldn't take something like this to make me call him.'

'If there's anything positive to come out of this, maybe that's what it is.'

There was a pause; the police lights down below continued to flash through the curtains. The lighting in the apartment was low. They could hear murmuring from next door, but other than that the room was quiet.

'What's his name?' Archer asked. 'Your son?'

'Peter.'

He went to reply but stopped. She noticed.

'What?'

Archer didn't move.

'What's wrong?'

He'd frozen.

'Listen.'

Helen paused.

She heard something too.

'What the hell is that?'

Two floors down, the main group was almost twenty strong, men with money and violence on their minds.

They were moving down 6, smashing their way into every apartment, searching for the group, kicking doors open and rampaging through rooms like a whirlwind of violence. They were armed with an assortment of handguns and knives; several had bats. A couple of them would only need their bare hands. On the 5th floor, two of them had stumbled upon the smoky scene of the first exchange between the balaclava-clad men and the group they were hunting. One of them had stolen Foster's .44 and his badge which he was carrying almost as a cruel irony. His buddy had taken the Glock.

Pockets of them were searching the rooms, trying to get the jump on each other and find the group first, working at an increasingly frenzied pace, determined to get their hands on the money and more than willing to kill for it.

A deadly, fired-up mob, working their way up the building floor by floor.

Apartment by apartment.

Upstairs, Archer and Helen were listening, trying to make sense of what they were hearing. Faint noise was coming from below, what sounded like thudding, thumping and shouting.

It was getting increasingly louder.

'What the hell is that?' Helen said quietly.

The door to the sitting room opened. Vargas appeared, Isabel holding her hand. 'What's that noise?'

Suddenly, Archer realised what it was. The two women saw it dawn on his face.

'Oh shit.'

'What?'

'We need to move! *Now!*'

He raced into the sitting room, followed by the others. Carson was on the couch, doped up, still staring at the ceiling with his mouth open. Slinging the M4A1 over his shoulder, Archer ran over to him, and reached behind him to pull him up, the wounded Marshal limp from the drugs in his bloodstream.

'Barlow, help me out,' Archer said. 'We need to move upstairs now!'

Barlow didn't respond.

'Barlow? Let's go. There're people com-'

He turned.

Across the room, Barlow still had his pistol in his hand.

But it was aimed at Vargas, Helen and Isabel.

TWENTY SIX

Archer didn't react at first. Disbelief accounted for that.

Then his hand slid for the USP in his belt.

'No, you don't,' Barlow said, swinging his pistol towards him. 'Toss it to the carpet. And the rifle. Now. One move from you Vargas and he dies.'

Archer stayed where he was, his hand inches from the pistol, looking at Barlow.

'What the hell are you doing?' he asked quietly.

'Toss the guns,' Barlow said. 'Or you die.'

Archer stared into his eyes for a moment.

They were wide, but in control.

Knowing he had no other option, he reached around and took the USP from the back of his waistband. He had no choice. A man doesn't have many when a loaded gun is aimed straight at him.

He threw it to the carpet, the weapon landing with a *thud*.

'And the rifle.'

Archer loosened it off his shoulders and placed it down carefully, the assault rifle joining the USP, never taking his eyes off Barlow, who stared back impassively. He then pointed his weapon at the women.

'You too, Vargas,' he said. 'The rifle and the pistol.'

'Jared, what the hell are you doing?'

'Toss the weapons.'

After a brief pause, Vargas complied. Barlow shifted his weapon back to Archer, beckoning him to move.

'Join the others, pretty boy.'

With no alternative, Archer walked over towards the other side of the room, Barlow taking a step back so he was out of arm's reach as Archer passed. Vargas had Isabel behind her back, protecting her. It didn't matter though. With four unarmed people against a loaded USP, there was only going to be one winner. Through the floor, they could all hear the sound of the smashing and shouting.

It was getting louder.

It was getting nearer.

Watching Barlow closely, Archer shifted the weight to the balls of his feet, slowly, ready to pounce on him and try to knock the USP from his hand. He couldn't shoot all four of them that quickly; it would take him time to work the trigger and aim.

Barlow saw what he was doing and aimed the gun straight at him.

'Don't even think about it,' he said. 'Or you'll be the first to die.'

'It was you,' Vargas said to Barlow. 'The ambush on the street. That's how they knew. You tipped them off.'

'Yes. It was me.'

'You son of a bitch.'

'You think I had a choice?'

'There's always a choice.'

'These people aren't who you think they are.'

Pause.

'How much do we make a year, Alice? Forty five grand? Before tax? And for this? You've been doing this for weeks. I've been doing this for years with no reward. You should see the amount they offered me. I couldn't say no. Putting my life on the line every day for this shit? No; not anymore.'

'You son of a bitch,' Vargas repeated, keeping Isabel behind her.

'I'm not going to die here. If I take you all out, they'll leave me be.' He focused on Vargas. 'I didn't want it to come to this, Alice. Really. I thought this would have been ended sooner.'

They all heard the noise of the mob getting even closer.

They were now on this corridor.

'It was supposed to be smooth as clockwork out there on the street,' Barlow said. 'No-one else was meant to get hurt. Especially not Jack.'

'And Foster. You killed him, Barlow.'

'Bullshit.'

'It's your fault. You may as well have pulled the trigger yourself.'

'Shut your mouth!' he screamed. He shifted his gaze to Archer. 'You had to stick your nose in and screw it up. You're going to die for that, asshole. I hope it was worth it.'

Archer didn't reply.

He'd slid a hand behind him very slowly while Barlow had been distracted by Vargas.

He grabbed a handful of curtain and bunched his fist.

'Anyway, I'm doing you a favour,' Barlow said. 'This'll be quick. You don't even want to

219

think about what they'd do to you if they found you alive.'

He looked at Vargas and shook his head.

'I'm sorry, Alice. You just weren't cut out for this.'

Archer suddenly swept his arm across and dragged the curtain open.

Pushing the others to one side, he dove to the floor.

Standing in the middle of the room, Barlow watched in bemusement, staring incredulously at him.

'What the hell are you doing?' he asked, chuckling. 'You think that's going to help?'

Then he realised.

He looked up and out of the sitting room window.

His smile vanished.

Eighty yards away, Joker had seen the sudden movement in the 8th floor window.

Looking down the scope, he saw one of the Marshals standing there, a gun in his hand.

Barlow.

He was their inside man but he needed to be eliminated.

He centred the crosshairs on the man's face and squeezed the trigger.

Barlow took the slug in the forehead, a small hole smashing through the window from the bullet, his head blowing apart. Vargas had pulled Isabel close and covered her so she missed seeing the impact, but she still screamed at the sound.

Barlow collapsed onto the carpet, spilling his weapon, and ended up splayed out in a heap on the rug. Not wasting a second and staying low, Archer belly crawled forward and dragged Carson from the sofa again.

He retrieved his weapons whilst Vargas grabbed hers, keeping their heads well down and out of sight from the window.

Outside the apartment, the thumping and shouting was so loud it had to be only a few doors away.

With Carson's USP in the back of his belt, the M4A1 in his hands, Archer crawled as fast as he could through to next door until he was out of sight of the window and then ran across the room, listening to the noise beyond the door and refrigerator. The kitchen curtains were drawn, protecting him from the sniper's vision, but he stayed to the side just in case the shooter tried his luck.

He heard a gang of people outside, shouting and smashing their way down the hallway. *A dollar opportunity.* The response team must have put a bounty on them and found some recruits from inside the building, doubling or tripling their numbers.

He spun and looked at the group waiting there, who'd followed his example and crawled out to the kitchen then got back to their feet, protected from the sniper's vision by the kitchen curtains. Helen and Vargas were dragging Carson, who was supported between them, hanging limp, Isabel standing beside Vargas and looking terrified.

221

A helpless child, an innocent nurse, a critically wounded doped-up man and a US Marshal.

Behind the door, the whooping, shouting and smashing was so loud it was almost in the room with them.

'They're coming for us,' he said.

Vargas lowered Carson then unslung her M4A1 and took off the safety catch, aiming the weapon at the door and keeping Isabel behind her.

'Get back,' she ordered.

'Oh my God,' Helen said, sheer terror in her eyes. 'We're trapped!'

TWENTY SEVEN

The horde kicked open 8H and poured inside. A black guy was lying on the couch, asleep with a bottle of whiskey on the floor beside his hand. The noise woke him and he stirred to find a gang standing over him, staring, two knives and a pistol shoved into his face. As he obviously wasn't who they were looking for, they turned away and left him alone, searching the rest of the apartment. The guy stayed where he was, blinking, totally confused.

The pace was picking up all the time; their initial cynicism and distrust of this offer had vanished, replaced by mob fever and money lust. Twenty grand a head was a hell of a lot of cash and they all wanted a piece of it. They'd almost cleared the corridor. Although they'd encountered a few people in the apartments they'd barged into, most of them were abandoned and empty. There was no sign of the targets. They'd find them though. There was nowhere to hide.

They knew their own building better than anyone else.

They piled back out of the door, heading for the apartment opposite. A big guy took the lead and didn't hesitate, kicking the lock off 8F as hard as he could. The door was no match for him and it splintered back. There were five apartments left to search on this floor. Some of the mob decided to give them a miss and ran into the south stairwell, heading up to 9 and getting a head start.

As he checked 8F with the rest of the gang, Castle's earpiece started going off. It sounded like Joker.

He was shouting something, but with the noise of the gang, Castle couldn't make out what he was saying.

'What?' he shouted back. *'Say again?'*

Inside 8A, Archer and Vargas checked their magazines and stepped back from the door, ready to go down firing. Behind them, Helen and Isabel stood there unprotected and terrified.

Archer flicked the firing mode to fully automatic, knowing this was it, their last stand.

C'mon, you bastards. Let's see how many of you I can take with me.

'Wait!' Helen said. 'What about the old laundry chute?'

'What chute?' Vargas said, not moving her aim from the door.

'I think there's a chute in the bathroom. It used to drop down to a laundry room somewhere below. All the apartments have them. They haven't been used in years, but it might still be there.'

Archer ran into the bathroom and saw she was right. There was an old grille covering a chute just above floor level, to the right of the bath. He hadn't noticed it before. He tried to rip off the cover but it wouldn't budge. He kicked it as hard as he could twice and it loosened enough for him to get his fingers around the top.

He wrenched it off, tossing it to one side.

The chute dropped down to a faint light a couple of floors down.

It was their only option other than to stay and die.

'Let's go!'

Behind him, Vargas and Helen carried Carson into the bathroom, shuffling in awkwardly under his weight.

'C'mon, honey!' Vargas said to Isabel, who followed them into the room, frightened and looking back at the front door of the apartment.

Hearing the mob so close they had to be just next door, Archer ran out of the bathroom and into the kitchen. Reaching behind the stove, he grabbed a pipe and pulled with all his might.

It ripped away from the wall; there was a quiet *hiss* as gas started filling the apartment.

He snatched something resting on the counter, then sprinted back towards the sitting room, ducking low and grabbing the second thing he needed from the window sill.

Pushing his way out through the crowd, Castle ran towards 8A, Joker shouting over the radio that the group were in the 8th floor south-west apartment. The lead members of the posse saw him running and followed, scenting money and determined to be in on the kill.

One of them forced his way ahead and pounded on the door but Castle didn't hesitate, kicking the lock hard and smashing it apart, the door giving way slightly. The men tried to barge their way in, but something was blocking from the other side. It was heavy.

Behind them, other members of the gang joined them, using their combined weight to force the door back.

Inside the bathroom, they were going down the laundry chute one by one. Helen and Isabel went first, Helen holding the girl tight in her arms. It was a diagonal drop, not too steep but enough to carry them down without any difficulty, and once they let go they slid out of sight, headed to the 6th floor.

Vargas helped Carson into the chute, a goofy, heroin-induced smile on his face, totally oblivious to what was going on and the level of danger he was in. She let him go and he slid down, disappearing.

Climbing inside, she could hear smashing and shouting at the door outside.

'Archer, let's go!' she hissed.

Just behind her, he locked the door. Taking one of the green grenades Vargas had stolen from one of the two gunmen upstairs, he slid the ring of the pin carefully over the door handle, then taped the grenade to the door frame with duct tape he'd grabbed from a drawer in the kitchen.

The gas was already filling the apartment, flowing out from the severed pipe. He could smell it in the bathroom as it seeped under the door. Vargas was half in the chute, holding on, waiting for him.

Outside, they heard the door smash open, the refrigerator falling down with a crash.

'Let's go!'

He turned and ran towards the chute. She let go and slid out of sight.

Jumping inside, he pushed himself off and followed her.

Splintering their way in, the horde poured through the door into the kitchen of 8A. There were twelve of them, more arriving every second.

Castle saw the door to the bathroom was shut and he smelt something in the air. He sniffed and smiled, then turned to the gang, who'd also picked up on it.

'No guns.'

A lot of them were armed with bats and they didn't wait, rushing into the sitting room.

'We got something!'

Castle ran forward and saw a man slumped on the floor, blood and brains sprayed on the wall behind him. Deputy Marshal Jared Barlow, their inside man. One of the mob saw his pistol on the carpet and ran forward to claim it. Another noticed the badge on his hip and ripped it loose along with the set of handcuffs tucked in a holster beside it.

'They're in there,' Joker's voice said in Castle's earpiece. *'I lost sight of them!'*

'This is Bishop. I'm on my way!'

Swinging his M4A1 around to his back, Castle grabbed a knife from a rack in the kitchen and moved to the bathroom door, wanting to end this once and for all himself. One of the thugs was already reaching for the handle but Castle grabbed him by the collar and pulled him back.

He moved up close to the door, listening. Smelling the gas in the air, he smiled. The Marshals thought they were being smart by rupturing the pipe but the gas meant they couldn't use their weapons now either, otherwise the spark would kill them all. They were as good as unarmed.

And this was now fifteen on four.

He tried the handle. The door was locked.

Behind him, the mob waited expectantly, weapons in their hands, ready to finish this off and earn their money.

Castle stepped back and kicked the door as hard as he could.

Archer had just made it to the bottom of the chute, two floors down on 6. The two women and Isabel were waiting for him across the old laundry room, with Carson on the floor beside them. The ancient grille that had blocked the chute had been kicked out of the way by Helen, the first one down.

Archer landed on an old dryer pushed up against the wall under the chute. Scrambling over it, he rushed forward and covered Vargas and Isabel, diving to the floor.

'Get down!'

The bathroom was empty. As two others followed him in, the group glanced around. Castle saw a chute in the wall to the right of the bath, the old grille that had covered it dumped to one side.

Shit.

They must have escaped down it.

As he stepped forward, something rolled across the floor and came to a stop by his foot.

He looked down.

Outside, Josh and Marquez were with the ESU Lieutenant when there was an enormous explosion from the 8th floor of the building.

As everyone ducked instinctively, a south-facing apartment erupted into a huge fireball, the windows blown out and fire billowing into the night, the wave of heat hitting everyone on the street, causing them to recoil.

Josh shielded his face.

'Jesus Christ!'

In the laundry room, Archer covered Vargas and Isabel as fire roared down the chute.

It burst into the room, an intense ball of heat that went over their heads, all of them lying face-down on the ground with their eyes squeezed shut. The fire sucked back up the chute almost as soon as it had arrived and the building alarm erupted again, that familiar wailing siren filling the air.

The group stayed low, coughing from the smoke, the laundry room dark and hazy around them.

Upstairs, the 8th floor corridor was filled with smoke, the fire alarm going off and echoing through the building.

Bishop had been running down the corridor from the north side when the explosion had happened. It had thrown him back down the hall, hitting him like a giant punch.

Staggering to his feet and blinking, he lurched his way towards the doorway of the apartment and looked at the devastation ahead of him, his ears ringing, smoke and dust stinging his eyes. The explosion had annihilated the interior of the apartment, the air filled with smoke, small parts of it on fire.

No one was coming out.

He tried to push the pressel switch on his vest but lurched to one side and vomited, dropping his assault rifle and falling to his knees. He felt as if he'd been hit by a freight train.

'What the hell's going on up there?' a voice asked in his earpiece. *'Report!'*

'They're gone,' Bishop said, his voice raspy, coughing and wiping his mouth with his sleeve and sucking in deep breaths as his lungs fought for air. 'They're gone.'

'The targets?'

'No. The back up.'

'How many?'

Bishop coughed, trying to clear his head and get his bearings.

'All of them. Castle's dead too.'

His radio went silent. Turning, he staggered down the corridor towards a fire extinguisher on a bracket on the wall, the fire alarm echoing around him, smoke still billowing from inside the destroyed apartment and burning the oxygen in the air.

TWENTY EIGHT

In the old laundry room on 6, the group were still coughing and recovering from the dust and smoke, which had flowed down the chute into the room and only now was withdrawing. It felt as if the explosion had rocked the entire building. The fire alarm in the corridors were still going off but suddenly went quiet, the echoes of the shrill siren reverberating in the air as the sound slowly died away.

Lifting his head and looking through the dusty haze, Archer saw rows of old washing machines and dryers standing against the walls around the room. The diagonal chute from 8A had deposited them on the east side of the building, facing all the cops on the street, the wrong side for the sniper who was firing from the south.

He pushed himself to his feet then moved over to the window, risking a quick look. It was still a sea of people, cars and trucks down there, a hub of activity. Foster's Tahoe and the car the street gunmen had pursued them in still where they'd been dumped several hours ago.

Blinking and coughing, he tried to make out Shepherd, Josh and Marquez in the crowd, but couldn't see them. Giving up, he turned back to the room.

'Everyone OK?'

He saw a series of nods and heard more coughing as his companions started to get to their feet, Vargas helping Isabel then Helen up. Archer walked over to check on Carson. Helen had thrown herself over him when the blast went off to protect him. He was lying flat on his back, still pretty doped up, but the smile on his face had gone. He looked confused, blinking, silent, the bloodied rags and makeshift bandages still packed onto his stomach. Archer patted him on the shoulder reassuringly; the last thing they all needed right now was for his heroin trip to go bad. Screaming and shouting from hallucinations wouldn't be ideal.

'So Barlow was the rat,' Vargas said, taking deep breaths, leaning against the wall with Isabel beside her. 'That's how they knew where we were. He got Foster killed and Carson shot.'

'He must have told them everything,' Archer said. 'They knew all your plans, your movements, everything. You might as well have painted a red target on your chests.'

'That son of a-'

She stopped herself, remembering Isabel.

'Bitch?' the child finished.

Vargas smiled, nodding. 'Correct.'

'Are you OK?' Archer asked the little girl.

She nodded, coughing, and gave a double thumbs up.

On the street, the gathered cops and Feds stared up at the south side of the building. Thick black smoke was billowing out of an apartment on the 8th floor, pouring out of the windows and drifting up the walls of the tenement block. The building's fire alarm had just been cut off.

Casting his eyes further down and now more than anxious, Shepherd looked over at the entrance. At that moment, an NYPD hostage

232

negotiator securely protected in a bulletproof vest and helmet was approaching the door slowly, keeping to the wall. He'd started making the walk just before the explosion, but after a momentary pause he'd continued on his way.

He had a metallic case in his hand, about the size of a slender shoebox, attached to a long cord; it was a phone. They needed to get talking to these people and try to resolve this issue without anyone else being killed.

Everyone on the street watched his progress.

Suddenly, there was a muzzle flash and a burst of automatic gunfire from the lobby windows. The negotiator shouted in pain as he was hit and went down, people ducking for cover. He collapsed onto the concrete then tried to drag himself away, leaving the phone.

Another man from his team moved forward, behind a protective shield, as more assault rifle gunfire burst from the window, hammering into the shield and knocking the man behind it back a step. Despite the onslaught, he made it to his buddy and grabbed him by the collar, pulling him back and keeping them both protected behind the riot shield.

Shepherd examined the entrance but couldn't see anything apart from another flash of gunfire. They were keeping away from the windows, firing from an angle well back inside. He wondered if the response team were working with the men who'd ambushed the Marshals on the street, or if they'd been taken out. Whatever the scenario, whoever had the entrance secured was making it as clear as daylight that they didn't want to talk. There were twelve dead cops and a dead pilot who were proof of that.

If the NYPD or Marshals were to get inside they'd have to do it by force, not negotiation.

Shepherd turned to Hobbs and Dalton standing beside him. Their earlier differences were long forgotten, a distant memory from when the course of the evening and resolution had seemed far more straightforward. Hobbs was still stunned after losing his entire team. Both men had been watching the negotiator approach and seen him go down; their eyes followed him as he was dragged safely back behind cover and attended to immediately by two medics.

Shepherd caught Dalton's eye; he motioned to one side with his head and the two men moved away.

'We've got to get in there,' Shepherd said, lowering his voice. 'Right now. We gave them the opportunity to talk.'

'I agree,' Dalton said. 'But not from above. We can't afford to lose another team. I'm not sending any of my Marshals up there into that.'

One of Dalton's people, a female Marshal, approached. The two men saw her coming and turned.

'What's the plan, sir?' she asked.

Dalton looked at Shepherd. 'We're going in.' He paused. 'I could use your opinion.'

Shepherd nodded, walking forward with him to join the Marshals' task force. The group were engaged in conversation concerning their next play, all of them keen to take action but broke off when Shepherd and Dalton approached.

Observing this but feeling frustrated and helpless, Josh turned to Marquez who was watching the smoke pour up the tenement block, like water spilling out of a tipped glass in reverse. He voiced what they were both thinking.

'You think he's still alive?'

She didn't reply, staring up at the building. After a long moment, she responded.

'On the call, Vargas said one of their Marshals had been killed by this response team. The lead Deputy, Foster. Did she mention how?'

Josh thought for a moment.

'She said they'd been taken off guard and he'd been hit,' he said. 'But two of the enemy went down too. It was a fire fight; you heard the gunshots in there. Why?'

Marquez didn't reply, turning her attention back to the building. She looked up at the south-east corner.

Then she shifted her gaze downtown.

'What is it?'

'Dalton told me about Foster. He was in the Army for over two decades, finishing as a Major, then was a US Marshal for the last eleven years. He was highly experienced; one of the best men they had.'

'So?'

'So, he was armed and ready. Expectant, prepared. They were barricaded inside an apartment, a handful of guns on the entrance, all of them poised to pull the trigger. If someone tried to come in, he'd grease them like baking paper. So how the hell did someone get the drop on him?'

She looked away, her eyes narrowing as she examined the city landscape south of the tenement block.

Josh started catching on to her train of thought.

He looked down the street. There were a series of other tall buildings, staggered down through Harlem and the top of the Upper West Side.

'You think there's a shooter?'

'You saw the way this response team arrived. They're professionals. What do you think?'

Josh looked at the buildings.

'OK, so they wouldn't be too far away,' he said. 'Not with the city wind and thermals. They'd be close.'

'Far enough to get a complete look of the building, but near enough to counter the city elements.'

Both sets of eyes settled on what looked like an office building on West 133rd, about eighty yards away.

It was the only place nearby with enough elevation and proximity.

The perfect position for anyone with a rifle.

Marquez nodded.

'That's where I'd be,' she said.

Without another word, the two of them turned away and started walking down the street, heading downtown.

As they left, a car suddenly screeched to a halt by the barriers ten yards away, and a stern-faced, dark haired man with five o'clock shadow climbed out, slamming the door behind him. He pulled his badge and showed it to the cop on the tape without even looking at him, and stepped

236

through a gap in the barriers. His name was Jake Hendricks; he was a Sergeant in the Counter Terrorism Bureau.

Hendricks was close to becoming a legend in the NYPD; he was just as well known to scores of criminals as to the rest of the Department. Built like a club doorman or a line backer, Hendricks didn't see things in shades of grey; he was fair but totally uncompromising, both judge and jury. If you did wrong or if he even thought you had, you were going down.

He'd been a cop for over fifteen years and had worked out of Precincts all over the city. One of the most well-known stories about him was his time working out of the 75th in Brooklyn, regarded as the most dangerous and challenging place for a cop to work in all of New York. Most officers only went there under orders, but Hendricks had put in a transfer requesting to go. His view was that if you were a cop you never backed down, you never took the easy way out and you fought criminality with a sledgehammer, giving no quarter. Some men were born to crunch numbers, or excel at sports, or work blue collar. Hendricks was born to be a cop; there were many criminals currently behind bars who would grudgingly agree with that statement. Some of them still walked with limps.

That particular Sunday, Hendricks had been off duty; he'd just been settling down to supper with his family at his house across the Hudson when they'd flicked on the television and seen the news. The reports were saying a gunfight had broken out in the street on West 89th between a team of Federal Marshals and five other gunmen.

Apparently there'd been a car chase uptown and they were now cordoned off in a building on West 135th and Broadway, the gang members successfully holding the doors. A helicopter of reinforcements had arrived, but rumours suggested they weren't part of the rescue effort. Efforts to take back the building had been resisted and countered; an ESU team had abseiled in, but police reports were saying they'd been all been killed.

When Hendricks had heard that last part, he'd stopped eating. He put down his fork, then without a word had risen from the table, grabbed his piece and shield, jumped in the car and burned it over here as fast as he could. This wasn't his jurisdiction and he was off duty, but a team of NYPD officers had died tonight.

That made it his business.

As he walked through the crowd, he saw a task force of US Marshals fifteen yards away, all of them vested up and carrying assault weapons, crowded together and examining what looked like several I-Pad tablets. Beside them, he suddenly spotted Shepherd.

Hendricks paused, both pleased and genuinely surprised. The two men were the closest of friends and colleagues; they both ran their own teams in the Counter Terrorism Bureau and had started out as rookies, training together in the Academy and then working as partners in the same squad car years back. Their families had even been on vacation together, and Shep had been Hendricks' best man at his wedding.

Shepherd saw him too. Leaving the group of Marshals, he immediately walked forward to meet him.

'Jake?'

'Hey Shep,' he said, shaking his friend's hand.

'What are you doing here? Did Franklin give you a call?'

Hendricks shook his head. 'I saw the news. Apparently an ESU team went down.'

'The chopper wreckage is in Riverbank State Park,' Shepherd said, pointing. 'And one of our guys is inside the building.'

'What? Who?'

'Archer.'

'He's in there?'

Shepherd nodded. 'That's why I'm here.'

'How the hell did he get caught up in this?'

Shepherd pointed south. 'The group of Marshals were ambushed downtown as they were getting into a car with a State witness they're protecting. Archer was on the street nearby. He saw what was going down and tried to intervene. He ended up having to go with them when they made their escape. There was a car chase which ended here when the Tahoe's tyres were blown out and it hit the hydrant.'

Hendricks looked over at the two vehicles still dumped in the street outside the building, all the doors open. Both were surrounded by smashed glass with shell casings on the ground beside each vehicle. The Tahoe had taken a hell of a lot of punishment, riddled with bullet holes.

'They duked it out,' he said, reading the scene. 'But the gunmen had superior firepower.

239

Something automatic. The Marshals and Archer took cover in the building.'

'Correct. They barricaded themselves inside an apartment. One of the Marshals has been shot, another has been killed, and we can't communicate with them; all phone lines are down.'

Hendricks frowned. 'Cellular too?'

Shepherd nodded.

'So what happened to ESU?' Hendricks asked.

'About thirty minutes after they went in there, a black, unmarked chopper arrived. We thought it was one of ours, but it wasn't. We counted ten men abseiling in, some kind of back-up response team. One of the Marshals managed to get to an emergency phone; she said whoever they are, this team are all heavily armed and inside to finish the job. She and Archer managed to kill two of them, but the others sure as hell aren't giving up. They took out the ESU team and the chopper with Claymores and a LAW. There've been sounds of gunfights and explosions from inside. We can't communicate with them so we have no idea where they are or their current situation.'

'Jesus.' Hendricks looked up at the tenement block. 'You think they're still alive?'

'They must be. The response team sure as hell aren't leaving yet.'

'So who the hell is this witness?'

'A seven year old girl.'

'A child?'

'Other than that, we don't know much more.'

'Nothing at all?'

Shepherd nodded towards Dalton. 'He won't give.'

'We'll see about that,' Hendricks said, striding over towards the US Marshal. Shepherd joined him.

Jake had a way of getting people to talk.

TWENTY NINE

Once he'd put out the fires in 8A, Bishop had stumbled his way down the north stairwell, leaving the smoky corridor behind him. He pulled back the door on the ground floor and moved into the lobby. He was still disorientated, unsteady and nauseous, his face blackened, dust and smoke in his lungs.

The others were momentarily taken aback when they saw him. King was reloading his M4A1, having apparently just fired off some rounds through the window. He turned and looked at him.

'What the hell happened?'

'I don't know,' Bishop said loudly, shaking his head to clear his hearing. 'There was an explosion. Castle was in there with most of the mob. They're gone.'

'Jesus Christ, I'm sick of this,' King hissed, as Spades, Diamonds, Knight and Braeten stood there in silence. 'All I'm hearing tonight is failure. Do you call this shit professional?'

Silence. None of the men responded.

'All of you, get your game-faces on and step up your shit. It's a kid, a gunshot Marshal if he's still alive, a hundred-twenty pound woman and some asshole wannabe street hero who's in way over his head. If they want a war, let's give them a war.'

Just then, there was a commotion on the stairs behind them. A handful of the remaining guys from the volunteer mob appeared from the north side doorway, all of them looking spooked.

The response team turned to them.

'Where were you?' Bishop asked, coughing.

'We were on 9, getting ahead,' one of them said, noting Bishop's appearance. 'What the hell happened?'

Bishop didn't reply, stepping to one side and shaking his head to try and get back his hearing. One of the guys from the stairwell walked towards King.

'We're leaving.'

'No, you're not.'

'You didn't say anything about us getting blown up. We're out of here.'

'No, you're not.'

'Try to stop us, asshole.'

Pause.

'Is this all of you?'

The man looked behind him. 'I guess so. Everyone else bought it upstairs.'

Without another word, King swung up his M4A1, aimed at the man's head and opened fire.

The guy didn't have a moment to react. The burst took half of his head off; as he dropped, the men behind didn't have time to move as King machine gunned them all, blood and bits of clothing spraying into the air. He worked the trigger, moving from right to left, as the assault rifle tore them to pieces, and he kept the muzzle climb low, expertly using every round to kill.

When the clip clicked dry, the air reeking of cordite and gun smoke, King looked down at the bloodied and torn bodies slumped in front of the stairwell.

Pushing the magazine release catch, he let it fall to the floor and slapped another one home from a pouch on his tac vest. He turned to the other men, who were standing back impassively.

'No-one's leaving. Neither them, nor us. Not until she's dead.'

Bishop stepped forward, beginning to recover, and retrieved his pistol from the man on the floor. He tucked it back into the holster on his thigh.

'Where are your guys?' King asked Braeten. 'Were they killed too?'

He shrugged. 'I think they're higher up, still looking. You said they had to earn their way out of here.'

'The door to 8A was barricaded,' Bishop said. 'And you all heard Joker. The Marshals were definitely in there just before Castle and co made it inside.'

'So where the hell did they go?' Spades said.

King didn't reply, pushing his pressel switch instead. 'Joker, sitrep. Give me some good news. What the hell happened?'

Hard to say. It's smoky as shit over there. I dropped Barlow. He's gone. But they were all in there just before the posse showed up.

'Maybe they went up in the blast?' Spades suggested.

King looked at Knight, who was tracing the building chart on the wall beside the elevator with his finger.

'East-side 6 is a large laundry room,' he said. 'It's connected to all the apartments on the 8th floor.'

The men looked at each other. Without another word, King took off towards the south stairwell.

The rest of the team and Braeten followed, sprinting after him up the stairs.

'They killed her entire family?' Hendricks said, incredulous, Shepherd equally surprised beside him. Dalton nodded. Another burst of gunfire from inside the building had shaken his resolve and finally loosened his tongue. He'd just filled Shepherd and Hendricks in quickly on who exactly 'Jennifer' really was.

'If the child had been killed, we never would have known,' he continued. 'It was a master stroke. Hell, it took us a while to be convinced ourselves; the detectives figured the girl might be suffering from PTSD. But then we realised the plan made perfect sense; Lombardi and Devaney control 99 per cent of illegal activity down there in Nolita and Tribeca. If Devaney's people are out of the picture, Mike Lombardi plays the grieving son and can take over without any competition.'

'And he tracked her down. That's what this is about.' Hendricks looked up at the tenement block. 'Is he inside?'

'No idea.'

Hendricks shook his head. 'This level of organisation. Premeditation. Weapons. Tactics. They had no idea this would end up in this particular building, yet they were able to react almost immediately with that kind of firepower

245

and entry. These are some seriously dangerous people.'

Neither Shepherd nor Dalton responded.

'So where are our guys right now?' Hendricks asked.

They looked up at the building. 'We don't know,' Dalton said. 'We don't even know if they're still alive.'

He stared at the smashed windows on the south side 8th floor apartment, smoke still drifting out and up.

'But if they are, I pray to God those men don't know where they are either.'

Inside the laundry room, the remaining members of the group were sitting by the south-side wall, Archer and Vargas on the outside ready to protect Helen, Carson and Isabel between them. All of them were sooty and covered in nicks, cuts and scratches, battered and bruised. However, they were still alive. Considering what they were up against and what they'd been through, that was a hell of an achievement.

Archer and Vargas had dragged a protective shield of the heavy washers and dryers in front of them to offer some kind of barricade in case the response team found them. Their exit point was a fire door leading to the south stairwell to their immediate left inside their barrier, which could only be opened this side. There was another door across the room, connected to the main 6th floor corridor. If the enemy came, that would be their point of entry. The west and north side of the walls were lined with grille-covered chutes at intervals, under which large baskets would have been placed once upon a time to catch the laundry. It was an ancient design, almost a relic. God only knew how long it had been since this building was renovated. After all the gunfire and explosions tonight, the solution would probably be a wrecking ball.

Carson was starting to groan, filling the quiet. Helen knelt down to check and comfort him. She looked up at Archer and Vargas, concerned.

'The heroin is wearing off,' she said. 'He needed to be out of here an hour ago.'

'What do we do? Should we dope him up again?' Vargas said, looking at Archer.

He went to speak but stopped, hearing something.

There was a clanging from the chute they'd come down on the other side of the room.

Archer and Vargas looked over their barrier of old machines.

A black shape suddenly dropped down into the room.

It bounced on the floor and rolled towards them.

A grenade.

THIRTY

Archer and Vargas reacted within that initial half-second, diving back for cover, taking Isabel down with them.

Their makeshift barrier saved their lives as the grenade exploded.

The sound was deafening, taking all of their senses and smashing them to pieces. The blast destroyed some of the washers, shrapnel and chunks of metal flying through the air, a few machines knocked over, others closer to the blast completely totalled.

Archer had covered Isabel's ears with his hands so his had been unprotected and the effect was catastrophic. It felt like the grenade had gone off inside his head.

Suddenly, everything was silent, like an interlude.

Releasing the girl's ears and seeing her move, confirming she was OK, Archer shook his head to try and clear it, the room as quiet as a church in prayer. The air was thick with dust and smoke, stinging his eyes. He'd dropped his M4A1 in the blast and saw it a few feet away, beside some rubble and pieces of washer. It was lying by the wall.

I need that, he thought.

He staggered to his feet, stumbling and falling back, wet liquid on his face. It felt like water; maybe a pipe had ruptured in the explosion.

He touched his cheek and his hand came away red.

Not water.

A grenade, Sam.

They know we're here.

They're coming.

Reeling, he made it to the wall and scooped up his M4A1. He turned and tried to aim at the doorway, falling into a wrecked dryer, blinking dust from his eyes, swaying as his brain frantically tried to recalibrate. Beside him, Vargas was still gathering her senses, trying to get to her feet but only having managing to get to her hands and knees. He saw a trickle of blood coming from her ear.

Through the haze, two figures suddenly appeared in the main doorway, looming out of the smoke and dust. Archer went to fire but stopped when he saw a small figure to his right, standing still, staring at the two men.

Isabel.

He'd turned his back for a second and she'd gone.

She was disorientated, and had stepped out from behind their protective barrier, walking right into the enemy's firing line.

The two men saw her. They had black assault rifles in their hands, inevitably full magazines inside, enough ammo to take on a squad of cops, let alone an unprotected seven year old child.

Two figures from a nightmare, black masks over their faces, guns in their hands.

That's it.

It's over.

She's gone.

The two men stared at the girl and lifted their rifles.

Then aimed them directly at Archer

They opened fire and noise in the room came back. Archer had already flung himself down as the bullets tore into the wall and machines, spraying more pieces of metal and chalk into the air.

Vargas swung her M4A1 forward and started to fire back through the gloom. Her aim was poor, her senses still affected by the blast, but it was enough to force the two men to duck behind the door in the hallway and buy Archer several vital seconds.

As Vargas kept her barrage up, he moved out from behind his cover and ran across the room, grabbing Isabel, scooping her up and taking her back with him, her screaming lost in the gunfire and smoke as Vargas emptied a magazine into the doorway, adrenaline speeding up the return of her faculties as she fought the muzzle climb, shell casings spraying out of the ejection port.

Pushing Isabel behind him, Archer took over the counter-firing as Vargas reloaded fast, slapping another clip into the weapon. The two guys on the other side of the door did their best to return fire, but they didn't have a chance to engage them properly as Archer kept up the onslaught, keeping them pinned down.

His mag clicked dry, Vargas taking over as the two men at the doorway fired a burst back. Pulling the empty clip from the weapon, he grabbed his last one from his pocket but turned as he did so to make sure Isabel was still behind him.

Then he saw Helen.

She was leaning against the wall, staring straight ahead, the noise and terror of the gunfight lost on her. If it wasn't for the thick piece of metal jutting out of her chest, she would have looked serene, as if she was taking a moment to absorb it all and watch the fight, like a spectator at Wimbledon.

As Vargas kept up her fire on the door, Archer moved over to Helen, his eyes stinging from the dust. She stared back vacantly, the light gone from her eyes, strands of hair hanging down either side of her smoke-stained face.

He looked down at the piece of metal; it was white, a piece of destroyed washer from the grenade blast.

It had pierced right through her, pinning her to the wall.

She was gone.

Grabbing Carson and dragging him towards the fire escape, Archer pushed the bar down with his elbow and kicked the door open. Vargas squeezed off two more bursts then scooped up Isabel and quickly followed them through the fire exit.

Just as they left, two more grenades were tossed inside from the other side of the room.

Vargas saw them early and slammed the door shut behind them, protecting them as they took cover in the stairwell.

Outside, everyone on the street heard the explosions and savage gunfight unfold. It was happening this side of the building, so they could see the muzzle flashes from the 6th floor

251

windows, the reports of the weapons echoing in the street.

Suddenly there was another explosion and more windows smashed out. As people recoiled, ducking down, Shepherd cursed, his patience at an end. He turned and kicked a car out of frustration, feeling totally helpless. Any NYPD officer or detective in peril made him anxious, but that concern went to a whole new level when it was one of his own people, someone under his command depending on him to come up with a solution.

He looked up at the building, more smoke coming from the 6th floor, and pictured Archer somewhere inside.

Just hold on, Arch, he thought. *Wherever you are. We're coming for you.*

Hendricks was standing beside him, his face dark, watching the apartment block. The gunfire ended abruptly, but the echoes from the shots and the explosions were still reverberating in people's ears, reporters behind the public barriers giving rapid updates, as shocked as everyone else at the speed of events. Hendricks looked over at Dalton and the Marshals team. They'd switched their attention from the apartment building and were now poring over the I-Pads, crowded round and peering at the screens.

It looked as if a frontal assault was imminent.

He glanced over at the lobby, *Claymores and an anti-tank rocket* echoing in his mind. If they had that kind of protection for the roof, God only knew what they had waiting for them behind that door. No way was the Marshals task force getting

252

in without many more, or even all of them, going down.

They needed to find another way to end this.

He turned to Shepherd. 'Remind me, who's the girl?'

'She's a State witness. According to Dalton, she's due in a matter of days. She makes the stand, she buries her brother and the team who killed her entire family.'

'Where are they based?'

'Walker Street. The family own a bar down there.'

Shepherd looked at Hendricks.

'What are you thinking?'

Hendricks didn't reply. He turned and stalked through the crowd instead, moving towards his car.

He ripped open the door and moments later was speeding downtown, dialling a number on his cell phone.

He needed an exact address.

Arriving on the 12th floor, Archer staggered down the corridor, Carson once again over his shoulders, his blood leaking over Archer's once white t-shirt and joining the black smoke stains.

Vargas was right behind him, holding Isabel's hand, her M4A1 in the other. On the way up they'd ducked into the corridor on 7, hearing running footsteps coming from above, and had just managed to avoid two gunmen sprinting down the stairwell. Once they'd passed, Archer and Vargas moved on as quickly as they could, trying to put as much distance between themselves and the laundry room.

12 was as far as Archer's legs would take him, his body still recovering from the grenade explosion. An apartment a third of the way down the corridor was open, on the east side so away from any potential sniper fire. Without even checking it first Archer ducked inside, followed by Vargas and Isabel; there was no one here.

They collapsed into the room, Vargas quickly shutting the door then locking it. Dumping Carson down heavily onto the floor, Archer did the same as before with the refrigerator, unplugging and dragging it into place as a barrier. This time it was much more of an effort, almost Herculean; he was exhausted. When it was in position, the door secured, they stepped back, sucking clean air into their lungs.

As he breathed in, Archer suddenly felt a searing pain. He looked down and saw some glass had hit him in the lower left of his torso, slicing through his t-shirt.

He stared at it for a few moments, then glanced at Vargas. She hadn't seen it.

Then he made eye contact with Isabel.

She had.

He pulled it out, coughing from the pain, and tossed it to one side with a *clink*, holding his M4A1 with one hand and cradling the wound with the other.

Downstairs, the gunmen were in the laundry room. Their boots crunched on the debris, their M4A1s sweeping the now empty space. King and

Diamonds had been the two men trying to force their way in, but the man and woman had held them off, despite three grenades.

King walked forward slowly through the smoke and saw a woman slumped against the wall.

She was dead, impaled. She had a chunk of metal the size of a man's forearm jutting out of her chest, her eyes blank and staring straight ahead. He had no idea who she was.

Spades and Knight reappeared from the south stairwell, panting.

'And?'

'We lost them.'

King stayed still for a moment.

Then he raised his weapon and unleashed a burst into the dead woman in frustration and fury, blood and shell casings spraying into the air.

THIRTY ONE

Josh and Marquez had just entered the south building on West 133rd. It was an office building, not an apartment block. They were intending to talk to the night security or whoever was behind the front desk, but there was no-one there. The pair of detectives looked around.

The place was empty.

'Where the hell is the guard?' Marquez said.

'Maybe he's off tonight. It's a Sunday.'

'Then why is the building still open?'

'Perhaps he's outside or upstairs watching the show.'

Marquez frowned and didn't reply.

Josh walked around the desk and looked down at several monitors. He glanced up and made eye contact with her.

'Security cameras are down.'

Stepping around the desk and re-joining her, the two of them walked forward, heading for the stairwell at the end of the lobby. Using the stairs was slower but the noise of the elevator could alert someone in the building that they had company.

If there actually was someone here.

As Josh pushed back the door to the stairwell, Marquez drew her Sig Sauer, pulling back the slide and glancing over at the abandoned front desk.

Something was wrong. Someone was here.

She knew it.

Inside a bar called *Lombardis* on Walker Street in Little Italy, a group of men were watching a hockey game on a television mounted above the long liquor shelf behind the bar. They each had a drink going and had been for some time, relaxed, secure on their own territory but each carrying a pistol on his person nevertheless.

On the screen, the Rangers were taking on the Penguins at the Garden and the game was squared at 2-2, the players skating fast around the ice, the puck flying back and forth, a quick flash of black on the white ice. There were several screens behind the bar; the one on the far right was flicked onto NY ONE, which was covering some kind of situation at a tenement block uptown in Harlem. No-one aside from one man paid any attention to it. Put a hockey game on alongside the news in here and there was only ever going to be one winner.

Sitting at the bar, Mike Lombardi drained his whiskey, watching the news report. Twenty five years old, tough and compact with swarthy looks passed down to him from his Milanese great-grandparents, he was still getting used to the fact that he was now head of his own New York crime family.

He'd always been an outsider. His mother had been a waitress who used to work in this bar; one night she'd caught his father Gino's eye. Gino had been married at the time and once his wife had found out the girl was pregnant and that it was his, she'd come down here and given her one hell of a beating, to within an inch of her life. Apparently there'd been plenty of people around that night, but none of them had intervened, not

257

when it was Gino's wife dishing out the punishment. His mother had been hospitalised but despite Gino's wife's best efforts Mike had been born six months later.

In the space between the beating and his birth, Gino's wife never let up. Although she never assaulted his mother again, she spent every spare moment making her life a misery, to the point that his mother soon quit working at the bar, frightened that the woman would assault her again or possibly order some kind of move against her.

Once Mike had been born, things still didn't improve. Although his father was a feared man, the word *bastard* had echoed in Mike's ears as a kid, both he and his mother ostracised, no-one wanting to get on the wrong side of Gino's wife. Mike lived with his mother whilst he was growing up, but had started to come down here when he was old enough, working tirelessly to impress his father and trying to gain his attention and respect. Gino had always acknowledged Mike as his son but as Mike grew older, ironically out of all of Gino's kids he began to most resemble his father in looks and temperament. He was the second youngest of six and although he was clearly the least favoured, that had started to change with time. When others saw Gino's acceptance and growing fondness for his youngest son, they'd followed suit and life had started to become a little easier during Mike's teenage years.

Gino had encouraged the boy's interest in the family business, despite his wife's intense dislike of him. To her, he was a constant reminder of her husband's infidelity. As Mike approached manhood, his dogged persistence had paid off. Unlike his half-siblings who grew up spoilt and lazy, Mike was a worker. In the last few years, he'd seen in the older man's eyes that he'd more than gained his respect. Gino was increasingly and pleasantly surprised by his bastard son; Mike had started out working the racketeering in the area and had risen to where he was in charge of controlling shipments coming in through the East Side Docks, paying off guys who worked there and the Union, and ensuring the cops, Coastguard or US Customs never got wise to anything in the freight containers.

However, it had all been part of a plan, years in the making. All the insults and abuse Mike had received as a kid had left some deep scars; a boiling hatred had grown inside him, like a steaming pressure cooker always on the verge of exploding. Mike was only half related to every member of this family. The only person in the world he truly cared for, his mother, had already passed on. He'd never shaken the hatred that had festered within him since he was a child, or forgotten the insults and the way his mother was treated, his father never going out of his way to put a stop to it which he could have done in an instant.

Looking at the world through a man's eyes, Mike realised his position as Gino's son gave him a major advantage.

It meant he could work his way up much more easily. Gain trust. Observe how the inner-workings of the operation functioned. Get a feel for the family; see who was happy and who was feeling misused. Blood was blood, and the one thing he'd inherited from his father was his ruthlessness. He'd shown hints of it already, kneecapping a guy who'd fallen asleep behind the wheel on a late-night job and consequently getting two of their guys busted. He'd also whacked three enforcers from the Devaney crew, chopping up the pieces and scattering them in the bay. Despite this violent streak, Mike was much more intelligent than he let on, and all this time had been planning his father's downfall.

And at the beginning of the month, he'd executed his plan.

Motioning at the bartender to refill his glass, Mike glanced up at the screen. Reading the teletext, he made out that there'd been some kind of gunfight in the Upper West Side and that a team of armed men were holding off a tenement block, some people trapped inside. The bartender topped up Mike's Jack as he watched the screen.

Suddenly, there was a screech outside the bar as a car pulled up, followed shortly afterwards by the sound of a door being slammed.

The men inside the joint glanced over at the noise.

Moments later, a big dark-haired guy dressed in jeans and a sweater strode in. He looked pissed. Two of Mike's men, Paul and Luca, put down their drinks and stepped off their stools, walking towards him with total self-confidence, knowing they were on their turf. Even if this guy was lost, he was still going to catch a beating. No one walked in here without an invitation or Mike's blessing.

260

However, the dark-haired guy didn't slow his stride or hesitate for a moment. He laid Paul out with a fierce right hook, a savage punch that almost put him into next week, then slammed Luca up against the bar as he went for his pistol, twisting his arm behind him and pushing his head down to the wood.

The others instantly reached for their weapons but the new guy pulled a gun from a holster on his hip, putting it to Luca's head.

'Throw them on the ground. Now!'

There was a pause, but the men complied, an assortment of handguns clattering to the floor, the men staring at him with vicious intent. Once the guns were on the floor, the guy slammed Luca's head into the bar, breaking his nose.

He collapsed to the polished floor in a heap at the newcomer's feet.

'You have any idea where you are?' Mike said. 'You're a dead man.'

'Is that right?' the guy said, pulling something off his hip and sliding it across the bar.

It was an NYPD badge.

Mike looked at it.

'Is that supposed to scare me?'

Moving forward, the newcomer grabbed the badge and slid it back into his pocket, then wrenched Mike off his stool, walking away and dragging him to the entrance, his gun buried in the mobster's side. Mike hid his surprise. He knew some members of the Department were ball-breakers, but this guy was acting like a mob enforcer, almost like he was on the wrong side.

'I don't forget a face,' Mike hissed. 'I'll find you.'

'Oh I don't think so,' the man replied, pushing him through the front door and outside towards his car.

Inside their new hideout on the 12th floor, Carson had been placed on the couch in the sitting room, safe from the sniper given that the apartment was on the east side. He was starting to double over and groan again, the cheap heroin all but worn off.

The sounds were passing through the thin wall, even with the door shut, and brought mounting concern, not just about the noise but over his condition. They'd been trapped inside the block for almost three hours now, with no medical aid.

If they didn't get him out of here soon, he'd be joining Foster, Barlow and Helen.

In the kitchen, Isabel was sitting on a chair as Vargas inspected some minor cuts on the little girl's face and arms, Archer watching her. Fortunately, Isabel hadn't been badly hurt from the blasts, Archer and Vargas protecting her and covering her from any shrapnel or debris. All three of them were blackened by soot and smoke, nicks and cuts peppering their arms and cheeks. The path of blood from Vargas' ear had dried. Archer now had the wound to his lower torso to contend with as well as a fresh cut across his eyebrow. The blood was trickling down his temple, just missing his left eye, and his ears were still ringing from the grenades.

Satisfied that Isabel was OK, Vargas looked over at Archer and saw him holding his palm to the lower left of his torso.

'You're hurt?'

'It's OK,' he lied. 'It's not deep.'

Pause.

Vargas swallowed.

'I saw Helen.'

Archer nodded. 'Yeah. Me too.'

He turned and watched the door, listening closely. With his back to the other two, he lifted his hand from the wound. The injury burned like hell. It felt as if he'd spilt hot liquid over his skin.

He rose and moved to the kitchen counter. Grabbing a towel from the table-top, he held it tight against the wound, staunching the blood as best he could. For the first time since they'd escaped, he thought back in detail to what had happened downstairs in the laundry room, replaying the entire sequence in his mind from the moment that grenade had clanged down the chute.

He suddenly went very still.

'What? What is it?' Vargas asked, watching him. 'Archer?'

He didn't move.

'Archer? Are you OK?'

Pause.

He turned slowly.

'What's wrong?' she said, seeing the look on his face.

'Downstairs. They had a clear shot at her,' he said, indicating to Isabel. 'They didn't take it.

He looked at Vargas for a long moment.

Then he leant back, sliding slowly down the counter and sitting on the floor.

Suddenly everything fell into place.

'What?' Vargas asked, pressing him. 'What is it?'

'I've been such a fool,' he said, shaking his head. 'This whole time, I never saw what this is really about.'

'What are you talking about?'

'Upstairs, earlier, when we took out those two guys on 22. You were staring at that man.'

'Yeah. So?'

'Not because you'd killed him. Because you recognised him.'

She blinked.

'They're not here for her, Vargas,' he said, nodding at Isabel.

He paused.

'They're here for you.'

THIRTY TWO

The room was silent.

Archer's statement had drawn no denial from her.

Instead, Vargas rose without a word and took Isabel through to the sitting room; Archer heard her tell the girl to lie down and promised she'd be just next door.

Then she re-joined him in the kitchen, closing the door to the sitting room so they were alone.

She sat down on the floor across from him, leaning against the wall, her M4A1 beside her. He saw the expression on her face.

The game was up.

'That story you told me earlier about Isabel,' he said. 'Was that bullshit?'

'No. That was all true. Every word.'

'But this isn't about her. They let her go. So who are you?'

Silence.

'Is Vargas your real name?'

'Yes.' Pause. 'I wasn't a United States Marshal until very recently.'

'How recently?'

'Been qualified for three weeks.' She paused. 'Before that, I was training in Glynco, Georgia.'

'And before that?'

'I was a cop.'

'Where?'

'Miami.'

'What division?'

'SRT. Special Response Team. Their SWAT unit.'

She paused.

'I finished my Academy training in LA just over two years ago. I did well, finishing at the top of the class, and spent the first twenty five months in a squad car working a beat in Inglewood. At the beginning of last year, I arrived at the Department one morning and was ordered by my Sergeant to meet with a police Commander. He started asking me about my background, what I wanted to achieve as a member of law enforcement, sounding me out. As the conversation progressed, it turned out that he wasn't from LA. He was Miami-Dade PD.'

'Why was he scouting you?'

'He had two SRT teams under his command, First and Second. Twelve people in each, male and female officers, units that performed the same tasks as LAPD SWAT. His Second Team were kosher, no problem. But he had suspicions about First. And these weren't just concerns about some detective who wasn't undercover anymore but still doing blow on the weekends. This was some high-level scamming; we're talking seven or eight figures worth of dirty cash and stolen product from legitimate raids and busts.'

Archer nodded. 'Go on.'

'He had a feeling that they were making more illegal money on the side than the guys they were busting. Drugs have been flowing through Florida like a river for the past forty years. You should see the amount of seized money, dope and cocaine that these officers have access to. It's

266

staggering, and their superiors are well aware of the temptation. They'd come up through the ranks themselves.'

She paused.

'The Commander had been working on finding out if these guys really were corrupt, but he hadn't succeeded. They were smart and covered their tracks effectively. Although they were under his official command, they worked together on a daily basis as a close unit, a tight-knit group. He'd tried sliding officers into the team who were working undercover for him, but none of them found any evidence of corruption. It even started making him think and look like he was just paranoid. However, he was a good man, and very experienced. Despite the lack of proof, he knew deep in his gut something was very wrong.'

Pause.

'He said his last two options were to bring in Internal Affairs, which would open a real can of worms and make his concerns public, or try one last undercover cop. The problem was, every applicant to SRT was assessed by a review board of current SRT team members and himself. The Master Sergeant of the First Team, Seth Calvin, had access to all their files, their history, their performance in training at the Academy. He knew weeks in advance before anyone applied to join his team what they were about. The Commander even tried sullying up a few applicants' records, but Calvin and his team smelt a rat, the officers joining their team unable to get close to any illegal activity.'

She paused.

'They were constantly on their guard, looking into Miami PD at anyone who could be set up as a mark to get inside their crew.'

She looked over at him.

'But they weren't watching the LAPD.'

His back against the wall, Archer listened closely, holding the towel close to the wound on his lower torso.

Vargas was ex-SRT, trained Special Response.

That explained the way she'd handled everything tonight. But he waited for her to explain the rest.

'I thought about the Commander's offer to go undercover and accepted,' she continued. 'It sure as hell was better than the alternative, working the beat in LA for five or six years hoping for a promotion and trying not to get killed. I packed my stuff and flew down there. But then it came to my cover story, which brought up a problem.'

'What was that?'

'Any applicant to SRT has to be a sworn Miami PD officer. We set it up so according to the file I'd been working Vice in Orlando but had requested a transfer to the Miami-Dade Department due to personal reasons. I was one of the best they had in Orlando, but for some reason I wasn't gelling with the team around me and needed a change of scene.'

She nodded.

'The story was solid. It held. They would have run some checks, but my dummy file was on the computer and I seemed legit. I then applied for SRT and went under the review board. I passed all the tests, mental and physical, and was at the top of my class in the training programme. But right then, we started to lay seeds. I was pretty abrupt and hostile to the other recruits. Didn't socialise. Deliberately caused some friction. When I was confronted about it in interview by the Commander, I said I didn't care what others thought of me, I just wanted to do my job to the best of my abilities. If they wanted a delicate chick, they should go to the beach. Then less than a week later, I was assigned to Calvin's team.'

She paused.

'At first, everything seemed legitimate. I began to think the Commander was imagining things. But after I smacked around a few suspects on some drug raids and bit back when the guys on the team started giving me shit, they began to relax. They included me more and more. And then I saw that the Commander wasn't just paranoid.'

She shook her head.

'Turned out this wasn't just a couple officers skimming a few notes off the stack. This was scamming that had been going on for years. Not including myself, there were eleven men in the First Team and every single one of them was in on it. A handful of others had retired on what they'd stolen, their replacements appointed by Calvin over the years, men who they knew they could trust and were secretly on the take. I relayed what I was seeing to the Commander and we began to build a case. On scores of busts, I saw them keep aside large portions of money and dope for themselves, tossing me a cut to keep me quiet. I hung out with a few of them at bars on the

Keys, shooting the shit and learning what they'd been up to all this time.'

'They weren't suspicious?'

'Take this from a woman. You wear a tight-fitting dress and act half-interested, a guy won't be thinking with his brain.'

'So what happened?'

'A separate task force from the Anti-Corruption Unit was set up to build a complete case on these guys. Surveillance, wire taps. I was wearing a fibre-optic on a couple of raids. Gathering weight on the older guys who'd retired was easy; they'd become complacent. They'd figured they'd already ridden off into the sunset and had gotten away with their crimes. None of these idiots understood the meaning of subtlety; they had five bedroom homes, speedboats. One of them even had a 230 thousand dollar Ferrari, fresh off the line. Nailing them was easy.'

'The others?'

'Not so much. The current officers were smart and had connections. Although they were screwing up, they were pretty slick and warier than the old guys. ACU couldn't find their stolen funds, and they only spoke about their dealings in person, never over the phone. However, at the end of November last year we figured we had enough with my first-hand accounts; the case was green lit and out in the open. The entire team was arrested, suspended and have been ever since, each of them still being brought in for questioning and grilled like tenderloin. So far they've admitted nothing, standing their ground, challenging us to provide any clear-cut

270

unquestionable evidence. Which is where I come in.'

'And it didn't take a genius to realise you were the one who gave them up,' he said.

She nodded. 'No. It didn't.'

'Once the Commander and his task force moved in, I was immediately pulled from SRT for my own safety,' she explained, as Archer listened closely. 'I was a jewel in the prosecution's crown. I'd been involved in some of this scamming and had seen first-hand the accused officers engaged in all sorts of illegal activity. Suddenly, I became extremely valuable but also a major target. The evidence against them was strong but not titanium. My testimony would carry considerable weight. If anything happened to me, there was a strong possibility the case could disintegrate. They've got powerful friends. If they got charged they'd get a few months, maybe a couple of years, maybe nothing at all if their lawyer played her hand right. If I didn't make the stand, they could get off pretty easy. They could even beat the charges.'

'The same as Isabel,' Archer said.

Vargas nodded. 'The Commander wanted me out of Florida. As I said, these cops had some powerful connections, including guys still on the force. The Commander had some himself, including Dalton, who was a former Miami PD Master Sergeant and an old friend of his. Given what I'd done, they asked me where I wanted to go, and the Commander suggested the US Marshals. He'd spoken to Dalton about the situation and provided I passed the training,

Dalton said I could join his office here in New York.'

'So they accepted.'

She nodded.

'Two days later, I was at the training academy in Glynco for seventeen weeks, laying low, living in camp, far from Florida and blending in with all the other recruits,' she said. 'Then I was assigned to Foster's team under Dalton's orders.'

'They didn't tell John who you really were?'

She shook her head.

'It was almost like witness protection for me; teams like Foster's live off the grid and always expect trouble. Although they thought they were protecting someone else, I'd have a three-man security escort wherever I went and no-one would know my story. For the past eight days, we've been laying low with Isabel, staying at DOJ safe-houses all over the State. It was killing two birds with one stone. I'd be part of Foster's crew protecting Isabel, yet they had no idea that they were also protecting me.'

'Jesus Christ,' he said. 'So these men are all cops?'

She nodded. 'Miami-Dade PD. Special Response Team. Including the sniper, that makes eleven men.'

'That explains their moves and obvious training. These guys know what they're doing.'

'Right now, they're all suspended as the investigation continues. The trial is set to start in eleven days. And guess who's due to testify against them.'

Archer considered the situation, mapping it out from the start to that very moment.

'They hired the street team to put you away. They're also in the area, but not on the trigger, wanting to lay low and away from suspicion but there in case anything went wrong. When the ambush didn't work, they came in themselves to take you out. Make sure you die so they walk.'

'Yes. These guys are cops; they know the drill. Their alibis will already be bought and paid for. They'll be able to prove they were nowhere near New York this weekend.'

She thought back in the evening.

'I don't know how the hell they found me. But however they did, they must have figured Barlow would be the weakest link on our team. Made him an offer. He must have told them everything; me, Foster, Carson. Who Isabel was. Our moves and location today. They set up an ambush to get me.'

Archer nodded.

'They knew any attack would appear to come from Mike Lombardi,' he said. 'And it would look like you got caught in the crossfire trying to protect her. The perfect plan.'

He paused.

'Jesus. These guys are supposed to be on our side.'

'Tell me about it.'

Taking it all in, Archer thought back to the gunfight on the 22nd floor. He remembered Vargas removing the man's balaclava and staring down at him when he grabbed her and said they had to go.

'Who was the guy you killed upstairs?'

273

'His name was Taylor. First Team's point man when they went in through the door. Real asshole.'

'You knew right then what this is really about.'

She nodded. 'Yeah.'

'So why didn't you say anything?'

'I've been sworn to secrecy and I was shocked. Besides, it wouldn't make any difference if they were after me or Isabel; we'd all still be in this situation. And I thought back up would get to us before I'd have to explain.' She saw the look on his face. 'Try to understand, Archer. I've spent the last thirteen months keeping a huge part of my life a secret; it's hard to shake that habit. Especially when there are a group of highly trained men searching for you and wanting to kill you.'

He thought for a moment.

'Well now we know for a fact who they are, we need to tell the people outside,' he said. 'This changes everything. They're wearing those balaclavas and using code-names for a damn good reason. Without them, their alibis count for shit.'

He grunted and rose, pulling the bloodied towel from his torso and pushing himself back to his feet. She joined him.

'So how do we contact them? The phones are down and they'll be guarding the lobby.'

'One phone isn't dead.'

She realised what he was thinking. 'The emergency line on 22.'

He nodded.

'We need to get back up there.'

274

THIRTY THREE

Downstairs, King, Bishop, Spades, Knight and Diamonds had reconvened on the 1st floor, near some sort of manager's office, having come back down from the laundry room on 6. Braeten had joined them, two of his guys elsewhere in the building hunting for Vargas. The man armed with the AK-47 was holding the front door.

Standing in the corridor with the surviving members of his team, King leant against the wall, his mood thunderous, going over the events of the evening in his head and wondering just how the hell everything that could have gone wrong, had.

His real name and rank was Master Sergeant Seth Calvin. Born and raised on South Beach and thirty three years old, he'd been a member of Miami-Dade Police Department for eleven years.

He'd been dirty for ten years and eleven months of them.

Most people in the United States didn't fully comprehend the amount of narcotics that flowed through the Florida Keys every day. Those old enough to remember Reagan's speech declaring war on the cartels figured the US Coastguard, Miami PD and the DEA had immediately leapt on the issue and had crushed the illegal trafficking in the thirty five or so years since that declaration. Back in the 1970s, Miami had become the drug gateway to the entire country. Pilots had flown in fresh product from Colombia and Cuba every day, huge quantities of cocaine and heroin that would sell for absurd amounts of cash. Once the cops wised up and started lying in wait, the pilots improvised, dropping the cargo in floatable bags into the sea. Runner speedboats would follow the flight path, scooping up the coke, and get it out of the water before the Coastguard showed up. South Florida had 8,000 miles of coastline; no matter how big the security operation or bold Reagan's statements had been, there were always cracks in the system and opportunities for drug cartels. To this day, they still ruthlessly exploited them.

The drugs flowed onto the streets to the dealers and junkies. Out of the Academy all those years back, Calvin and his partner Denton had been assigned a beat in West Grove, a rough part of town that offered way more in the way of risk than it did reward for a rookie police officer just starting out. Cop shootings in Miami were common, especially by drug dealers. One month into their partnership, the two men had answered a neighbour complaint call and ended up finding a man shot dead inside a house, two rounds in his forehead and the sitting room torn to pieces, the killer obviously searching for something. Checking the rest of the house, they'd found three keys of dope and ten thousand dollars taped to the inside of a shelf in the kitchen. Neither of them had ever held that much money in their hands in their entire lives.

It was at that very moment that the two men realised they could make this work to their advantage.

When back-up arrived, the body was removed and the drugs and cash were booked, three keys and eight thousand dollars of drug money. Calvin and Denton had given their reports and left the scene with a stack of bills tucked inside their waistband under their uniform.

The two cops had popped their cherries.

And they'd liked the way it felt.

They'd started out small and subtle, keeping their records and their reputations clean whilst learning the ropes and working the beat, familiarising themselves with the players and the drug trade. Detectives and officers on busts all over the city would seize large quantities of powder and all of it ended up going through the Miami PD lock up, the money eventually parlayed back into circulation, the drugs taken to a lab and destroyed. Calvin got to know two of the guys running a shift down there, Markowski and Fowler, two men who had millions of dollars worth of dope within arm's reach and who, Calvin soon discovered, shared his and Denton's sentiments on capitalising on their privileged position. They couldn't touch the money that had been booked, but they sure as hell could go after the powder.

The four men started to take a key here or there and replace it with a substitute, selling it back on the street at a jacked up price. No-one around them was ever the wiser; they had so much of the shit going through the cages at the Department that none of their superior officers ever noticed.

They also knew for a fact that they weren't the only ones doing it.

That was almost eleven years ago. Since then, Calvin and Denton had done their time in West Grove then applied, trained and been accepted to SRT, joining one of their entry teams and getting a slight rise in pay. Despite their secret doings, both men were proficient, intelligent officers and had quickly risen through the ranks, Calvin making Master Sergeant in the First Team of SRT three years ago and Denton Sergeant below him. They kept up their racket along the way but they'd had to be ever more subtle and on their toes, scores of clean officers around them who could never be swayed and were therefore treated with utmost caution. On occasion, after clearing a residence during a bust, the two men had found dope or cash and left it where it was hidden. If it was discovered by any detectives or CSU, no-one would know they were aware of it.

If it wasn't, they would come back for it later.

As Calvin grew more senior in SRT, so did his influence on who made his team. Markowski and Fowler had applied and joined the task force, followed by more guys whom Markowski had recommended, assuring them they were reliable and up to extracurricular activities outside of official police business. Each man was pissed off watching the criminals they were trying to bust living movie-star lifestyles whilst they put their lives on the line for little reward, and they all wanted a share of it, any good intentions they'd ever had as cops erased like chalk on an old school blackboard. Calvin developed a system. Whenever one of the older guys moved on or retired, he would handpick a carefully vetted newbie from the candidates who he knew he and his men could trust.

Slowly and surely, the percentage of officers on the First Team who were corrupt grew from 20 per cent to 40, from 60 to 80. Soon, it was all but one man. Being SRT, they were the smash and grab teams that came in through the front door, fully armed and with warrants to search wherever the hell they wanted before any detectives and forensic teams got there. Many of the police seizures and drug busts were monumental. Miami was still ground zero for most of the cocaine coming into the United States, and Calvin and his peers constantly had the shit running through their fingers, like putting their hands under a huge tap of powder that never stopped flowing. They stole large amounts of cash and product, finding fifty keys and only reporting forty, discovering half a million dollars and handing over four hundred thousand, taking vast quantities of blow and selling it back to the cartels or dealers at a hiked-up price. If anyone the other side threatened to talk, they were taken care of. Police raids were as common as knocks on front doors in Miami and not all of them went peacefully.

Calvin had joined the force at 22; by the time he was 26, he was on his way to becoming wealthy. By his 28th birthday, he was a secret millionaire. And the whole time, he covered his tracks and made sure all his guys did the same.

Amongst all the dirty activity, the team also performed some legitimate high-profile busts and provided security for VIPs visiting the city as part of their responsibilities as an SRT team, mixing the lawful operations in with all the scamming, to keep their reputations clean and avoid any unwelcome attention or suspicion. It worked. The newspapers, the city, the Mayor and the rest of the Department viewed them as loyal public servants. Men of honour. Although money laundering was now illegal, if a man was smart with the stolen cash and either banked it off-shore or invested it the right way, the funds could never be traced.

The war on drugs had spoils, just like any other conflict. The same as the soldiers who raided Hitler's retreat once World War Two was over, Calvin and his men were making the most of a highly profitable situation. It was ideal. Collectively they had millions of dollars stored away from years of skimming. You make a few legit busts and take down a few collars, the Department superiors and the press applauded you for doing a great job. No one would ever think you were dirty.

It had worked like a dream. In the almost eleven years Calvin had been a cop, he'd earned close to four million dollars in illegal drug money.

And that was just his share, not including the cash the rest of his guys had taken.

Although the vast majority of the cops in Miami-Dade PD were clean, Calvin and his team weren't the only ones abusing the system. Some of these other officers were about as intelligent as third graders. They didn't take sufficient precautions, got careless about paying off the right people, left a trail that a child in the woods could follow. Internal Affairs were always hanging around the Keys on the hunt for these guys and it was like sharks with blood in the water when they found them. They knew how tempting all that money and coke could be to someone with a gun and authority. They were always on the prowl.

The Department tried to keep quiet about guys who got popped for corruption; most of them were shunted into retirement and threatened with severe consequences if they talked. Others were made an example of and ended up in the State pen, sharing a cell with the same people they used to bust.

But Calvin and his team were smart. He had an instinct for those who would never take a cut, and he could sense the SRT Commander had some reservations about him and his team. In eighteen months they successfully worked around a handful of officers who'd been assigned to his squad as definite marks and from whom they needed to keep their activities well hidden.

But then they screwed up.

They got comfortable.

And Officer Alice Vargas joined the First Team of SRT.

*

Inside an NYPD safe house downtown on Remington Street, Hendricks finished cuffing Mike Lombardi to a chair. It was a single room in a Lower East Side apartment, often used for meet-ups with undercover cops or as protection for anyone laying low in wit sec, not for working over mob bosses and extracting information. This was definitely a first. The place had one window, which had been covered over and the two men were alone.

Hendricks pulled a bag off the man's head, tossing it to the floor.

In the seat, the Mob leader blinked as his eyes readjusted to the light, filling with defiance as he looked up at Hendricks, who drew his pistol and pulled the slide.

'You realise what you're doing?' Lombardi said, without fear. 'You know who I am?'

Hendricks leaned in close.

'These walls are soundproof. That means no-one will hear you scream.'

Reaching into Lombardi's pocket, Hendricks pulled out a cell phone and held it up.

'You're gonna call your team right now and tell them to come out of the building. Weapons thrown out of the door first, followed by all of them, hands on their heads, fingers interlaced, walking slow.'

Lombardi frowned. 'What the hell are you talking about?'

Hendricks's face darkened.

He put his gun against Lombardi's groin, burying the barrel into the fabric of his jeans.

'Make the call, asshole.'

'Whoa! Wait! Wait! I don't know what you're talking about!'

'Yes, you do!' Hendricks shouted, pushing the gun down. *'Make the call!'*

'What people? What the hell are you talking about?'

'The building. The Marshals!'

'What Marshals? That thing uptown?'

'Yes!'

Hendricks dragged back the hammer of the pistol, the barrel buried in Lombardi's groin.

'Last chance. Don't think I'm joking.'

'*I don't know anything about that!*' Mike shouted. '*Why the hell would I want to kill some people in some building?*'

His finger halfway down the trigger, Hendricks looked in the man's eyes.

They were as wide as dinner plates but there was an honesty there that only a gun to the balls could bring.

This wasn't the first time he'd used this particular interrogation method; it had a knack of cutting right to the truth.

'The girl,' he said, quieter and slower. 'In the building.'

'*What girl?*' Mike shouted back.

Hendricks's stared into the Mob leader's wide eyes. There was a long moment, filled by panicked breaths from Lombardi.

Then Hendricks withdrew the gun from the man's groin, easing the hammer down. He looked away, thinking fast.

Then he turned and started walking away towards the door.

'*Hey!*' Lombardi said, jerking his arms, the handcuffs rattling and locking him in place. '*Hey! Uncuff me! Hey!*'

Hendricks ignored him, walking out of the safe house and slamming the door shut behind him, heading for his car.

THIRTY FOUR

Taking a seat inside the maintenance office on the 1st floor of the tenement building, his M4A1 still in his hands, Calvin cursed himself at his stupidity, thinking back to the beginning of last year when he'd let Vargas join his squad. He'd fallen for a well-planned set-up, taken the bait and that was all it had taken for over a decade of work to completely fall apart.

And now, they were in the deepest of shit.

Just over a year ago, a member of First Team, Hayworth, had been leaving Miami and SRT for Arizona and they'd needed a replacement. Hayworth had been a choirboy, Calvin and his team working around him for just over a year, and they were all sick of doing so. They wanted an officer who they wouldn't need to hide everything from; it took too much time and energy so they decided to go fishing from the pool.

Out of all the current prospective candidates who'd put in applications and were accepted for SRT training school at the time, Vargas had stood out. She'd seemed legitimate; five foot four, a buck-twenty with a nice ass and a bad history. He and Denton had done extensive checks on her background but she seemed to be the real deal. She'd transferred from Orlando and had a high-ranking friend who put in a good word and got her a position at SRT school.

There were rumours that she'd been investigated for racketeering, though there was nothing on the file.

She was abrasive and tough, and Calvin had been completely deceived; at her sit-down interview with the committee, he'd watched her closely. The physical aspect of their work meant there were fewer female applicants than male, but she looked hardy. She wasn't green or unabatedly loyal to the Department like many other recruits. He'd requested she join his team and after a cautious feeling-out process, Calvin decided to test her and see if she could be trusted. If she reacted badly or refused, they'd made plans for that.

However, she'd been game, not surprised at what they were up to and saying she'd keep her mouth shut if they made sure she wasn't left out. With that, he shrugged off any remaining doubt.

It proved to be the biggest error he'd ever made.

In late November, Calvin and his team had been arrested on a night raid at each of their homes. That pint-size package of misery had buried five of Calvin's ex-colleagues, and got every single current officer on his team brought in wearing handcuffs. It turned out the Department had been investigating a case against them for corruption and had brought in an Anti-Corruption task force from Internal Affairs to assist, more heat on the SRT First Team than the midday Florida sun. They got out on bail by the skin of their teeth, largely because of a top flight lawyer but assisted by the fact that prior to the arrests they'd all had great reputations. They'd been suspended for four months, and would remain so until the case went to trial in eleven days. Vargas had ruined a lot of lives by what she did.

And if you did that, you'd better sleep with a gun under your pillow and one eye open for the rest of your life.

By the time the team realised she was the mole, Vargas had vanished; she'd left Miami, with no-one having any idea where she was. The moment he was granted bail, Calvin had set out to find her. As the collection of evidence continued, he redoubled his efforts, feeling the pressure mounting and knowing he was running out of time. He spent a lot of money attempting to track her down; he even hired a cartel team to find her and take care of the situation, but she was nowhere to be found. It wasn't just personal; as he was interrogated and questioned, his entire record as a police officer being examined, he realised that the entire case was largely dependent on her. His precautions of keeping a clean record had paid off; without her sworn testimony, the Department couldn't make anything stick.

However, he'd almost given up hope of finding her and resigned to his fate. Then, eight days ago, they got lucky. Ridiculously lucky, all things considered. Denton had made it home after a long-ass day of questioning by IA and switched on the television last week, flicking onto the news.

Vargas had just made a huge mistake.

He'd called Calvin who'd flicked onto the news and seen the shot. Vargas was with a security team, US Marshals or Feds, ushering a small girl into a car in what looked like Police Plaza in New York.

She was in the background, but it was her.

Calvin might have been under review but he still had some powerful friends. Two pay offs later he discovered that Vargas was now qualified and operating as a US Marshal until their case went to trial. She'd been transferred to a three man team protecting some kid who also had a target on her chest from an on-going case in New York.

They needed to act fast, making the most of an opportunity they never should have had. Calvin knew how much those folks made; not a great deal, especially considering the danger they were constantly exposed to. He pulled files on the agents and figured Barlow was their safest bet. As it turned out, the man was in a lot of debt, largely due to the fact that he'd recently been divorced and had been hit with some hefty maintenance payments.

The timing couldn't have been better. When they'd put an offer on the table, he'd snatched at it and told them everything; schedules, routes, routines. Who the kid they were protecting was. What car they were driving. He did all this on the condition that he get paid first and only Vargas was taken out, none of his guys taking a hit. He didn't know her and had no affinity with her. They could cover it up to make it look like she got caught in the crossfire trying to get the kid.

It could be blamed on the Irish crew trying to get the child.

Better and better.

Now they had a plan, they needed execution. Calvin had hired a hit-team one of the Miami cartels liked to use for any work they wanted carried out against New York clients who stepped out of line. Nonetheless he'd also insisted his entire team be in the area as back up, just in case the shit hit the fan. This was a one-off opportunity and the stakes were too high to just leave it all to an unknown group. He'd ordered the entire squad up to New York for today, Sunday, all of them buying off alibis as Calvin used a pool of their stolen cash to obtain weapons, clothing, tactical gear and potential transportation.

He'd had to tread carefully; his phone was tapped and there were cops watching his house and following him around Miami in case he tried to run. He'd ditched them, the same as his guys, by going to a Panthers hockey game last night and disappearing into the crowd. They'd had two cars waiting for them outside; they floored it and headed up the East Coast overnight. The journey had taken twenty one hours, but they made it, holing up at their safe house in New Jersey where they found their equipment, pilot and chopper waiting. Calvin had paid damn good money for everything to be there, working anonymously with an East Coast cartel he knew of from his SRT experience. The pilot had seen all their faces, but he wouldn't give them up; he'd been paid well, plus he was more crooked than they were.

As it turned out, all his preparation had proved more than necessary. Braeten and his team had failed. Vargas and the Marshals had taken cover in a building.

If she was going to die tonight, they were going to have to kill her themselves.

They'd geared up, choppered out and made their entry, but so far the whole operation had been a disaster. Five of his guys had been killed, along with a stack of residents inside this dump. An ESU team and pilot had been taken out, which meant there were going to be huge ramifications and consequences once this was done.

And worst of all, Vargas was still breathing. Some asshole they hadn't known about was helping her and it was clear from the body count that he knew what he was doing. What was supposed to be a simple insert, eliminate and extract was now turning into a situation quickly spiralling out of control.

And if the NYPD got inside before they could gather their dead, they would be making some fascinating discoveries once CSU started fingerprinting the corpses in the combat fatigues.

Like how they were all Miami PD officers currently being investigated for corruption.

Calvin was already working out his escape. He knew that even after Vargas was killed and the fear of prosecution removed he could never go back to Miami. His five guys who'd been killed here tonight had put paid to any return. He had no family, and had over three million dollars in a private off-shore Cayman account. When the bitch was finally gone, they'd chopper out and disperse in New Jersey before the cops could get to them. The pilot worked in the drug trade; he spent his life circumnavigating the US Coastguard and dropping off cargo. He'd buy them a window of escape, however brief.

Calvin would then head north and make his way to the Canadian border. He'd be a wanted man but he knew how to disappear. Even if they put two and two together early and realised he'd organised this, they'd never find him. They'd search for him in the south first, figuring he'd head back to Florida and lay low or maybe try for Cuba or Mexico, staking out his apartment, his girlfriend's place, any of his old haunts. Truth be told Calvin was sick of the heat; he'd lived down south his whole life. He'd go somewhere where there was no risk of anyone recognising him, and he could live off the fruits of his corruption for the rest of his life.

But none of that could happen until they took care of Vargas. Calvin cared about his men a hell of a lot. They were his brothers; she'd had a hand in killing five of them tonight. Now, it was more than personal.

He looked over at his team beside him in the corridor. They all looked tired and demoralised, and rightly so. None of this had gone to plan. And once they left here they'd have to get out of the country immediately, every man for himself.

'So what now?' Knight said.

'We need to get the hell out of here,' Spades answered. 'We're in so much shit, I say we call the chopper and bail. Screw Vargas.'

'What are you, a pussy?' Knight hissed. 'Five of our guys died and you just want to quit?'

'You think the Feds outside are going to wait much longer?'

'She's taken out half our team, asshole. Friends of yours. That alone means she has to die.'

'If the NYPD get in, so will we.'

'Shut up,' Calvin ordered, as the two men confronted each other. 'Let me think for a moment.'

Silence. He thought of his men who'd been killed; Queen, Clubs, Hearts, Pawn and Castle. Markowski, Patterson, Taylor, Gibbons and Kosick.

'Taylor and Gibbons were taken out on 22, right?'

Knight nodded. 'Yeah. Both took a burst to the chest.'

'So what the hell were the Marshals doing up there?'

His men looked at each other and shrugged.

'The roof?' Spades suggested.

King looked over at Diamonds, who'd first discovered the two dead men with Knight. 'You see anything up there?'

'Nothing. Just the door to the roof. Only other thing I saw was a fire box down the corridor.'

'Fire box?'

'Yeah. Red thing. Stuck on the wall.'

Calvin's eyes widened; he moved over to the building chart on the wall inside the office and traced it with his finger.

'Holy shit.'

'What?' Knight asked.

'There's a fire phone on 22. That's what they were doing. We missed a phone line.'

THIRTY FIVE

With Isabel between them, Archer and Vargas were in the south stairwell, just passing 13 as they made their way upstairs, Vargas clearing ahead with her M4A1, Archer doing the same behind.

They'd left Carson on the couch in the apartment with his Glock and a promise they'd be back soon. The cheap heroin had worn off now and his pain was becoming more extreme once again. He'd been lucid enough to understand them, nodding at their instruction whilst gritting his teeth in pain.

As they moved up to 14, Archer checked the corridor through the window on the door.

Empty.

He was about to continue sweeping behind them when he noticed something out of the corner of his eye.

Someone had dumped a cardboard box on the stairwell landing ahead of them.

Suddenly, his arm shot out, past the child, grabbing Vargas by the leg.

'Don't move!'

Vargas froze.

He was looking down at her feet.

Her body not moving a fraction, she followed his gaze.

A thread was drawn across the stairs, one end wrapped around a small nail driven into the wall, the other tied around the railing that ran up the stairwell. It was almost imperceptible, a translucent piece of wire.

Vargas's shin was pushed right up against it, the wire bent back, about to give.

'Don't move, either of you,' he repeated.

They followed the wire with their eyes. It ran directly under the cardboard box just above them resting against the wall of the stairwell.

Taking the utmost care, Archer moved past Isabel, stepped over the wire and approached the box. He grasped the edges and lifted it away slowly.

Underneath was a Claymore mine. *Front Towards Enemy* was printed on the side facing the trio, the blasting cap attached to the tripwire.

'Holy shit,' Vargas said.

Vargas eased her leg back slowly, the tension on the wire loosening a touch, taking the pressure off the blasting cap. The wire unbroken, they both exhaled.

They made eye contact; she gave him a shaky smile and a nod of thanks.

He went to speak.

Before he had a chance, the stairwell suddenly erupted with the sound of automatic gunfire as plaster and dust sprayed violently from the walls around them.

Archer and Vargas fell to the side, taken completely off guard.

As they did, Isabel stumbled, losing her balance.

Vargas lunged for her, but just missed her, and the girl fell backwards.

Archer watched in horror as Isabel tumbled down the stairwell, coming to a hard jarring halt on 13. Vargas went to go after her but another burst of rapid gunfire made her recoil, keeping her where she was. They were sprayed with chalk and dust as bullets shredded the walls. Three guys in camo fatigues were working their way up the stairs.

Although Archer and Vargas were now firing back , they were hampered by the fear of hitting Isabel and were forced to withdraw, being totally exposed in the stairwell. The attacking fire was too strong. The onslaught forced them to duck into 14, no other choice. The wall where they'd been standing was shredded to bits by gunfire, dust, chips of plaster and chalk falling down around the Claymore on the landing.

Risking a glance round the wall, Archer watched as one of the cops grabbed Isabel, scooping her up.

'Vargas!' the girl screamed, helpless.

As the man turned and ran off with her, the girl's screaming audible in the breaks in gunfire, Archer and Vargas ducked out and fired at the other two through the gap in the middle of the long flight of stairs.

'No!' Vargas screamed.

Below, Isabel fought and thrashed under his arm but the guy was too strong. He disappeared down the 13th corridor and out of sight, closely followed by one of the other men. Archer and Vargas went to follow, but the third man had stayed where he was, keeping up his assault rifle fire, forcing Archer and Vargas back behind cover.

They heard Isabel's screaming from the floor below.

It was fading.

The remaining gunman kept firing up on them, sensing an opportunity to end this himself. Archer went to return fire but his M4A1 clicked dry.

'Shit!'

He snapped back, plaster spraying off the wall near him, and reached to his pocket but he was out of ammo. Beside him, Vargas was also out. He dropped the M4A1 and drew Carson's USP from his waistband, taking off the safety.

As more gunfire ripped into the wall, Archer suddenly remembered the Claymore on the landing in the stairwell.

With the gunman stalking up the stairs towards them, still firing, Archer fired off a few rounds with his USP, grabbed his empty M4A1 and moving to the edge of the corridor, hurled the assault rifle up the stairs at the tripwire.

Whilst it was still in the air, he grabbed Vargas and dove to the floor with her down the corridor.

The mine exploded; there was a *thump* and then hundreds of tinkles of metal ball bearings as they smashed around the stairwell.

Eventually they came to a halt, some rolling down the corridor, joining Archer and Vargas on the floor.

Then suddenly, it was quiet.

The gunfire in the stairwell had stopped.

THIRTY SIX

Archer and Vargas were alone in the 14th floor corridor, chalk, dust and cordite in the air, their ears ringing, shell casings and ball bearings littering the stairs and the edges of the hallway.

The mine had done its job and annihilated the guy in the stairwell. Archer moved out from the corridor, down the flight and retrieved the dead man's weapon, which had clattered further down the stairs. The dead guy had one spare magazine, which Archer stuffed into the pocket of his jeans, pushing Carson's USP into the back of his waistband with the safety on. Everything else on the gunman's person had been destroyed; he'd taken hundreds of metal ball bearings front-on which had smashed holes in both him and his equipment. The used plates of the blown Claymore were scattered on the steps in front of him, joining the other metallic debris and the body slumped down the stairwell.

The white, chipped wall behind him looked like a horror movie set.

Archer ran back up the stairs to the 14th corridor. Vargas was kneeling, tears streaming down her face as she took gasping breaths, in momentary shock. He knelt beside her, thinking fast whilst checking left and right, making sure no one else got the drop on them.

They were exposed either side of the hallway. It would only take one unexpected arrival and burst of fire to put them both down.

296

Vargas was sobbing, covering her mouth, tears sliding down through the dust and cuts on her face.

'*They took her*,' she whispered under her palm. '*They took her. They'll kill her!*'

Kneeling beside her, Archer frantically searched for a solution. He was drawing blanks. He and Vargas were outnumbered, low on ammo and now the response team had Isabel.

He continued to sweep back and forth, protecting them both sides whilst desperately trying to think what to do next.

Suddenly, he heard a noise from the north side and spun, the sights of the M4A1 trained down the corridor.

He walked down towards it, willing one of the response team to appear.

Nothing.

'I know how we can end this,' Vargas suddenly said, from behind him, still sobbing.

Archer turned.

She'd drawn her Glock and was holding it to her temple.

Her hand was shaking, tears running down her smoke-stained face, creating small paths in the dirt and dust.

'If I die, you two and Jack will live,' she said, her chin quivering. 'They'll let you go.'

He didn't move. Her finger was tight on the trigger, the harsh metallic barrel against her smooth skin.

'No. They won't.'

There was a pause.

He stepped forward.

She stepped away and pulled back the hammer, her arm and lip trembling.

'C'mon, Vargas,' Archer said. 'Put the gun down.'

'This is all my fault.'

Her finger moved a fraction on the trigger.

'No, it's not. Alice. C'mon.'

He approached her painfully slowly.

She didn't move.

He kept coming closer until he gently took her hand, the gun still against her head.

He carefully lifted the arm so the gun pointed in the air. Tears were sliding down Vargas's cheeks.

She dissolved with emotion and he held her.

The corridor stretching away beside them.

Long and empty.

King carried the girl under his arm downstairs to the 1st floor; Spades was beside him, pulling out an empty magazine from his M4A1 and slapping another into the weapon. The kid was thrashing but she was no match for King's strength.

Knight and Bishop appeared up the stairs from the lobby with Braeten and one of his guys; they'd been keeping the entrance secure from the Feds and the NYPD whilst King, Spades and Diamonds went up to 22.

All four sets of eyes narrowed when they saw the kid.

'What the hell happened?'

'We found them on 14,' King said. 'And look what we picked up.'

He passed the girl to Spades beside him, who slung his rifle and took her.

'Take her to the lobby. Wait, where the hell is Diamonds?'

'He stayed, sir,' Spades said, taking the kid. 'I heard an explosion in the stairwell. Sounded like the Claymore.'

King pushed his pressel. 'Diamonds, report.'

Nothing.

'Diamonds?'

No response.

As Spades headed downstairs with the kid, King turned to Knight, Bishop, Braeten and his guy with the AK, his mood thunderous.

'Split. Two men, either side, north and south stairwells. Change magazines and get ready. She'll be coming for the kid.'

As they moved off, he stepped into the manager's office. The building intercom was there on the wall just inside the room, a microphone panel beside a switch.

Smiling to himself, he pushed down the button.

It was time to end this thing once and for all.

Upstairs, Vargas was still distraught, Archer embracing her, when the silence of the building was suddenly broken.

'Look what we have down here,' a voice said, filling the hallways.

They both froze.

The accent was American, non-regional; the electronic intercom made it sound disembodied and sinister, echoing down the hall.

'I'm sure you know who we are by now and why we're here. The kid's cute, Vargas. But she

299

*won't be when we're done with her. There won't
be anything left.'*

Vargas covered her mouth.

*'I know you can hear me. And you'll be able to
hear everything we do to her. You wouldn't want
that now, would you Vargas?'*

Pause.

*'You got four minutes to get down here, bitch.
Hands up, no weapon, backing down. Surrender
or we start on the kid. We'll make it last all night.
You can listen to every second.'*

Pause.

'The clock's ticking. 3.59. 3:58.'

Vargas looked at Archer, total fear and abject
hopelessness in her eyes.

She blinked, tears sliding down her sooty
cheeks, cutting paths through the dust.

'I have to go.'

THIRTY SEVEN

Knight and Bishop were in the south stairwell,
Braeten and his guy down the other end of the
corridor in the north.

Braeten was crouched just inside the 1st floor
corridor, aiming up the stairwell with his pistol,
hearing the leader's voice echo around the
building. Beside him, his guy kneeled, pulling out
the mag of his AK and checking it was full. He
slotted it back inside and aimed at the same spot
as Braeten, exactly where anyone coming down
the stairs would appear.

Finally, hours after the shit storm on the street,
they were going to finish this job. Braeten was
keen to kill the woman himself, more out of hurt
pride than anything else. Never in a million years
would he have thought this operation would be
this difficult. A shitload people had died tonight,
including Hayes, but she was still alive.

But not for long.

They waited. It had been almost three minutes,
but there was no sign of the female Marshal yet.

Braeten smiled in anticipation; he hoped she
came down this side. He'd never killed a Fed
before.

'One minute, bitch!' the leader's voice shouted
over the intercom.

'Time to earn your freedom,' Braeten
whispered to the man beside him, who nodded,
pulling the stock and racking a round.

They were ready, just waiting for the woman to
appear, anticipation in their trigger fingers. She

wouldn't just leave the kid to suffer. She was a woman, full of maternal instinct and all that bullshit.

They kept the sights of their weapons trained on the stairwell, their ears straining to hear any indication that she was coming down.

But no-one came.

'Thirty seconds!'

They waited.

'C'mon bitch,' he whispered, preparing for a last second rush.

Nothing.

'Ten!'

'Nine!'

'Eight.'

Not a damn thing.

'Three. Two. One!'

Silence.

'Anything?' the leader shouted from the doorway to the office.

'No sign,' Braeten shouted back.

'None here either,' someone called from the south stairwell team down the hall.

Braeten watched the leader disappear back into the office.

'OK, bitch, your choice. We'll start with her fingernails. She'll scream so loud the cops on the street will hear it.'

Down the hallway, King released the intercom and pushed his pressel switch

'Spades, get the kid up here.'

He waited and smiled. No way could Vargas hold out with the girl screaming over the intercom and filling the hallways. He meant what he'd threatened; Vargas was going to die tonight. That was the only way this was going to end and he'd do whatever it took to ensure that happened.

Once the girl's screams started echoing down the corridors, Vargas would lose it. She'd run down, full of guilt and despair, and eat a magazine from one of his men or the hit-team on the north side. The asshole with her would die too; not because he knew anything, but because he'd stayed with her and helped kill Markowski, Patterson, Taylor, Gibbons and Kosick. He'd pay for that. Calvin knew the type from Miami; heroic pricks, full of honour. He'd had to work round assholes like that when they were assigned to his task force, people like Hayworth.

Calvin smiled again, but it faded when he realised Spades hadn't appeared with the kid yet. He pushed down the pressel on his uniform again.

'Spades, get up here. I'm waiting.'

He waited.

Nothing.

'Spades, get your thumb out of your ass and respond.'

Nothing.

Grabbing his M4A1, King ran to the south stairwell, joining Knight and Bishop who were still aiming up the stairwell.

'Stay where you are,' he ordered, running down the stairs to the lobby.

When he got there and ripped open the door, he saw Spades.

He was slumped on the floor in a limp heap, his weapon beside him.

And the girl was gone.

THIRTY EIGHT

Inside the elevator shaft, Archer and Vargas climbed as fast as they could, gripping the steel bars of the service ladder on the wall, moving up and up.

On Archer's back, Isabel clung tight like a small limpet, her eyes squeezed shut as she held onto him. The rungs of the ladder led all the way up to 22. Aside from weak light from the panels in the doors on each floor, the shaft was pretty dark save for one source of light from above, the doors on 14 which had been dragged open all the way.

Archer knew that they'd have both stairwells covered, waiting for Vargas to appear. He was never going to let her walk to her death. The tears in her eyes and the satisfaction in the voice of the man on the intercom as he described what he was going to do to the child had lit something in him, a fury he'd only ever experienced once before. When it had struck him back then, he'd beaten a man to death with a door.

No mercy, no other emotion except white-hot rage.

As the voice counted down, Vargas preparing to go to her death, Archer remembered Helen's voice from earlier when Foster had asked her about the building.

The elevator's been busted for weeks.

With just over three minutes to go, he'd raced into an open apartment on 14 and reappeared moments later with a thick knife he'd found in the

305

kitchen. Sprinting down the corridor to the elevator shaft, he'd worked the blade in between the doors, opening them a fraction and releasing the lock, then put his fingers into the gap and prised them all the way apart.

Tossing the blade to the floor, he looked down into the darkness, all the way to the basement.

He'd turned back to Vargas who was watching him; she realised what he was thinking.

Inside the shaft was a service ladder to the right of the doors that seemed to lead all the way down.

Slinging his M4A1 over his shoulder, he'd swung onto the ladder and started to climb down rapidly, Vargas following him and doing the same.

The voice on the intercom was muffled but still audible inside the elevator shaft as they headed down into the darkness.

The elevator was lodged in the basement, left there gathering dust until they got round to repairing it. That meant when they reached the bottom of the ladder and stood on the top of the elevator, they were looking directly into the lobby.

Through the dirty glass, they saw Isabel and one of the anonymous men holding her by her hair.

Both of them were close to the elevator, less than six feet away.

The man had a pistol in his other hand.

But he also had his back to them.

Placing his weapons down quietly, Archer had gently released the interior lock. Then he and Vargas had each grabbed one of the manual handles fitted to the inside of the static doors and eased them open slowly.

They'd slid apart easily with the locks disabled, but the cop had heard something behind him and turned.

Archer had been already been making his move. He'd hit the guy with a huge uppercut that took him completely off guard and lifted him to his toes. The force and surprise of the blow meant the man let go of both his pistol and Isabel, the punch knocking him to the floor.

Archer didn't give him a moment to recover. He'd leapt on him, clamping a hand over his mouth as Vargas moved forward and grabbed Isabel, hurrying her towards the elevator. The anonymous corrupt cop was dazed but fought back; Archer buried his forearm into the man's throat and suffocated him, the countdown from the intercom echoing around the lobby, the man's boots scrabbling and slapping on the floor as he thrashed and choked.

Once all movement ceased and he was sure the man was dead, Archer rose and ducked back into the elevator shaft, joining the other two, less than a minute to go. He and Vargas had pulled the doors back and secured them. Vargas then swung both M4A1s over her shoulders and started to climb the ladder as quickly as she could. Archer knelt down, hoisting Isabel onto his back, and had started to follow her up, scaling the ladder fast, knowing it was just a matter of time before they were discovered.

Right now he was almost at 11, his body exhausted but adrenaline giving his arms more strength than he'd had in months. He glanced down and saw a small pair of arms, one across his neck, the other under his armpit. He also noticed the shirt bandage on his right bicep and remembered that first fight in Helen's apartment hours ago.

Above him, Vargas had already made it to 12, pushing off the interior lock and dragging open the doors with the handles one by one. They weren't going back to 14. Carson was down this hallway and they needed to get back inside the apartment with him. Vargas quickly checked the corridor and then stepped out onto the floor. The moment she did, she turned back and watched the other two, willing them closer.

'Don't look down, honey,' Vargas whispered to Isabel, who was clinging to Archer's back.

Two rungs later, he was within arm's length. Vargas reached down and took hold of the little girl, helping her up to join her on the 12th floor corridor. Archer realised the countdown on the intercom had ended.

It had gone quiet.

Suddenly, he heard shouting and the elevator doors down below in the lobby being wrenched open.

'Shit!'

Clenching his teeth and using every fibre of muscle in his arms and back, he raced up the remaining three rungs, hurling himself into the corridor as gunfire suddenly lit up the dark shaft, the men below firing straight up, bullets tearing into the brickwork.

Knowing they couldn't waste a second, Archer staggered to his feet. Vargas had taken Isabel's hand and the two of them were already running

308

down the corridor to the apartment holding Carson.

Archer went to follow.

Suddenly, plaster sprayed from the wall behind him from two gunshots within a hair's breadth of him, followed by a *click* as a weapon clicked dry. A man had burst from an apartment beside the elevator, a pistol in his hands, having heard the gunfire from down the elevator shaft. The slide was back, the clip empty.

Archer's hand flashed for his USP but the guy charged and smashed back him into the wall, knocking the pistol out of his hand. Turning and grappling with the guy, Archer saw he was one of the original attackers who'd jumped the Marshals on the street.

The guy was clawing at his face, trying to gouge his eyes, but Archer gripped his arms, pulled them apart and head butted him with the top of his head but didn't have enough room to really do any damage. The man reeled but hit Archer back with a wild right hook and they smashed back into the opposite wall, the fight not clean or smooth, a life or death brawl.

Fighting to stay on his feet, Archer saw that the lift doors were open behind the man. Clutching the back of the guy's head with his left hand, Archer fired two hard right uppercuts into his face, the man's grip loosening enough for Archer to break free and push him back a step.

The ambusher gathered his balance and launched himself straight back.

And Archer kicked him in the chest as hard as he could.

The force of the blow knocked the guy backwards into the elevator shaft. He scrabbled in the air as he tipped back into nothing, desperately trying to save himself, but with his back to the steel lift cords, there was nothing to grab.

He plummeted down twelve floors of dark emptiness, his screams echoing in the shaft as he fell.

King and his team were still firing up the shaft when they heard the noise.

'Get back!'

The body hit the top of the elevator hard with a hard *thud*, a cloud of dust punched into the air, the response team momentarily recoiling. The impact killed him instantly.

Nevertheless, Knight aimed with his M4A1 and put three rounds in his chest. They looked closer and saw it wasn't Vargas or the guy she was with. It was one of Braeten's crew, his body smashed from the impact, his head lolled to the side and blood spilling out of his mouth.

'Shit!'

Upstairs, Archer heard the man land and the burst of gunfire that followed it. Pulling the elevator doors shut and falling back against the wall, he sucked in deep breaths then scooped up his USP from the floor.

Moving forward, he ran towards Vargas, who was anxiously waiting for him in the doorway of the apartment. Once he made it inside, they pushed the door shut and locked it instantly, then dragged the refrigerator back into position before they could pause for breath.

THIRTY NINE

Reunited and safe, Vargas turned and dropped down to hug Isabel, checking her for any injuries, both of them tearful as they clung to each other. Staying low, Archer made sure the curtains were still secure, then knelt down beside them.

'Are you OK?' he asked Isabel.

She nodded, strands of hair clinging to her face from dried tears, her arms wrapped tightly around Vargas, not letting her go.

'I knew you'd save me.'

Archer smiled. Seeing that she was unhurt, he rose and moved into the sitting room, approaching Carson who was lying on the couch just where they'd left him. The heroin had worn off now and his face was screwed up in pain, his Glock in his hand.

'There…you are,' he said, grimacing, clutching his stomach. 'Thought…you'd left.'

'No way,' Archer said, placing his weapon on the floor and kneeling by the injured man. Beside him, Carson coughed.

'Did you…get to the phone?'

Archer shook his head. 'We ran into trouble. Long story. Put one of them down though.'

'How…many…left?'

'I don't know. Still more than us.'

'You're…bleeding.'

Archer glanced down and saw blood on the lower left of his white t-shirt from the glass he'd taken out earlier.

The patch had grown.

'Makes…two of us,' Carson said, using most of his strength to force a smile.

Archer looked closer at the padding on Carson's stomach. Rule number one with compression bandages was don't remove them; the bottom ones had probably stuck to the wound and removing them could get the blood flowing again. They seemed to have done as good a job as they could under the circumstances. He glanced at Carson's face. His eyes were sunken, dark rings around them from a combination of blood loss and the aftermath of the heroin. They flicked up past Archer; Vargas and Isabel had joined them.

'Hey,' he said. 'You're both a sight…for sore eyes.'

Vargas stepped forward, putting her hand to his brow. Isabel moved closer too. Carson looked at her and forced another smile.

'I…could use…another makeover right now,' he said to her.

'Hang on just a bit longer, Jack,' Vargas told him, gripping his hand. 'Dalton and the crew will get in here soon. There're medic teams down on the street, waiting to come in. They'll fix you up.'

He nodded with as much conviction as he could muster.

'Where's Barlow?' he asked.

Archer and Vargas glanced at each other.

'Tell you later,' she said.

As Archer rose, Vargas suddenly noticed the blood patch staining the lower left of Archer's once-white t-shirt. He had his hand half-over it, but not enough to fully hide the red.

'Hey. You're hurt.'

He didn't move.

'Let me see.'

She reached for his arm and took it away gently.

His palm came away red from the blood-soaked fabric.

'Jesus,' she said. *'Next door. Now.'*

Down on the street, Hendricks screeched to a halt as close as he could get to the barriers on the corner of West 135th Street. Jumping out of the car, he cut through the crowd and made a beeline for Shepherd, who saw him coming and stepped forward to meet him.

'What happened?' Shepherd asked his friend.

'The men in there aren't Lombardi's people. He had no idea the kid and the Marshals were inside.'

'How can you know that?'

'I put a gun to his balls and pulled back the hammer,' Hendricks replied, looking up at the tenement block. 'This is about something else.'

'So someone else must want the kid dead,' Shepherd said, thinking. 'But who else would want to kill a seven year old girl this badly?'

Silence.

The penny dropped.

'It's not about the kid at all, is it? They're going after another member of the group.'

'It must be one of the Marshals. Or Archer.'

'Not Arch,' Shepherd said. 'I've heard what eye-witnesses from the gunfight on the street have said. It was pure coincidence he ended up in this. He was just passing by.'

'OK, one of the other three then. One of Dalton's team.'

'So why the hell would someone go to all this trouble for a US Marshal?'

Both men shifted their gaze to Dalton, who was talking with his team, finalising their assault plans. Either he was lying about the girl or he hadn't told them the full story.

But it was time for some answers.

'Are you kidding me?' Calvin screamed. *'Are you kidding me?'*

The men were all standing there, having gathered in the large lobby. None of them thought it wise to respond. Spades' body was lying in a heap by the elevator doors behind them. No-one had bothered to move him.

Braeten had seen one of his own guys sprawled dead on the roof of the elevator just before they secured the doors. He'd fallen to his death, Vargas or the asshole with her knocking him into the elevator shaft. Out of all his guys, he was the one he was closest to. It had put him in a foul mood.

Calvin shot his cuff and checked his watch.

'We should have handled this two hours ago. You think the cops are just going to keep waiting outside for us to resolve this?'

'So let's get the hell out of here,' Bishop said. 'Let it go, boss. We tried. It didn't work.'

'We're staying,' Knight said.

'What more can we do, brother?' Bishop replied. 'We've torn this place apart looking for her.'

Frustrated, Calvin looked around the lobby. He knew Bishop was right.

'Let's cut our losses and get the hell out of here while we still can,' Bishop said.

King didn't respond. His eyes settled on the black holdalls they'd brought with them, full of equipment, dumped in the corner of the lobby. His breathing slowed.

Then the solution came to him, like clouds parting to reveal sunlight.

It had been staring him in the face the entire time.

It was something he and his team should have done the moment they'd arrived.

The others noticed the change in his demeanour.

'Boss?' Knight asked.

He turned and smiled.

'What is it?' Knight asked.

King looked at Bishop

'You're right. I think it's time we got the hell out of here. We're leaving.'

FORTY

With Carson watching Isabel and weapons close to hand, Vargas was patching Archer up for the second time that evening. This time however, they were in the kitchen, beside the table near the window.

Although they were on the east side, the curtains were still drawn, memories of how Foster and Barlow had died still vivid in their minds. Archer had pulled up the lower portion of his shirt, Vargas cleaning the wound the best she could. Unlike the superficial cut to his arm, the glass had buried itself deeper here.

And unlike the previous apartment they'd taken cover in, there was no first aid kit in the bathroom. Vargas was having to improvise.

'What was it?' she asked.

'Piece of glass. Got it from the laundry room when the grenade went off.'

'Why didn't you say?'

'Why didn't you tell me what this was really about earlier?'

She looked up at him, concern on her face.

'It went deep, Archer. I need to clean it.'

She rummaged through the cupboards and drawers, searching for anything she could use. No luck; she pulled open the fridge and paused. Reaching inside, she drew out a small bottle of vodka, half-full. She unscrewed the top, taking a quick sniff, then re-joined him.

'This is going to sting.'

He nodded apprehensively and she poured some directly over the wound. His teeth clenched like he was being electrocuted, grunting in pain, his body tensing up. It was one of the most painful things he'd ever experienced; he felt like he was going to pass out. She covered the wound with a relatively clean towel she'd found in a drawer by the sink. The alcohol was still burning into the wound, killing any bacteria, and Archer took slow breaths, trying to work through the pain.

'Guess this counts as a third date,' he said through gritted teeth.

She chuckled, shaking her head. 'You got a girlfriend?'

'No.'

'I'm surprised.'

'I'm not. I'm like a revolving door. People come and go. No-one stays.'

'I have.'

He looked over at her and found himself smiling. He'd only known her for a few hours, but she had a point. He decided not to mention that she hadn't had a choice.

He took over holding the cloth to the wound, and she withdrew. She wiped her hands on another towel then tossed it to one side and took a seat near him. They sat there in momentary silence, the curtains drawn, the lights low. The wound on his torso burned like hell.

Archer looked over at her. She was sweaty and tired, blood and dirt all over her white shirt and dark jeans. Her hair was hanging down, jet black, covering the stained rivulet of blood coming from

318

her right earlobe. She still looked great. Using the moment of quiet, she took her Glock from her holster and pulled back the slide. Withdrawing the magazine, she laid the weapon on the table and started popping bullets out onto her lap, counting ammunition. Holding the cloth to the wound on his torso, he watched her work.

She paused and looked up at him, thinking.

'You ever think of doing something else?' she asked.

'What, other than being a cop.'

She nodded.

'I don't know how to do anything else. For better or for worse.' He paused. 'What about you?'

'I'm a US Marshal now. Once the trial is over, that isn't going to change.'

He nodded.

'You know, ninety nine per cent of people wouldn't have intervened on the street,' she said. 'They would have stayed low, taking cover, looking after themselves.'

'That's not who I am.'

Pause.

'Most people switch on the news and see that something bad happened to a good person. Maybe they were mugged. Maybe they were shot or stabbed. They see those things and think how unfair it is. How unlucky that person was.' He looked down. 'But it's always been more than that to me. It always will be. I see something like that and it really pisses me off. It makes my blood boil.'

He glanced up at her.

319

'That's what I felt when I saw those guys coming for you on the street. That's what I felt when the mob were heading for the apartment. That's what I felt when they took Isabel and that man was taunting you on the intercom.'

She watched him, still paused in her ammo count.

'I've thought about it,' he said. 'But right now, I don't want to do anything else. I'm not leaving it to another person to fight people like this for me.'

'You can't win forever,' she said. 'Eventually you'll die.'

'We all will. And if that happens, at least I died for something.'

'That's enough?'

'It is for me.'

Pause. She observed him in the dim apartment.

For the first time today, she noticed a different look in his eyes.

He fixed her gaze.

'When they come, I'll be right beside you,' he said. 'That's a promise. I'm not going anywhere.'

Silence. She watched him, bloodied and bruised, blood leaking from a cut over his eyebrow, his hand holding the makeshift bandage to the wound on his torso.

'Can I ask you something?' she said. He nodded. 'If you could go back, would you still have intervened on the street?

He grinned. 'In a heartbeat.'

'You're that sure?'

'Otherwise I wouldn't have met you.'

He'd replied instinctively then paused, realising what he'd said. Watching him for a moment, Vargas smiled.

She went to respond but paused, frowning. There was a noise coming from the sitting room; Archer heard it too. It sounded like Carson was calling for them.

He got up and followed her as she opened the door.

'Oh shit!'

Isabel was on the floor, fitting, her body jerking and spasming, her eyes rolled back in her head.

Vargas dropped down and went to hold her but the girl had stiffened out. Archer threw his towel bandage to one side and dropped down to try and help.

'What's wrong?' he asked.

'She's epileptic!'

In the office building directly south of the tenement block, Marquez and Josh were still searching each floor. It was painstaking and tedious work. Josh had always trusted Marquez's hunches but that's exactly what this was, a hunch. Foster could have been capped off by a lucky bullet inside the building.

They met by the north windows on 12. Both of them looked out at the building eighty yards away. Smoke was still streaming from the destroyed apartment on the 8th floor. There was a fire crew on the west side of the building, having finished hosing down the wreckage of the ESU chopper.

Josh looked down at the mass of people on the street; he wanted to get back down there and re-join Shepherd and Hendricks. He and Marquez had been gone for a while. Peering closer, he saw the Marshals task force were gathered close, poised for action.

'This is a waste of time,' Josh told her.

She shook her head, looking around the dark building.

'There's someone here,' Marquez said. 'I know it.'

'How can you be sure?'

She pointed at the building.

'Look at that. It's like range practice. And where's the guard?'

'Where we should be. Outside. We need to get back downstairs.'

'And do what? Stand there and watch.'

He looked at her for a moment. 'I'm leaving, Marquez.'

She turned on him.

'There's someone here, Josh.'

'No. There isn't.'

He turned without another word and walked towards the stairwell, pushing open the door and disappearing, the sound of his footsteps fading and leaving her alone.

Isabel's fit had just subsided, her body softening, the muscles relaxing after the fit had contracted and locked them tight. She was lying on the floor, her head on Vargas' lap; she seemed confused, blinking and looking at them, not saying anything.

322

'Stay still, honey,' Vargas said, reassuring her. She checked her watch. 'Shit.'

'What is it?'

'She missed her medication. She takes it twice a day, morning and night. The flashes from the gunfire must have triggered a reaction.'

'Does she have any medicine with her?'

Vargas thought for moment.

'It's in my bag. I left it downstairs in Helen's apartment.'

Archer looked at her, then at the little girl. Vargas was holding her head either side as she recovered.

'What happens if she doesn't take it?'

'These attacks will come and go. They could go on all night.'

He looked down at her and took a deep breath.

'I have to get it then. The moment we fire a gun, it could happen again.'

Archer pulled the mag of his M4A1, checking there was ammo inside, and slid it back into the rifle. Helen's apartment was on 5.

Seven floors down.

And this time, he was going out there by himself.

FORTY ONE

Moments later, he was back in the corridor on 12, alone, his M4A1 in his hands. He focused his hearing as hard as he could; the close-proximity gunfire had left a dull ringing in his ears which wasn't helping at all.

Clearing both ways, he moved down the corridor. He slid into the south stairwell, immediately checking up and down, already missing Vargas' protection watching his back.

He started moving down as quietly as he could, looking out for any tripwires or hidden Claymores.

When he got to 11, he stopped by the door then swept across, making sure there was no-one lying in wait.

No-one was there.

He did the same on each floor.

10, 9, 8.

Then 7.

Then 6.

When he made it to 5, he paused, then eased out into the corridor. It was empty. He moved slowly, constantly checking behind him, his heart racing.

If he got ambushed right now, he'd be vulnerable from both sides.

Any unexpected or sudden gunfire would shred him to pieces.

He arrived beside the doorway to Helen's apartment, their first hideout hours ago. Well aware the sniper was surely still out there somewhere, he dropped to the floor and inched into the apartment slowly, making sure not to move the door and alert the sharpshooter that there was someone inside.

There was enough of a gap for him to crawl through as he wriggled along the floor.

The fridge was still on its side; behind it were the two dead bodies of the men in fatigues who'd followed up the sniper fire. *Two dirty cops,* Archer thought. No wonder their moves had been so practised. He crawled past them, trying to avoid the blood and milk pooled on the floor but getting some on his jeans, feeling it soak into the fabric. He made it to the doorway to the sitting room. Staying close to the wall, he worked his way inside, trying to ignore the throbbing pain from the cut just above his waist.

Foster was still slumped against the wall, the bullet hole in his forehead, in the same position that he'd been in when they left him. Archer noticed with anger that both his weapons and his badge were missing.

He looked at the dead Marshal, the first of their group to be killed. They'd all been caught completely off guard, no idea then of the lengths the other side were prepared to go to in order to kill Vargas. They could never have suspected a group of professionally trained men armed to the hilt and with a sniper were coming here to take her out.

Although he hadn't known Foster before tonight, in that brief time he'd been hugely impressed by him. His response to the ambush on the street and his actions inside the building had been instrumental in saving their lives. At least he'd gone out on his shield, protecting the group and doing his job.

From the few intense hours he'd known him, Archer guessed that's how he would have wanted it.

He crawled forward and saw Vargas's black bag across the room on the floor. He reached over, taking hold of it. He opened it and found the box of tablets inside. *Carbatrol* was printed on the box, along with a white prescription sticker just below.

Miss I Lombardi. 200mg x2 daily.

Sliding them into his pocket, he left Vargas' bag and shuffled back towards the doorway the way he'd come.

Moving back into the kitchen, he stayed low and headed towards the door, wanting to get the hell out of here.

Then he heard someone coming.

Moving out of the stairwell, Knight and Bishop turned and headed towards 5B, the apartment where Joker had killed Foster and where Markowski and Patterson had been whacked soon after.

Arriving at the door, they tried to push it back further but the frame jammed against the refrigerator lying on the floor inside.

The two men slid through the gap in the door, moving into the apartment.

Aside from the bodies, the place was still. Looking down at Markowski's body at his feet, Knight shook his head. Knight's real name was Sergeant Ben Denton, an eleven year man with

326

Miami PD and Calvin's oldest friend and police partner. Thirty three years old, he was one of the original ringleaders of their operation along with Calvin, Fowler and Markowski. During the course of his career he'd personally acquired over two million dollars in dirty cash and had beaten several charges of misconduct and one of sexual harassment.

Denton had a special dislike for Vargas. He'd made a move on her once outside the locker room at the station, having had his eye on her for a while; she'd given him a black eye and almost broken his arm. He was the man who'd seen her on the television eight days ago when he'd got home from a grilling at the Department. Tonight, although he knew he could never go back to Miami, he was more than invested in killing her out of principle and revenge. He wasn't leaving this building without making sure she was dead. After that, he'd stay with Calvin, laying low and getting over the border into Canada. Denton had screwed over a lot of people over the years, both police and criminal. If he went down, he knew he wouldn't last a week in the joint, shacked up with a load of guys he'd busted.

Failure tonight wasn't an option.

There was only one way this was going to end.

He watched Bishop, aka Fowler, across the room rummaging through Patterson's overalls, searching for what they were after. Pools of blood were starting to dry under both bodies, colleagues of theirs and close friends.

Denton swore. Fowler looked up and knew what he was thinking.

'Rather them than us, right,' he said, as he frisked his way through the dead man's fatigues.

'That bitch is going to pay for what she's done. I swear to God.'

Fowler nodded, continuing his search. After a few moments, he found what he was looking for.

'Bingo,' he said, holding up the item he'd pulled from Patterson's vest. 'Unharmed.'

'Good.' Denton paused. 'Let's get out of here and get moving.'

Fowler rose and pointed to a black holdall slung around Denton's shoulder.

'Might as well dump that shit. You're not gonna need them anymore.'

Denton thought for a moment; he had a point. The contents were heavy and he'd been carrying the bag around all night.

He slipped the holdall off his shoulder, leaving it on the floor.

Fowler rose, scooping up his M4A1, and the two men ducked back out of the door.

Inside the bath, Archer didn't move, his M4A1 resting on his thigh, pointing down between his feet.

He heard the two men exit.

He shifted to one side to sneak a glance over the rim. The bathroom was half-destroyed, the walls torn apart from the gunfire.

His movement disturbed a piece of tile from the wall above him.

He saw it, almost in slow motion, drop away from the ruined wall.

It fell towards the floor.

Outside in the hallway, Denton and Fowler heard it.

They stopped in their tracks.

The two men swung round and doubled back, looking through the sights of their M4A1s.

They re-entered the apartment, looking left and right silently. They cleared the kitchen and sitting room, ending up with their weapons aimed at the bathroom.

Denton examined it; the room had been half-destroyed by gunfire.

The bathtub was against the far wall, standing on a step, riddled with dents.

The wall above had taken most of the onslaught, with few tiles remaining.

He pushed his pressel down. 'Joker.'

'Yeah?'

'You see any movement in the apartment on 5?'

'No. Nothing.'

The two men stayed still for a moment, listening.

As they stood there, a small piece of tile above the bath fell off the wall, smashing to the rim of the tub, mirroring the noise they'd heard from out in the corridor.

Both men smiled.

'What a dump,' Denton said.

'Think they improved it,' Fowler joked, pointing at the half-destroyed wall. 'Let's go.'

Inside the bath, flat on his back, his fingers curled around the grip of the M4A1 and ready to fire, Archer held his breath.

329

He heard the men leave the room but didn't move for at least a full minute, making sure they'd actually gone and weren't lying in wait.

Then, hearing nothing, he exhaled.

Taking the utmost care, he climbed out slowly.

This time, no pieces of tile fell.

FORTY TWO

Archer made it back to the 12th floor apartment safely and without incident, re-joining a relieved Vargas, Carson and Isabel in the sitting room. The girl had taken a dosage of the medication under Vargas' watchful eye and was now curled up in an armchair, still recovering from the seizures. She'd been sick a couple of times during Archer's absence and was pretty out of it; Archer had never encountered anyone with epilepsy before, so he followed Vargas' lead and left the child alone, giving her some room and letting the aftermath of the seizure run its course. Apparently that was the best thing to do.

Watching Isabel, Vargas turned to him. 'You see anyone down there?'

'Don't ask.'

'What's in the bag?' she asked, pointing to his side.

On his way out of Helen's apartment, Archer had noticed a black holdall dumped on the floor, left by one of the two men who'd almost found him in the bathtub. Archer had quickly unzipped it, checking what was inside; after seeing what it contained, he'd decided to take it with him.

He unslung it carefully off his shoulder, lowering it to the floor, and unzipped it again so Vargas could see the contents.

Two Claymore mines were sitting inside the fabric, nestled side by side.

'Jesus.'

'Guess they didn't need them. They might come in handy.'

She frowned and saw the detonator already connected to the blasting wire inside the holdall by a length of wire.

'Wait, are they armed?'

He shook his head. 'Just the clacker and the wire. Relax. It's all good. You need to fit the blasting cap for it to explode.'

Placing the bag safely out of the way, Archer walked across the room to the sofa, kneeling by Carson.

The wounded man was still conscious, but only just.

'Welcome…back,' he forced.

Archer nodded, patting him on the arm.

'What's…the situation…down there?'

'We made it to the lobby through the elevator shaft earlier. I saw they've booby-trapped the door. They've used Claymore mines, the same as they did up on the roof. And there was something else against the wall.'

'What…was it?'

'It looked like an internet hub. I think it's a phone jammer.'

'You…need to turn it off,' Carson said.

'Jack's right,' Vargas said. 'We need to warn the people outside. If they try a frontal assault, they'll be cut to pieces.'

Archer checked his watch. It was just past 9 pm.

'They've lost a lot of their guys,' he said. 'They'll be getting desperate. You know who they are. Their dead buddies are scattered all over

332

the building. Once CSU IDs them, the whole group will be convicted. They've got nothing to lose now.'

He paused.

'Or they'll cut their losses, gather up their dead guys and bail.'

'No way,' she said. 'I know them. Not when I still have air in my lungs.'

There was a pause. In the quiet, they all noticed something, a sound coming from the hall.

Archer turned and looked at Vargas.

'You hear that?'

They listened closely. It was coming from the corridor.

'What the hell?' she said.

He thought for a moment then rose, moving out of the sitting room and making his way quietly towards the main door.

'Wait!' she hissed, following him. He turned to her, standing in the sitting room doorway; she shook her head.

'It's OK,' he whispered.

He pulled the refrigerator back a foot and unclicked the lock.

The door opened a slit.

Archer looked through the slender gap.

The corridor was empty.

But there was a sound coming over the intercom; it was muffled, but was constant and monotonous, electronic, some kind of beeping.

Vargas joined him, listening by the jamb.

'What the hell is that?' she said.

Listening for a few moments longer, he eased the door shut and locked it.

'I don't know.'

Vargas looked at him, confused, then turned and took a quick look out of the window. She stiffened.

'Oh shit.'

'What?'

'I think my people are coming in.'

He moved over and joined her; she was right.

Down below, he could see a cluster of US Marshals in vests and with assault weapons. They were in a huddle which broke, people checking their weapons and moving towards the building.

'They try to come in through the front door, the mines will kill them and half the people on the street.'

'We can't just walk down there and tell them to hold off.'

'We stay here, they die!'

'We move, we could die.'

They looked at each other; neither option was appealing.

'We've got to do something!' she said.

They rushed back into the sitting room; Carson was looking over towards them anxiously.

'What's…happening?'

'A Marshals task force outside are preparing to come in. We need to stop them. They'll get blown to pieces.'

Isabel had stirred and was blinking up at Vargas, who looked down at the little girl.

'We need you to stay here with Jack, honey. We won't be gone long.' Isabel tried to sit up.

Vargas moved forward, kneeling down and hugging her. 'What we're doing means we can get out of here once and for all. Jack will protect you.'

By the couch, Archer looked down at Carson. 'Sure you're up to it?'

Gritting his teeth, Carson nodded. 'I could...do with giving some...payback.'

Hugging Isabel one last time, Vargas rose. The two of them hustled to the door. Vargas looked back as Isabel moved off her chair and joined Carson by the couch, the wounded man holding his Glock in his left hand. He reached over with his right and took her hand, the girl looking over at Vargas, unsure.

'We'll be back soon,' Vargas said. 'I promise.'

FORTY THREE

Down on the street, the Marshals team had finally had enough. Hobbs had been on the phone for most of the past two hours, first explaining to his senior officers what had happened to his team on the roof and the chopper, then trying to figure out a plan for a secondary approach. The Police Commissioner had arrived, been filled in on the situation and was talking with the senior NYPD men on the ground, also trying to come up with a solution to the stand-off. Two other ESU teams had arrived but they were being ordered to hold back; no more NYPD choppers were going near the building unless ordered, and that sure as hell wasn't going to happen anytime soon.

Dalton's group was a separate issue. They were a Federal team and had jurisdiction here, and he'd decided it was time to get inside the building once and for all. Their two helicopters were back from an operation in Long Island, but after what had happened to the ESU vessel, the pilots were understandably reluctant to fly anywhere near the building carrying a team on what could well turn out to be a suicide mission.

That meant they were going in from the ground.

Dalton was mid-briefing when Hendricks and Shepherd approached him. He sensed their urgency and broke off from what he was saying, motioning to his team to give him one moment.

He moved off to one side with the two men, Dalton's team watching him expectantly.

'What's going on?' Shepherd asked.

336

'We're going in.'

'That's not wise. They put down ESU with Claymore mines and a rocket launcher,' Shepherd said. 'Who knows what kind of weapons they've got in there?''

'We have no alternative. It's time to end this thing.'

'Listen. These men aren't after the child,' Hendricks said. 'This is something else.'

Dalton looked at him. 'How could you possibly know that?'

'I went downtown; grilled Mike Lombardi. He has no idea what this is about.'

'Are you kidding me? You went down there and told him the whereabouts of our only witness in his trial?'

Hendricks didn't reply. Dalton's expression changed, hardening.

'You know what, from now on we'll handle this,' he said. 'This is a Federal situation; stay the hell out of it.'

'Listen to him, James,' Shepherd implored. 'These men aren't who we thought they were. They're here for one of your people.'

'What? Why?'

'I don't know. But I think you do.'

Dalton didn't reply.

Behind him, his team waited expectantly, ready to go.

'Stand down and stay the hell away,' he repeated. 'That's a Federal order. We're going in.'

On the 12th floor, Archer and Vargas were in the corridor, the two of them standing back to back, covering each other in the now familiar pattern. The hallway was quiet but they both felt vulnerable, as they'd done the entire damn time they'd been here. Being inside one of the apartments gave momentary protection and slight security; out here, there was nowhere to hide.

There were no more people left on this floor; the place was eerily empty.

And in the quiet, the constant beeping over the intercom continued.

They couldn't waste a second; if the Marshals managed to breach the front door, the Claymores hidden behind the desk would blow them to pieces.

Moving fast, the pair entered the stairwell and started making their way down, ready and fully prepared to encounter the SRT team or the guys from the street and take them out head-on.

Hendricks and Shepherd watched Dalton re-join his team.

'This isn't smart,' Hendricks said. 'They annihilated the ESU task force. They'll do the same to them.'

'What else can we do, Jake? He won't listen.'

'Last time they came in from above,' Hendricks said. 'This time, they know it'll be from the ground. It'll be a massacre.'

Shepherd glanced at his friend and saw him staring up at the top of the building.

He realised what he was thinking.

Hendricks turned to him.

'You with me?'

Shepherd nodded.

Without another word, the two men ran from the sea of NYPD vehicles and jumped into Shepherd's car, Hendricks pulling his cell as Shepherd fired the engine.

They needed a chopper ASAP.

Archer and Vargas moved down the stairs quickly. By now they'd become accustomed to each other's movements and patterns, strangers from mere hours ago who were now relying on each other to stay alive.

5.

4.

3.

The lower apartment block was like a ghost-town. Everyone was either gone, hiding out or had been killed in the gas explosion on 8 when the mob of residents had found them.

Pausing on the 3rd floor stairwell, they both glanced down the corridor.

It was deserted.

There was no-one about.

Including the response team.

FORTY FOUR

Down on the street, Dalton's task force stepped past the barriers and shot-up cop cars, moving slowly forward. Four men at the front of the group were holding bullet-proof riot shields, the same type that had saved the Hostage Rescue man's life when he'd tried to get a phone inside earlier. The raids and busts they performed as an agency often weren't smooth and they were accustomed to this kind of drill. They were approaching in a group like a Roman tortoise, an ancient defensive manoeuvre but still highly effective.

Watching them approach the building, Dalton realised Hobbs was beside him, looking anxious. Any cause for argument they'd had earlier had been blown up with the ESU team and their chopper.

Dalton glanced at Hobbs.

'Here we go.'

Archer and Vargas arrived onto the 1st floor.

It was empty, no-one around, like all the others.

However, they knew the team of Miami cops were using these floors, so Archer pulled open the door, Vargas going through, wanting to clear it quickly before they continued down. Halfway along the corridor, Archer passed a room with an open door that looked different. It was some kind of maintenance office, no one inside.

Expecting an ambush at any moment, he ducked into the room, followed by Vargas. They both saw an intercom panel on the wall, but the button wasn't pushed down.

There must be another somewhere else in the building, Archer thought.

Vargas looked at him and pointed down. He nodded. They couldn't waste any more time. They quickly cleared the rest of the corridor and the north stairwell.

As they moved down to the ground floor, ready to fire, they saw a load of dead bodies slumped on top of each other. They'd all been shot, blood on the floor and on the walls behind them.

Climbing over them, with no time to spare, Archer and Vargas paused by the door.

He looked at her and nodded.

Ripping the door back, they aimed into the lobby, ready to fire.

But none of the gunmen were there.

The man Archer had strangled was still dumped in a heap by the elevator but there was no-one else. The place was deserted. Archer looked over at the mass of Claymores aimed at the door and winced.

He approached the jammer by the wall and flicked a switch; it seemed to shut down.

Vargas had already pulled her phone, looking through the shattered window, seeing a task force of Marshals approaching the door.

'Put your hands up!' one of them bellowed, seeing Archer through the gap and aiming at him with a shotgun.

Outside, the Marshals were eight yards from the door. Behind the cop car barrier twenty yards away, Dalton watched.

Suddenly, his phone rang.

They were two yards from the door.

'Hello?'

'Sir, it's Vargas! Do not enter! I repeat, do not enter! The door is rigged to blow!'

Dalton took off and started running towards the building with no regard for his own safety, people watching from the crowd and wondering what was happening.

The Marshals team were at the door.

'Stop!'

The other side of the door, Archer saw the Marshals task force by the blown-out glass. Two of them were training their weapons on him.

He saw a dark-haired man suddenly appear from behind, running forward and shouting at his team to lower their weapons. He had a phone to his ear. *Dalton.* Vargas saw him and ended the call, moving forward as close as she could get without touching the Claymores.

'You can't get in here, sir,' Vargas told him. 'There are enough Claymores here to kill everyone on the street.'

'Are you OK?' Dalton asked. 'Where's the child?'

'She's upstairs. She's fine. These men are the cops from Miami; they're here for me.'

Dalton stared at her. 'You're sure?'

'Positive. This door's trip-wired, sir. You'll have to come in from the roof!'

342

Inside the lobby, there was a noise from the north stairwell. Vargas spun and swept up her M4A1, pointing it at the door. She and Archer both eased their way towards it.

Pulling the door back, they aimed their weapons up the stairs past the dead bodies, but no one appeared, no other sound except the continuous beeping.

'Where the hell is that coming from?' Archer said.

Vargas withdrew to the lobby, checking the detailed building plan on the wall.

'The basement,' she said. 'I'll check it.'

As she turned, Archer heard what sounded like movement again, from somewhere just up the stairwell.

He took a step forward, aiming up the flight, as Vargas moved down the stairwell to the floor below, her M4A1 in her shoulder, easing her way downstairs.

Alone in the office building downtown, Marquez arrived on 13.

The layout was the same as the floor below, lots of dark cubicles and desks with computers and keypads, everything switched off. It was strangely quiet for a place so normally infused with noise and activity.

She wasn't mad at Josh for leaving; neither of them had any idea if Archer was still alive. All the gunfire and explosions from the tenement block over the course of the evening seemed to have eroded his patience and frayed his nerves.

She was very fond of Archer but knew Josh viewed him as family.

Suddenly she spotted something and walked forward to take a closer look, heading towards the north side of the building.

As she moved closer, the hairs on the back of her neck rose.

A silenced rifle was laid on a table, pointed at an open window.

It had been abandoned, but she caught a hint of aftershave in the air.

Someone had just been here.

Reaching to her pocket, she grabbed her phone and started scrolling for Josh's number, her Sig Sauer in her other hand.

But the pistol pushed into the back of her neck made her freeze.

Vargas crept down into the basement.

There was a hum from the boilers, the air much warmer, the corridor wider to accommodate the machinery. Sweeping either side with her M4A1, she heard the beeping get increasingly louder the further she headed along the corridor.

She stepped forward quietly.

The beeping got even louder.

Up ahead, a large puddle of water had settled on the tiles, water dripping from an old leaky pipe running across the ceiling. The severed cords of the phone lines were dangling in the water, a death trap, beside a fire axe that had been dumped there.

Just before the water, to her right, was a metal box with a glass panel that had equipment or wires inside. A maintenance map of the building was beside it, stuck to the wall.

Just above the box was the intercom.

It was taped down, the light turned green.

Beside it was something else, beeping monotonously.

The digital receiver for a detonator.

She froze, then glanced up.

C4 had been packed all around the joists above her head.

She looked to her left and saw it had also been pushed into the corners of the ceiling.

Plastic explosive.

Enough to blow the entire building.

Her blood ran cold when she realised what was going to happen.

It was almost as cold as the steel of the gun that was pressed into the back of her neck.

FORTY FIVE

'Drop the weapon,' a familiar voice said.

She didn't move, staring at the wall in front of her.

'Drop it.'

She let it fall to the ground, still facing the receiver.

She didn't need to turn to recognise who was holding the weapon. His name was Denton, Calvin's old partner, a Sergeant in SRT and a creep. He'd made a move once, and after she'd rejected him and kicked his ass that lust had been transformed into pure hostility.

Facing the wall, she sensed him lean in close.

'I knew you'd come down eventually,' he whispered into her ear. *'Inquisitive bitch.'*

She felt his other hand touch her lower back.

It slid lower and she tensed.

'Don't move,' he said. 'I'm thinking I might have some fun before I pull the trigger.'

She suddenly coughed, momentarily loosening the gun from the back of her neck as her head jerked down. She deflected his arm, twisted and kicked him as hard as she could in the groin, driving her shin upwards like she was taking a goal kick.

He recoiled as he took the blow, dropping the gun and yelping in pain. She swung her M4A1 around but he recovered enough to grab it and wrench the weapon out of her hands, the assault rifle clattering to the floor as he slammed her up against the wall.

He had about eighty pounds on her and he knew what he was doing. He wrestled her to the ground, using his superior strength and size advantage, and started strangling her. She smashed the heel of her palm up into his nose desperately, which loosened his hands.

Pinned under him, she frantically scrabbled for anything within reach that she could use as a weapon; she cut her hand on some glass from the smashed phone-line panel.

Ignoring the pain, she grabbed the shard and slashed it across his face. He immediately recoiled and released her, shouting in pain. She hit him again with the heel of her palm, this time breaking his nose, and managed to roll away as he rocked back, clutching his face. She scrambled to her feet and reached for the pistol on her hip.

Wiping blood out of his eyes and lurching to his feet, Denton saw the puddle of water behind her with the ruptured cord from the severed phone lines hanging in it.

He lunged forward and kicked her back, the force knocking her into the water.

There was a *whump*. The force of the electric shock threw Vargas back against the wall and she dropped in a limp heap, collapsing to the ground just out of the puddle.

Denton spat blood out of his mouth and wiped it out of his eyes then reached for his M4A1.

Scooping up the rifle, he buried the stock in his shoulder, pulled the slide and aimed at her head.

Suddenly he was thrown forward as a burst of assault rifle fire hit him in the back, the muzzle flash lighting up the dark basement.

Seeing the man fall, Archer ran down the corridor past him and dropped down by Vargas, who was lying motionless on the floor.

He felt her neck for a pulse.

There was none.

Quickly laying the M4A1 to one side, he started CPR, constantly checking either side of him. Under his hands, Vargas jerked lifelessly with each push on her sternum, her body limp, her weapon dropped to the side.

'C'mon, Vargas,' he said.

He pushed harder, willing her to come back.

'C'mon!'

He breathed into her mouth and continued the CPR.

Suddenly a figure appeared from the north stairwell, one of the original gang members who'd ambushed Foster and his team on the street.

He had a gun in his hand.

Archer swept up his M4A1 fast and pulled the trigger.

Click.

It was empty.

Dropping the rifle, he threw himself to one side as the other man fired, hitting the air where Archer's head had just been. Archer had already pulled Carson's USP from his belt and fired from his back, putting two rounds in the guy's sternum a half inch apart.

Archer pushed himself back to Vargas as the dead man hit the ground, pressing with even more force, continuing the compressions rhythmically and firmly.

'C'mon, Alice.'

He pushed but she wasn't responding.

She was limp.

'Stay with me.'

He pushed hard.

'Let's go, Vargas.'

Nothing.

He pushed.

Nothing.

He pushed.

Nothing.

'Let's go Vargas!' he shouted, pushing even harder.

She suddenly took a huge breath, her eyes wide with panic, and started scrabbling, gasping, coughing and whimpering.

Archer grabbed her and held her close, giving her time to recover and realise where she was. Sucking in air, her chest heaving, she hugged him, looking over his shoulder at the darkly lit corridor, her eyes wide in panic, gripping onto him like they were floating out at sea and she couldn't swim.

'It's OK. It's OK. He's gone. I'm here.'

She panted for breath, clutching him close.

Suddenly, another of the gang members appeared from the south stairwell, a pistol in his hands. Archer had his back to the man and didn't see him. Still holding Archer, Vargas desperately whipped her Glock from the holster on her hip and fired a split-second before the gunman. She hit him in the leg then fired again and hit him in the chest. He collapsed to the floor and was still.

She tried to keep the Glock up but it fell from her fingers and she clung onto Archer with both arms, sucking in deep breaths, recovering from the electric shock. As she did so, he turned and checked over his shoulder.

The guy she'd shot was dead.

They sat there in the basement, her chest heaving, both of them bloodied, bruised and beaten up.

And above them, the detonator kept flashing, hooked up to the C4 that would demolish the building at any moment.

FORTY SIX

Downtown on West 30th Street, Shepherd car's swept into an estate, Hendricks having just quickly shown the guard on the front gate his badge.

As they sped into the compound, the two Sergeants saw the rotors of an NYPD Agusta A119 helicopter already whirring at full speed; Hendricks had ordered it to be ready and waiting, the vessel flying over from the NYPD's helicopter base in Floyd Bennett Field, Brooklyn.

Screeching to a halt, the two men stepped out, slammed the doors and moved around to the rear of the vehicle. It was a Counter Terrorism Bureau Ford, not Shepherd's own car, so it contained the standard issue weapons and equipment stowed in the back. Shepherd ripped open the trunk and they both started pulling on bulletproof vests, locking them in place, *NYPD* printed on the front and back in thick white lettering.

Pulling two Mossberg shotguns from stowed positions in racks inside, Hendricks grabbed a box of ammunition and passed one of the weapons to Shepherd, who slammed the door shut.

The two Sergeants ran across the tarmac towards the chopper, pulling open the door and climbing inside. Securing the door behind them, Shepherd grabbed a headset and pulled it on as Hendricks started loading his Mossberg, pushing shells into the breech.

Up front, two pilots from the Aviation Unit were ready to go. Both of them were looking over

351

their shoulders, peering at the two Counter Terrorism Sergeants.

'We going to the building?' the lead pilot asked over the helicopter intercom.

'Make it fast, Lieutenant,' Shepherd said.

'You sure that's wise?'

'We have people trapped inside. They're running out of time.'

The pilot looked at him, well aware of the ESU chopper that had been dropped. Then he nodded. Loading his own shotgun, Shepherd watched the helipad shrink as they rose into the air above the rooftops, the lights of Manhattan suddenly appearing as they lifted higher and higher.

Hendricks racked the pump on his Mossberg and held a support grip, the vessel turning and heading uptown fast.

On the 20th floor of the West 135th tenement block, Calvin, Bishop and Braeten were almost at the roof. With his M4A1 in one hand, Calvin looked at the detonator in the other.

When the solution had come to him downstairs, he couldn't believe he hadn't considered it sooner. With the pace of events, the gunfights and explosions, he'd completely forgotten about the C4 explosive, timer and control switch they'd brought in one of the black holdalls.

That was the answer.

Demolish the building.

The moment he explained the plan to the others, their eyes had lit up. They'd lost six of their guys tonight; by blowing the place, they could abandon Vargas and chopper out. The moment they were within safe distance, they'd detonate. It didn't matter where she was, the whole building would be destroyed, reduced to a heap of dust and rubble. She'd go down with it and they'd be out of here, making their escape.

Calvin smiled as he moved up the stairs, thinking of her hiding somewhere in the building, barricaded in with the asshole helping her and the kid, figuring if they just waited it out they'd be saved.

The three men arrived on 21, passing Gibbons' body in the stairwell, lying in a pool of blood. Stepping over their dead colleague, Calvin and Fowler saw Taylor, aka Hearts, sprawled in the corridor where he'd been shot. The demolition would also take care of their bodies; CSU would probably find enough to ID at least one of the dead cops, but by then Calvin, Fowler and Denton would be out of the country.

Breathing hard, they raced to the stairwell that led to the roof, pushing open the door and running up the final set of stairs. When they arrived, the trio ran towards the heap of dead ESU officers in the centre of the roof. They grabbed them, dragging them out of the way to make space for their chopper which was already on its way. Denton had remained downstairs, fixing the explosives and insisting on lying in wait until the last minute in case Vargas appeared. He wanted to shoot her himself, not blow her up. Calvin knew Denton had something personal to settle with her, so he left him down there, telling him to not wait long and haul ass when he hit the stairs.

Calvin checked his watch; he'd better be on his way up by now. They sure as hell weren't going to wait for him. Two of Braeten's guys were still down there too, hunting for her. It still wasn't too late for one of them to hitch a ride out of here with Calvin and his team. He couldn't care less either way.

Checking his watch, he pushed down the pressel on his vest.

'Knight, where the hell are you?'

He waited.

Denton didn't come back.

'Ben, get your ass up here! We're not waiting!'

He looked over at Braeten, who was dragging the last ESU officer out of the way by his heels, the body leaving a trail of blood on the concrete behind it.

'Where the hell are your guys?'

'I don't give a shit,' he shouted, well aware of the time. He dumped the body to the side then pulled his pistol out of the back of his waistband. *'Let's go!'*

Running into the lobby, Archer pulled his cell and dialled Shepherd, following Vargas. They smashed into the north stairwell and climbing over the pile of dead bodies, started running up the flights. If it was just the two of them, they could break a 1st floor window and climb out.

However, they had Carson and Isabel ten floors up, both completely unaware of the sudden new level of danger they were in.

As he raced up the stairs, Archer felt faint and dizzy but willed his body to give him one last spike of adrenaline. The wound on his stomach burned but he ignored it. He could feel hot blood leaking into the waistband of his jeans. He'd never felt so tired, but he fought his way up the stairs, his lungs bursting, his thighs full of lactic acid.

In front of him he saw Vargas was struggling too, still recovering from the aftermath of the electric shock.

4.

5.

6.

The phone was to his ear, still ringing.

Then Shepherd answered.

'Archer! Talk to me!' he shouted. The background noise on his side of the call was loud and intense.

'They're cops, sir!'

'Say again?'

'They're all Miami PD!' he said, sprinting up the stairwell behind Vargas, who was grimacing and struggling in the aftermath of the electric shock. 'They're planning to blow the building!'

'Hendricks and I are on our way in a chopper. Get to the roof!'

FORTY SEVEN

The black unmarked helicopter that had brought Calvin and his response team to the building was approaching from the west. The pilot moved across the Hudson and headed towards West 135th. Up ahead, he saw the smoking wreckage from the ESU chopper in Riverbank State Park by the water. Two fire trucks and some NYPD squad cars were surrounding it in a cluster. There were no other choppers around the building, which made him smile. It seemed what had happened to the ESU team had deterred any other pilots from risking taking a hit. It would make their escape a hell of a lot easier.

His eyes narrowed in satisfaction as he looked at the roof. All the bodies of the dead cops had been moved, which would give him room to land.

He saw three men standing there waiting for him, all of them armed, Calvin, Fowler and some guy with blond dreadlocks. He must have earned himself a ride somehow.

'I see you,' he shouted into his radio. 'Stand back!'

'Hurry up!'

Suddenly, there was a loud *clunk*.

Clunk. Clunk.

Alarms started going off in the cabin, red emergency lights flashing. Fighting with the controls, the pilot wrestled with the stick, confused. Looking over his shoulder, he saw black smoke billowing from the side of the vessel.

Jet fuel was leaking down the side of the chopper, all the alarms in the cabin howling, gas spraying into the air from the ruptured fuel tank.

He fought with the stick as hard as he could but he couldn't control it. The helicopter started to spin.

'Shit! I'm hit!'

In the office building downtown from the tenement block, Marquez aimed through the scope of the Vintorez and hit the chopper's fuel tank twice more, putting five bullets into a grouping the size of a cup and saucer, smashing a window of the office building as she fired.

Fuel was bleeding out and the chopper was starting to spiral, same as the ESU vessel earlier.

Beside her, the response team sniper was dead. She'd assumed she'd been done for when the gun was pushed into the back of her neck, the man holding the weapon ordering her to drop her own pistol. She'd closed her eyes, knowing she was about to die, when there'd had been a gunshot.

She'd stayed still then slowly opened her eyes.

Turning to her left, she saw the sniper was dead. Josh was standing there, his pistol in his hand.

He'd changed his mind.

After making sure she was OK, they went to call it in. They tried Shepherd, but they couldn't get through, the line engaged. Josh had been inspecting the dead sniper for any ID and Marquez examining the weapon when they'd suddenly seen a helicopter approaching from the other side of the Hudson. Both of them immediately identified it at the same vessel that had delivered the response team earlier, definitely not one of theirs.

Marquez had dropped down behind the man's rifle and aimed directly at the fuel tank.

Time for some payback.

Now she watched the vessel spinning, going down. Below, the fire team hosing down the smoking ESU chopper were already running for cover.

The second chopper hit the ground twenty yards from the first and exploded on impact.

On the roof, the three remaining gunmen had swung round in her direction. They realised what had happened and immediately started firing at the windows of the building. Briefly ducking her head as some of them smashed around her and Josh, she took aim and fired, hitting one of the gunmen in the shoulder and punching him off his feet.

The others returned fire, running back and taking cover behind a thick air vent duct, the wounded man staggering up and joining them.

Marquez aimed where she figured they would be and fired twice more, putting two holes in the metal duct.

Arriving on 12, Archer and Vargas sprinted down the corridor. They burst into the apartment, the refrigerator already pulled back out of the way from when they'd left. There was no time to lose.

Running into the sitting room, Vargas raced over to Isabel as Archer moved to Carson, who was lying on the couch in the same position as when they'd left him.

'C'mon, we've got to go!' he said.

He pulled him forward to lift him in a fireman's carry.

Carson didn't react.

'C'mon, Jack.'

Nothing. His arm was limp. Slowing, Archer withdrew and looked at him, Vargas joining him and staring down at her fellow Marshal.

His chest wasn't moving anymore.

His eyes were open, looking at the ceiling.

For the first time since Archer had first seen him on the street, his face looked natural and relaxed.

He was gone.

'Oh Jack,' Vargas said, tears in her eyes, Isabel standing beside her. She noticed a small amount of glitter still on his collar from earlier.

Not wasting another second, Archer grabbed the black bag and USP, running to the front door.

'Let's go!'

Vargas was right behind him with Isabel; they raced into the corridor and turning into the stairwell the trio began their desperate ascent up the building.

They moved up the flights quickly, but were hindered by having to go at Isabel's pace. Although she was going as quickly as she could, it was still a lot slower than Archer and Vargas could have managed alone. They were both wounded but adrenaline and survival instinct were masking the pain and driving them on, racing up flight after flight. They didn't waste a second clearing any of the corridors.

With the place about to blow, none of the response team would be hanging around.

They continued up, legs burning, the stairs seemingly endless, knowledge that the C4 could explode at any moment fuelling every desperate step.

The deserted apartment block was quiet now, save for one sound.

They hadn't turned off the intercom when they were down in the basement and the beeping continued, constant, monotonous, terrifying.

His legs full of lactic acid, his lungs on fire, Archer willed the noise to continue.

FORTY EIGHT

Isabel hadn't been injured and despite being so much smaller she kept up well. However, by the time they got to 17 she was exhausted and slowing, not really aware of the terrible danger they were in.

Stopping momentarily, Archer threw Vargas his M4A1, who slung it across her shoulders on the strap. He swept Isabel up and carried on, adrenaline giving him one last burst of strength, Vargas leading the way, fighting her way up.

18.

19.

20.

21.

When they staggered onto 22, they saw the man Vargas had shot earlier in the corridor up ahead. Demolishing the building would destroy the bodies; by the time CSU managed to pull an ID, if ever, Calvin and his team would be long gone.

Vargas pulled open the door to the roof, taking huge breaths, pausing for a moment to recover.

Lowering Isabel, Archer pulled his USP and followed her up the stairs, Vargas taking Isabel's hand and keeping her close as they quickly cleared the roof.

Not seeing anyone, they moved forward out towards the centre.

Shepherd and Hendricks were coming in from the south in the NYPD chopper, forty yards away.

Shepherd looked down and saw Archer on the roof.

He had a dark-haired woman with him, the little girl between them. Hendricks had the Mossberg in his right hand, gripping the hand support with his left as they swept over the buildings of the Upper West Side.

'What the hell?' the pilot suddenly shouted.

Looking down, he and Shepherd saw the wreckage of another chopper the other side of the building. It was engulfed in flames, close to the ESU vessel that had been totalled earlier.

Ignoring it and focusing on the roof, Shepherd tapped the pilot's shoulder and pointed.

'Get down there!'

Standing on the roof, bloodied, bruised, battered and totally exhausted, Archer, Vargas and Isabel saw the NYPD helicopter approaching.

Finally out of strength and energy, Archer moved forward, willing it closer. There was no one else up here apart from the pile of ESU bodies; the Miami cops must have already been picked up by their chopper and left.

Which meant the building would blow any moment.

'C'mon!'

But then to his horror, the NYPD chopper suddenly veered away.

Archer shouted, waving his arms.

'Hey! Hey! Come back!'

Watching in desperation, stranded in the middle of the roof as the chopper backed up, he suddenly froze.

Standing there, his hair and shirt billowing from the chopper's rotors, his instincts started screaming at him.

He was being watched.

He turned slowly.

Two of the enemy and the gang member with blond dreadlocks had appeared out of nowhere.

One of the Miami PD SRT cops had been hit in the shoulder, blood staining his fatigues; however, he had a LAW 66 rocket launcher resting on his other shoulder, aiming it at the NYPD chopper, the reason it had withdrawn and couldn't get closer.

The other man had an M4A1 in his shoulder, the guy with dreadlocks a steel pistol.

The weapons were aimed straight at him, Vargas and Isabel.

FORTY NINE

Archer stared at the muzzles of the guns. The lead man also had a control switch in his left hand which he tossed to the ground angrily. Archer recognised the switch from interactions with the EOD in London; it was a detonator.

The fact it had been discarded indicated the men were in no rush to leave.

They couldn't get out of here in time themselves.

He shut down the explosives.

Beside him, the other man was tracing the NYPD chopper with the LAW, keeping it from getting any closer, his left arm hanging limp at his side. The man who'd held the switch ripped off his balaclava angrily, tossing it to the ground.

Tanned and brown-haired, his face was a mask of fury and nothing but pure hatred.

Beside him, Archer heard Vargas whisper *Calvin.*

He was the SRT Master Sergeant, the leader of the response team.

'Finally got you, bitch,' he said to Vargas.

'That's what Denton thought,' she hissed back, full of defiance.

Calvin's eyes narrowed. 'Where is he?'

'Where do you think?'

Archer was beside Vargas and Isabel. His legs felt like cooked spaghetti, his vision hazy, his hearing impaired from all the explosions and gunfire.

In front of them, fifteen feet away, Calvin smiled, looking down the sights of his M4A1.

'There was only one way this was ever going to end,' he said, grinning.

'Shit!' Shepherd said from the helicopter as they veered away. *'Get closer!'* he shouted at the pilot.

'No friggin way,' the lead pilot said, pointing at the man tracing their movements with the anti-tank rocket launcher. *'He hits us with that thing, we join the chopper graveyard down there.'*

Shepherd and Hendricks watched helplessly, seeing Archer, the woman and the child encircled on the roof. Swearing again and dumping the Mossberg to one side, Shepherd unclipped his belt and moved into the back, ripping open an equipment case.

There was a Barrett M82 sniper rifle and ammunition inside, two magazines with ten .50 12.7x99 NATO rounds inside, huge ammunition for a powerhouse of a rifle. After 9/11, NYPD choppers were equipped with the Barretts to shoot down aircraft, which meant it would decimate the Miami cops on the roof.

He pulled it out and slapped the mag into the weapon, racking the bolt and extending the bipod legs, lying down in the cabin.

He didn't have time to sight the weapon, but prayed to God it shot straight.

'Hover straight!' he shouted at the pilot, as Hendricks ripped open the door.

'They've got them!' Marquez said, looking down the scope of the rifle in the building eighty yards downtown.

There were three men, two in combats, one with dreadlocks. Archer and the woman looked like hell, covered in cuts and bloodstains, makeshift strip bandages on his arm and her leg. The angle meant she could just see the response team man's head; he seemed to have momentarily forgotten about her.

Marquez centred the crosshairs on his face.

The rifle was a straight shooter; she'd nailed the fuselage on the chopper exactly where she'd aimed.

She slowed her breathing.

He was talking, his head bobbing slightly, looking down the sights of a black assault rifle.

She pulled the trigger.

Click.

'Shit,' she said. 'No ammo!'

Josh ran back to the dead sharpshooter, frantically searching through his pockets for spare ammunition.

Marquez watched helplessly through the scope, praying she'd be in time.

'C'mon, hurry!'

Archer looked at the three men about to kill him. Glancing at the guy with dreadlocks, Archer thought back to the street hours ago, sitting on the bench and seeing that man crossing the street intending to murder Vargas.

A perfect afternoon destroyed by violence and now with so many dead as a result.

Archer stared at the man's face, trying to focus.

He was unsteady; he felt his pistol slip and drop out of his hand, clattering to the concrete. He glanced down at it. Under his feet, the concrete was blood-stained from earlier in the night, some stray ball bearings still scattered around on the roof. He wanted to lie down.

Beside him, he felt Isabel pressing against his leg, shaking.

Vargas picked up the girl, shielding her as much as she could, holding her close to her chest and turning her body from Calvin. It was futile. She knew it would be scant protection when the moment came.

'You think you could do what you did and get away with it?' Calvin said, his eyes boring a hole into Vargas.

'I should ask you the same thing.'

'You betrayed your own. Now you're going to die, bitch.'

'Look around, asshole,' she said. 'You took off your mask. Your boys are scattered all over the building. No way are you getting away with any of this.'

'That doesn't matter anymore. I don't even care. I just want to watch you die.'

He paused and grinned, looking at Archer, who was staring at the ground slightly ahead of him, blood staining the lower left portion of his t-shirt.

'Speaking of which, it looks like your friend is already on his way.'

Vargas glanced at Archer beside her; his face was pale, his eyes fixed on the ground.

But out of the corner of her eye, she noticed something else.

His right hand was inside the black bag slung across his shoulders.

FIFTY

When Archer had dropped his pistol and looked down, feeling dizzy, he'd noticed debris from the explosion earlier.

Ball bearings.

Claymore mines.

The he realised something.

He still had the black bag over his shoulder.

As Vargas had spoken to Calvin, unknowingly distracting him, Archer had slid his hand slowly into the open bag, feeling for the blasting cap already attached to the wire.

He'd found it and slowly screwed it into one of the mines, Calvin's attention fixed on Vargas, savouring his victory and not noticing what Archer was doing.

He willed them to keep talking.

Finally, the cap locked into place.

The mine was now armed.

He felt the shape of the weapon. *Front Towards Enemy* was on the convex side. If he got it wrong, he'd kill himself, Vargas and Isabel in an instant.

'Time to say goodnight, bitch,' Calvin said, hitching up his M4A1 and aiming at Vargas' forehead.

Archer's fingers curled around the clacker, taking the utmost care not to close it.

'Hey Seth,' he said.

Calvin paused.

The use of his first name took him off guard.

'Catch.'

Archer suddenly whipped the bag off his shoulder and threw it towards Calvin, who didn't have time to step back.

It hit him in the torso and he instinctively caught it, the other two men watching with surprise.

All three saw a length of wire disappearing inside the bag, the other end connected to the detonator in Archer's hand.

Front Towards Enemy.

Calvin looked up as realisation dawned.

Archer shielded Vargas and Isabel with his left arm and squeezed shut the clacker in his right hand as hard as he could.

The moment the Claymore inside the bag got the detonation signal, the bag *whumped* and the side facing Calvin exploded

They'd been standing in the shape of a triangle, him at the front. The explosion dropped the two cops and the dreadlocked guy, smashing the glass in some unbroken windows on a building immediately behind them. The ball bearings cut them to pieces, using their own weapon against them.

They fell where they stood, their weapons clattering to the roof top, killed instantly. The bag ended up in rags on the concrete, blown apart, the smoking plates of one of the mines visible through the damaged fabric. In front of it, what was left of the three men was all over the tarred concrete.

Then, suddenly, it was still.

Slowly opening her eyes, Vargas blinked, waiting for any delayed pain, Archer holding her and Isabel protectively. She looked down; she wasn't hurt from the blast.

She glanced up over Archer's arm and saw that the men were all down, annihilated by the anti-personnel mine. The weapon was effective at up to 100 metres and Calvin had been holding the bag.

She was shielding Isabel, who had her head buried in her shoulder. Sensing it was quiet, she lifted her head an inch, opening her eyes.

Standing together, silently, the wind ruffled their clothing and hair.

'Are we safe?' she whispered.

'Yes,' Vargas said. *'We're safe.'*

She looked up at Archer, who was staring ahead across the roof.

'Archer.'

He didn't reply.

'Sam?'

Then she looked down and saw the spreading blood stain on his shirt.

The next thing he knew he was falling. He didn't even feel the ground as he hit it but it felt comfortable when he got there.

He lay down and rested for the first time all day. It felt good, finally, after leaving the gym all those hours ago. Now he was looking up at the night sky. He couldn't see any stars; apparently you couldn't in New York from all the city lights.

He saw Vargas above him, kneeling, saying something, her jet black hair hanging down over her face. He examined the cuts, nicks and dirt on her cheeks and upper body; to him, they made her seem even more beautiful.

She was saying something but he couldn't hear her.

As he stared up at her and realised what was happening, her voice from earlier suddenly echoed in his mind.

Is that enough for you?

Flat on his back, she and Isabel finally safe, their eyes met.

As hers welled with tears, he smiled one last time.

Is that enough for you?

It is for me.

FIFTY ONE

Almost a month later, Matt Shepherd was sitting at his desk inside the Counter Terrorism Bureau on Vernon Boulevard in Queens, lost in thought and momentarily alone.

It was a Saturday morning, sun streaming in through the windows of the Department. Dressed in the Bureau-issue navy blue polo shirt and a pair of jeans, he leaned back in his seat, a cup of coffee in his hands.

He had a copy of *The New York Post* on the desk and was looking at the top story. The last funeral for a member of the ESU team who'd died on the roof that day had just taken place. The photo was from the service. Beside it, in a linked report, was the news that the city had decided to completely renovate the Harlem apartment building on West 135th. It had only taken twenty years or so.

Shepherd stared at the paper, his mind reliving the events of that night twenty seven days ago, his emotions mixed. After they'd seen the three enemy gunmen get taken out by a sudden explosion, the pilot of the chopper carrying Shepherd and Hendricks had immediately moved in, followed shortly afterwards by more back up. The NYPD'S Bomb Disposal Team had dealt with the C4 rigged up in the bottom of the building, as well as the sea of Claymore anti-personnel mines set up by the door. Vargas' call to Dalton had saved more than just the Marshal rescue task force's lives; the disposal specialist said if they'd gone off, the Claymores would have killed scores of cops and detectives further back on the street. They secured the weapons and unlocked the door.

Finally, for the first time that evening, the NYPD and Marshal teams could get inside. They'd found bodies littered all over the building, some of them identified as the renegade cops, many of them not. Including the sniper Marquez and Josh had found, there'd been seventeen men involved in the plot to murder Vargas: a five-man hit-team, a ten man response team, a sniper and a drug-running pilot who'd been killed when his chopper went down beside the Hudson. Every single one of the response team and the sharpshooter were current members of the Miami-Dade PD Special Response Team, an entire unit of dirty cops. This had caused a great deal of consternation and some very awkward questions being asked from the top.

The Miami press had wanted answers for what had happened, especially details of what the stand-off inside the building was about. After review and conversation with the Florida Police Commissioner, it was decided to give them what they wanted. It would be impossible to conceal what had happened; it had all played out in full view anyway, so the decision was taken to tackle it head on and give them the facts. A press conference conducted by the heads of the Miami Dade Police Department named all twelve disgraced officers, as well as revealing their involvements in corruption and the stolen and illegal funds in their auxiliary bank accounts that were being seized as a result of an undercover officer's diligent work. A major review was underway, involving the Senate, the highest ranks of the Department, ACU and Internal Affairs, law-abiding officers who'd interacted with the team shocked at the extent of the corruption that had been going on under their noses for so long. Extra safeguards and extensive background checks were already in place to ensure something like that could never happen again.

He sensed someone approach and turned. Josh walked over to his desk, joining him, holding a foam cup of tea.

He was dressed in the same outfit as Shepherd, his pistol and badge on his hip.

'Morning sir.'

'Morning.'

'Everything alright?'

'Yeah. I guess. All things considered.'

Josh saw the paper on the desk. He tapped it. 'Did you see page 4?'

Shepherd nodded. 'I did.'

With the case against Mike Lombardi and his crew ironclad, one of his men had come forward two days before trial and said he'd testify against the others in exchange for a reduced sentence in a secure facility out of the State. Called Luca, he'd taken to the stand with two black eyes and a broken nose. Rumour had it an NYPD Sergeant and close friend of Shepherd's had been responsible, but there was no proof. Luca was so desperate to escape serious time, he let it go. Shepherd had watched from the back of the court and listened as Luca gave his testimony.

Apparently, Lombardi had been looking for a chance to make his move for a while. It had needed meticulous planning, no witnesses, no-one left alive to talk. The East Hampton gathering had been the perfect opportunity. As family, Mike had been invited to the party but had politely declined, setting up an alibi and secretly arranging with three of his most trusted men, with the promise of significant financial reward and roles in his new organisation, to take out the entire group. He'd already sounded these guys out about a potential takeover; all of them were on board.

It was time for the old guard to move on.

The job couldn't have gone more smoothly. Gino's villa was pretty secluded, located beside the beach. They'd come in from the water and walked right into the house, Gino and the family pleasantly surprised to see them. Each man was carrying a gift, parcels wrapped under their arms.

They'd walked in and then opened fire.

Hosing the entire group had taken just over a minute. The first ten had gone down before they even knew what was happening; Mike had fired through the package and dropped five of them himself. They were armed with silenced sub-machine guns packed with ammunition from weapons they'd lifted from some of Devaney's muscle, and they annihilated the entire family. They'd found two more upstairs, both women who were unarmed, one of them with a phone in her hand about to dial 911. They'd been taken care of, killed where they stood. When it was done, the men checked they hadn't left anything incriminating or anyone alive.

Satisfied, they'd taken to their boat and left.

Their alibis in place, the murder weapons dismantled and dropped in the sea, Mike had been at home that night when he got the expected knock on the door. A blue and white had taken him to the local Precinct and he'd used all his acting skills, feigning horror and anguish at the atrocity. There was only one group of suspects he was told, and they were bringing them in. Casings had already been found with prints from the Devaney crew; if they could prove the hits were ordered, they could send down Frankie Devaney himself.

Four weeks later, seemingly recovering from his grief, Mike started to assert control over the family operation. Too soon, and the cops would smell a rat. Too late, someone else would take his shot. Everything was in place; everything had been accounted for.

Save one thing.

The girl.

Luca said Mike had attended the funerals for his family; they'd had two joint services, nineteen caskets eventually going into the ground, all of them different sizes for the men, women and children killed that afternoon. However, Mike's hit list had included twenty names; standing there in his suit at the second of the two funerals, the priest talking, he suddenly realised there was a coffin missing and started to panic.

Who did we miss?

Mike had been quick to realise who it was: his seven year old half-sister, Isabel, the youngest member of the family, the apple of her father's eye who'd been an unplanned surprise to them all when Gino's wife had announced she was pregnant again at the age of forty three. Isabel's coffin wasn't there. He'd checked with his guys if they remembered capping her off, but none of them could. *She probably wasn't at the villa,* he told himself. *She was at a friend's place. The police have her in protective custody in case the Devaneys try to finish the job.* His suspicions were confirmed two weeks ago when he caught a news bulletin of the girl being ushered towards a car in DC; she was alive. He didn't order any moves on her though; they'd wasted everyone at the villa and checked every room. She didn't see anything.

How wrong they were.

Shepherd chuckled, remembering Mike and his crew's face when the child was brought in as a witness. The Court had to provide a box for her to stand on so the jury could see her as she gave her testimony which she gave clearly, her high pitched little voice condemning them to a life inside.

Four weeks on from the building siege, the child was recovering but still had a long path ahead of her. She'd seen more violence in the past few weeks or so than most people experienced in their entire lives. Nevertheless, with Vargas sitting near Shepherd and smiling at her reassuringly, the girl had told the courtroom what she'd seen that day and had unhesitatingly identified her brother and his crew as the shooters.

Game, set, match.

It was one of the worst acts of violence committed in living memory by a New York crime family. Although he had nothing to do with what happened at the building on West 135th, Mike Lombardi and his team, save for Luca, received several life sentences each on nineteen counts of murder. The story on page 4 was to do with them; apparently, there had been some kind of incident at Riker's yesterday involving four new inmates during yard time. An investigation was underway, but no murder weapons had been found and apparently no-one had seen who jumped them. Mike Lombardi and his team were out of the picture for good. Street justice, if ever such a thing was appropriate. Here, it definitely was.

You reap what you sow.

Shepherd and Josh stood there in silence, the building around them at work but not busy, the weekend shift putting in their time. Looking at the paper, the same person came to mind, someone who should have been standing there beside them.

Shepherd rose.

'C'mon. We've got work to do. Franklin's got a new op for us. And I've finally found a replacement for Jorgensen.'

'Really?' Josh said, intrigued.

'You, me and Marquez will lay out the audit first upstairs. They'll meet us all in the city later and you can make introductions.'

He rose, patting Josh on the shoulder as he passed. Josh looked down at the newspaper's headline for a few moments. Then he turned and followed Shepherd up a metal flight of stairs leading to some Conference Rooms used for briefings on the floor above.

Marquez was already in there, waiting for them with Rach, an analyst. She nodded to the two men as they both took a seat. Shepherd was damn proud of her; it turned out she'd had a hunch that the response team had a sharpshooter. Josh had joined her but lost patience and left her to it, thinking she was imagining things. However, she'd found a rifle soon after he left, just before she had a gun pulled on her from behind. The sniper was about to shoot, but Josh had returned just before he pulled the trigger and dropped him. Apparently on his way out Josh had noticed something leaking out from a store closet in the stairwell. Pulling open the door, he'd found the dead body of the guard from the front desk inside. She was right. There was a sniper there.

Marquez had used the dead man's rifle to put down the enemy chopper as it came in from the Hudson. If she hadn't, the building would have been detonated. Once again, his team had outdone themselves.

And he had a feeling their new fifth member would fit right in.

'Morning Rach,' Shepherd said, settling into his chair.

'Morning sir.'

'So what do you have for us?'

'Checkmate.'

Vargas examined the chess board in front of her. Her opponent was right; she'd lost all her pieces and the King was done.

Across the small circular table in Bryant Park 42nd Street, Isabel reached over and knocked it over.

'You win,' Vargas said, smiling ruefully. She'd allowed it to happen, but managed to look suitably crestfallen.

Across the table, Isabel grinned back. She went to respond but something caught her attention over Vargas' shoulder. Vargas turned and saw another small girl waving at them. She was with what had to be her parents on the lawn, the adults taking a seat and enjoying the sun.

'Do you know her?' she asked Isabel.

She nodded keenly. 'Can I say hi?'

'Go for it.'

Isabel was already off her seat, running over and hugging her friend. Moments later, the two girls were doing cartwheels and handstands on the lawn, getting rid of some of their seemingly limitless energy.

Vargas leaned back in her chair and watched.

Now they were approaching the end of April, the good weather was here to stay and the city looked spectacular. She still had a small bandage over her eyebrow and was walking with a limp from the shrapnel wound to her thigh, but other than that she was in pretty good shape, the other bumps, cuts and bruises all but healed. She'd had some minor heart palpitations as a result of the electric shock she'd sustained, but the doctor told her those would settle and pass with time.

However, psychologically she felt much better. She now knew for a fact that everyone involved in the corruption in the Miami PD Special

Response Team was either dead or in jail. For the first time since she could remember, she wasn't undercover or looking over her shoulder, worrying if the guys she busted had found her.

Surviving the ordeal on the street and inside the building had earned her a hell of a lot of respect in the Marshals service as well as in the Miami-Dade Police Department, especially considering she'd not only kept her witness alive but had also taken down the four gang members and the ten-man response team with Archer's help. Isabel had made the stand and buried her brother and his crew. They were all going away for several life sentences.

Mike Lombardi had been picked up on Monday morning having been found handcuffed to a chair inside an NYPD safe-house in Midtown. He was shouting and hollering that a dark-haired cop had put a gun to his balls and assaulted some of his people at their bar in Tribeca. He'd kept up the complaints all the way to the stand, but no-one took any notice and Isabel's testimony finished him. As it turned out, he had more than a few enemies inside. Reports had come through that he and his four friends hadn't made it past their second night; Gino Lombardi's influence had reached out from beyond the grave and for some men, you didn't need to share the same blood to be considered family.

The funeral services for the fallen ESU team had all taken place. Funerals for Carson, Foster, Barlow and Helen had also taken place around two weeks ago. She'd missed Barlow's for obvious reasons. The body count from that Sunday night had been high. A number had been killed in the explosion on the 8th floor apartment when the mob had come hunting but few people mourned them. After long debriefing and extensive statements from all parties, the DOJ had officially let it be known how impressed they were with Vargas's performance in keeping the child and herself alive.

However, she'd made it very clear how it hadn't all been down to her.

Not by a long way.

As she cast her mind back to that evening, she remembered the conversation she'd had with Archer, before they ventured downstairs and realised the building was about to be blown up. She'd seen the look in his eyes; he knew he was going to die. He'd stayed with her and brought her back from when Denton had electrocuted her. No-one had ever made those kinds of commitments to her. Ever.

She felt emotion rising in her throat, but swallowed it back down, blinking as she thought of him.

Glancing to her left, she saw someone approaching, moving through the people wandering around the Square. He was a young guy, early twenties, and was walking directly towards her. She'd seen him before, in a photograph.

She rose and they shook hands. He had his mother's eyes.

'You made it,' she said.

'Of course.' Pause. 'I'm Peter.'

'Alice.'

383

He took a seat beside her. Together, the two of them watched Isabel in silence; she was having a good time, playing with her friend. Since that evening she'd been up and down, suffering from bad nightmares and delayed stress. A psychiatrist had warned things could get worse. However, he'd also offered some hope; although children were easily scared, they didn't know the way the world worked yet. They were able to recover from trauma surprisingly well, given the right nurturing and care.

Time would tell.

'That's the girl?'

'That's her.'

There was a pause filled by background noise from the Park and neighbourhood.

'They told me a piece of shrapnel killed her,' Peter said.

Vargas nodded. 'That's right. From a grenade explosion.'

Someone nearby heard this and looked up from their paper. Vargas caught his eye and smiled; the man returned his attention to the New York Post.

'Must have been quick,' Peter said.

'Yes it was. She saved all of us. When we first took cover in there, she didn't hesitate or tell us to leave. She let us in right away. If she hadn't, I wouldn't be here. Neither would Isabel.'

Pause.

'I heard her talking when we were trapped up there. She was talking about you. How much she missed you and regretted what had happened.'

The young man blinked and swallowed.

'But we're alive because of what she did.'

Pause.

'Have you spoken to your father?'

'Not recently.'

'Maybe give him a call.'

A pause. Their conversation was never destined to be a long one; she could see the young man struggling with emotion but holding it together. He was tough, just like his mother. He stood up and turned to her.

'It was a pleasure to meet you,' he said, offering his hand.

Vargas shook it. 'You too.'

He walked away and she watched him go.

As he moved down the path, headed out of the Park, he passed another man who was coming the other way.

Vargas' breath caught when she saw him.

Apart from a butterfly stitch over his eyebrow and some nicks and cuts on his arms, he looked normal. She watched him walking over; he was wearing a white t-shirt. As he moved, a gust of wind pushed the fabric against his stomach and she caught the outline of the bandage strapped to his lower torso, across the jagged wound which was healing nicely.

A pair of kids raced past him, almost knocking him over, but he swerved just in time and took a seat beside her. He looked over at her and smiled.

'Hey Vargas.'

'Hey Archer. You made it.'

'Of course. I love this place.' He glanced at the table beside them. 'Let's skip the chess, though.'

She smiled. 'Agreed.'

He'd passed out on the roof from blood loss and exhaustion. An NYPD helicopter had arrived on the roof shortly after he'd fallen unconscious. Two men ran over, one of them saying his name was Shepherd and that he was Archer's sergeant. They'd carried Archer onto the helicopter, watched anxiously by Vargas and Isabel, who'd climbed in after them.

With the girl safely on her lap, Vargas had watched the building shrink as they moved away, the bodies of Calvin and the other two splayed out on the roof. Archer had regained consciousness in hospital the next day, an IV in his arm, his wounds cleaned and bandaged. Apparently they'd got him there just in time. He'd been discharged two days later and had been taking it easy since, letting his body heal up.

Vargas had met his NYPD partner Josh at the hospital, who told her Archer's physical state after police operations was becoming a bit of a running theme. Apparently he'd been off for three months since Christmas and had been due back in the field the day after the incident at the building. Josh had taken to calling him Lazarus, but amongst the jokes and ribbing she'd seen how relieved he was that his friend was OK. *That son of a bitch never gives up,* Josh had told her the night Archer had been admitted and was unconscious, both of them sitting by his bedside.

After everything that had happened, she could certainly agree with that.

The two of them watched Isabel doing cartwheels, sunbathers and people on office lunch breaks sitting around the pair of girls as they played on the grass. A kid having fun, far from danger and bloodshed. No-one watching would have any idea who she really was and what she'd been through.

That was the way it should be.

'So she's all yours now?' Archer said.

Vargas nodded.

'No surviving family. No other guardians. It was me or the foster home. Something else I'm new at. Guess I'll just have to figure it out.'

'You'll be fine. You've already done more for her than anyone else in her life ever has.'

Silence fell as they watched her play. Vargas turned to him.

'So what now for you?'

He looked back at her. 'At least my cough's gone.'

The way he said it made her laugh.

'I just got a text from Shepherd. He wants me in tonight. Apparently an op just came in. Some kind of security audit for Cinco de Mayo. Finally back on field duty.'

'The building didn't count?'

'That was just a warm up. I needed a bit of practice.'

She smiled. 'I meant what now for you. Right now.'

Pause.

He smiled and glanced at his Casio.

'I've got a few hours to kill. I guess I could hang out here for a while.'

'I'd like that.' She motioned at Isabel. 'I think she would too.'

'I'll go grab us a drink. I never did finish my Sprite just before I first met you.'

He rose and she watched him walk off. Slipping her hand into her pocket, she withdrew her cell phone.

She had a new message, a small envelope in the corner of the screen.

It was from Matt Shepherd.

Her new Sergeant.

4:00pm, SE Union Square. New op for CdM.

She looked down at it and smiled. She tucked the phone back into her pocket, past the new NYPD Counter Terrorism Bureau badge and Sig Sauer on her hip.

Twenty feet away, Archer was at a stand, buying three cans of Sprite.

She'd wait until later to tell him.

She was sure he could handle one last surprise.

THE END

###

About the author:

Born in Sydney, Australia and raised in England and Brunei, Tom Barber has always had a passion for writing and story-telling. It took him to Nottingham University, England, where he graduated in 2009 with a 2:1 BA Hons in English Studies. Post-graduation, Tom followed this by moving to New York City and completing the 2 Year Meisner Acting training programme at The William Esper Studio, furthering his love of acting and screen-writing.

Upon his return to the UK in late 2011, Tom set to work on his debut novel, *Nine Lives*, which has since become a five-star rated Amazon UK Kindle hit. The following books in the series, *The Getaway, Blackout, Silent Night, One Way, Return Fire* and *Green Light* have been equally successful, garnering five-star reviews in the US, UK, France, Australia and Canada.

One Way is the fifth novel in the Sam Archer series.

Follow @TomBarberBooks.

Read an extract from

Return Fire

By
Tom Barber

The sixth Sam Archer thriller.
Now available on Amazon Kindle.

*****

ONE

Lying alone in the large bed, the dark-haired woman's eyes suddenly flared open.

She was on her left side, facing the balcony and as her sleepy brain recalibrated, she found herself staring out at the night sky through the open French windows. The thin curtains were fluttering gently, having been pulled back to allow what faint breeze there was to whisper into the room, the night hot and close, the street below quiet.

The bedroom was on the 2nd floor of the villa, facing a coastal road, and although there was the occasional noise from outside that wasn't what had woken her. Taking a deep breath, she pushed herself upright and ran her fingers through her hair, doing her best to rid herself of yet another nightmare.

Twenty eight years old, tanned and lithe, she had long black hair, hazel eyes and skin the colour of dark caramel, a perfect blend of her Brazilian and American heritage, her natural tan enhanced and made richer by her exposure to the Mediterranean sun over the last few days.

As the mists of sleep started to clear, she bowed her head and closed her eyes, taking a few deep breaths.

She was a tough woman, mentally strong, and until the last few months had never really had any trouble sleeping, at least not that she could remember. However, during the past four months and especially over the last seven days, her nights had been as fragmented as the aftermath of a glass vase dropped onto a hard floor.

There were two reasons for that.

The first was she was still having regular flashbacks from a job she'd worked on four months ago; employed by the United States Marshals service to protect a witness, she'd been trapped inside an apartment building in New York, the group she was hiding with being hunted by a team of determined and ruthless killers.

The second reason was a person.

And he wasn't here tonight.

She'd met him that day back in March after he'd been trapped in the Harlem building with her and he'd ended up saving her life. Since then, the bond that had developed between them during those intense few hours had deepened, and now they were both living and working together. She'd fallen for him hard and had been delighted when she'd found her feelings were reciprocated.

But right now things between them weren't good at all. They'd had a massive argument just before she'd left New York a week ago, which had started out as something pretty innocuous then developed into a full-on shouting match. She'd said some things in the heat of the moment that she now deeply regretted, and had spent all week wishing she could take them back. She'd been constantly checking her phone and email for missed calls or messages, but there hadn't been anything from him, not one word.

Opening her eyes, she glanced over at the empty space beside her.

In ten hours, she'd see him again.

And she genuinely didn't know if things were going to work out.

With those same thoughts squirrelling around in her head, just as they'd done all week, she slid out from under the covers, grabbed her cell phone from the bedside table and padded across the wooden floor to the door, quietly pulling it open.

The villa beyond was dark and quiet, the only other person in the house fast asleep. The young woman was dressed in a grey crop top and a pair of small grey shorts, light sleep-wear given the night time heat, and as she stood there she felt a welcome whisper of wind across her bare skin, fanning her for the briefest of moments.

She walked out of her room and moved down the twisting stairs slowly and silently. Arriving on the ground floor, she padded across the cool tiles and double-checked the front door was locked, which it was. Although there was no reason why it shouldn't have been, nevertheless she felt a quick moment of relief; the ordeal inside the Harlem housing block had left her with a variety of scars both mental and physical, and one of the former was an increased anxiety concerning security.

Standing there alone in the darkness, she saw the hands of a clock on the wall indicate it was 2:19am. Her flight home was at 10:30am, so she figured she could afford four or five hours more sleep before she'd have to rise, shower, grab a quick breakfast then take a cab to the airport.

Satisfied the house was secure, she quickly checked her phone again for messages or missed calls.

Nothing.

Tucking the phone into the pocket in the back of her shorts, she headed into the kitchen and poured herself a glass of water from the tap, her mouth dry from the night-time heat. After taking a few sips, she tipped the rest away and retraced her steps, heading up the stairs quietly, moving back into the guest bedroom and closing the door behind her with a soft *click*.

Walking over to the bed, she slid between the thin covers, pulling the top sheet back over her body and looking out through the open French windows to her left again, at the moon and stars up in the night sky. His image reappeared in her mind and she started thinking about what she would say when she saw him at JFK, wondering which one of them would be the first to extend the olive branch. She so hoped she hadn't blown it.

Despite the heat, she shivered; as so often happened at night, all of her fears began to magnify, intensified by the quiet.

Maybe he doesn't want to reconcile, she thought.

Maybe we're done?

Shit; are we done?

Settling deeper into the pillow, she closed her eyes and tried to clear her mind.

The three men waited, giving her time to fall back to sleep.

Then a few minutes later, the door to the small bathroom behind her slowly opened.

The trio, all dressed in dark clothing, moved noiselessly into the bedroom. Standing together by the right side of the bed, they stared down at the woman lying between the sheets with her back to them, completely unaware that they were there.

The man on the left was holding a roll of duct tape, the man on the far right a case containing some equipment.

The guy in the middle was the leader. His hands were free.

As the other two looked at him, waiting for the order, the leader studied the woman in the bed, noting the delicious smoothness of her tanned skin and her complete vulnerability as she lay there with her back to them.

Then he turned and nodded to each of his companions.

Time to begin.

****

Made in the USA
Middletown, DE
13 November 2015